# NOT YET LOVE

"You aren't in love with Lindsay," Andrew said boldly, making no move to release Claudia from his half-embrace. She began to protest, but he silenced her by placing a finger on her lips. "You know it is true."

"He has been very kind to me," she said. "I owe him loyalty and more."

"That isn't love, but duty," Andrew said, and brought her even closer to him. "It isn't duty that brings you to me."

"You do flatter yourself, my lord," Claudia said with outward coolness, but her pulse was beating faster.

"Oh, I know you aren't in love with me either," Andrew said softly, his lips very close to hers. "Not yet." And he brought his lips down on hers . . .

ELIZABETH HEWITT, who came from Pennsylvania, now lives in New Jersey with her dog, Maxim, named after a famous romantic hero. She enjoys reading history and is a fervent Anglophile. Music is also an important part of her life; she studies voice and all of her novels for Signet's Regency line were written to a background of baroque and classical music.

# A
# *Private*
# *Understanding*

*Elizabeth Hewitt*

A SIGNET BOOK

**NEW AMERICAN LIBRARY**

A DIVISION OF PENGUIN BOOKS USA INC.

SIGNET TRADEMARK REG. U.S.PAT. OFF. AND FOREIGN COUNTRIES
REGISTERED TRADEMARK—MARCA REGISTRADA
HECHO EN DRESEN, TN, U.S.A.


SIGNET, SIGNET CLASSIC, MENTOR, ONYX, PLUME, MERIDIAN
AND NAL BOOKS are published by New American Library,
a division of Penguin Books USA Inc., 1633 Broadway,
New York, New York 10019

First Printing, January, 1990

1 2 3 4 5 6 7 8 9

PRINTED IN THE UNITED STATES OF AMERICA

For Catharine,
who also understands the passions
and plagues of love

# 1

Claudia Tavener glanced at the small delicately crafted watch—a gift from her stepfather—which she wore pinned to the bodice of her sensible gray cotton round dress. It was just after twelve and wanted scarcely an hour before the children's luncheon would be served. She glanced at her charges, Jane, Lydia, and Thomas Bingerley, and saw that they were happily engrossed in a story being told to them by Susan the nurserymaid as she folded freshly washed and ironed clothes and placed them in the nursery cupboard.

It was rare that a governess found time to herself until late evening after the children were in bed, and Claudia took advantage of this unexpected freedom to return to the schoolroom. Pushing the door to the nursery nearly shut, she went at once to the window where the light was best to read the crossed, recrossed, and nearly undecipherable letter she had received that morning from her mother, who resided in Woodstock near the town of Oxford.

Claudia was so engrossed that she was unaware she was no longer alone until a small sound startled her and she looked up to find her employer standing beside her. She was annoyed at the interruption and didn't scruple to hide it. "You startled me, Mr. Bingerley," she said rather coolly. He made no reply, but drew her roughly into his arms, crushing Claudia's fingers and the letter between them.

His action took her so by surprise that she made no protest, submitting, if not responding, to his embrace. She was more exasperated than alarmed. It was not the first time that Bingerley had attempted this feat in the six months since Claudia had been governess at Bingerley Court, but it was the first time he had caught Claudia sufficiently off guard to succeed in his design.

Claudia let the letter drop to the floor and managed to get her palms against his chest, intending to push him away, but before she could do this, a high-pitched scream rent the air and he released her so abruptly that she fell against the low windowsill, bruising the backs of her thighs.

At the door leading into the nursery stood Mrs. Bingerley, her china-blue eyes wide with horror. "George," she said in a disbelieving whisper, and then crumpled gracefully to the floor in a dead faint.

The brief moment of silence that followed this was the last Claudia was to know for some time. Susan came running into the room followed by the young Bingerleys, who, upon seeing their mother stretched out on the floor, broke into wails of distress. The maid also began to weep loudly and they were quickly joined by Mrs. Ramsett, Mrs. Bingerley's mother, who added her own share to the din and confusion. It was operatic histrionics fortissimo.

Bingerley did nothing. He moved back against the window and looked appalled, leaving Claudia to deal with the chaos. Ignoring the pointless, contradictory commands issued by Mrs. Ramsett, Claudia went over to kneel beside Emeline Bingerley and in a few moments had slapped her into consciousness. The lovely eyes clouded and filled with tears as Mrs. Bingerley added her sobs to the cacophony.

"I think you had best take your wife to her room, Mr. Bingerley," Claudia said with more than a suggestion of command. She helped Mrs. Bingerley to rise, but when Bingerley approached, his wife shrunk away from him and clung to her mother, sobbing into Mrs. Ramsett's well-cushioned shoulder.

"If it's you that's done something to overset my girl,

Bingerley," Mrs. Ramsett said in a minatory way, "I warn you you shall have me to deal with."

Bingerley looked quite wretched and Claudia thought with some satisfaction that well he should; dealing with Mrs. Ramsett was never easy at the best of times. He made some sort of half-mumbled reply to his mother-in-law, but Claudia didn't wait to hear his explanation. She herded Susan and the children back into the nursery and firmly shut the door to the schoolroom. It took her the better part of half an hour to quiet the excitable maid and to reassure the children that their mama was not sick or dying, but at last quiet again prevailed.

It proved only to be a brief respite for Claudia. She had just returned to her own room when there was a sharp knock at the door. She opened it to find Miss Pricey, Mrs. Ramsett's dresser.

"The mistress sent me to fetch you," Pricey said, and Claudia knew she did not refer to Mrs. Bingerley, who was mistress in name only of Bingerely Court. "She wants a word with you in Miss Emmy's sitting room." Her features were set in the indifference of servitude, but there was a gloating light in her eyes that confirmed what Claudia had already feared, that somehow the blame for the uproar that had occurred would be put on her head. Suppressing a sigh, Claudia thanked the dresser in a perfunctory way and went downstairs to Mrs. Bingerley's rooms.

Mrs. Ramsett was clearly in command now both of herself and of the situation. She wasted no time asking Claudia for her version of what had occurred; Claudia's culpability was clearly unquestioned. Mrs. Ramsett began by informing Claudia that she regarded her as a viper nurtured in the bosom of her family. "I never thought I should live to see my trust so betrayed," Mrs. Ramsett said, clutching a fine lawn handkerchief to her ample breast. "It is beyond everything infamous."

Her daughter was stretched full on the chaise longue sobbing faintly into an embroidered pillow. "How c-could you, Miss Tavener?" she said between sobs. "How could you?"

"You are mistaken, Mrs. Ramsett," Claudia said with quiet assurance. "I have done nothing to betray either your trust or Mrs. Bingerley's. To do so would be to my own dishonor."

Mrs. Ramsett made a sound rather like a snort. "Don't try to gammon me, miss. My Emmy told me how she caught you red-handed making up to Bingerley. He wasn't putting up much of a fight, no doubt of it, but he's a man and weak like all of them. But you, miss, with all your fine connections and education know better and there's no excusing you."

Claudia sat at the edge of a straight-backed chair and said nothing, swallowing the ire that rose into her throat like bile. She knew that any attempt to defend herself would be pointless. Both mother and daughter wanted to believe that it was she who had thrown herself at Bingerley's head. It was so much easier and more comfortable to do so than to believe that George Bingerley was a philanderer who did not scruple to attempt to seduce females who ought to have had claim to his protection.

Claudia's glance rested for a moment on George Bingerley. He sat slumped in the chair nearest the door. He had tried to slip out of his wife's sitting room when Claudia came in, but his escape had been foiled by a piercing glare from his mother-in-law that had skewered him to his chair.

The look with which Bingerley met Claudia's was one of helplessness. Claudia knew she would find no assistance from the head of the house, for the title was an empty one; Bingerley was no match for his mother-in-law. The outcome was inevitable, and she came to the conclusion that at the least she could save herself unnecessary verbal abuse. She rose and calmly walked toward the door that Bingerley hadn't had the courage to use.

Mrs. Ramsett, who was delivering her considered opinion of Claudia's character and morals, broke off in midword to stare at Claudia in astonishment. "Where do you imagine you are going, miss?" she said, her arms akimbo and her upper torso thrust forward belligerently. "I'm not finished with you."

Claudia turned slowly and fixed her cool, dark-blue gaze

on the older woman. "No? I thought you had made yourself quite clear, Mrs. Ramsett. I presume my employment in this house is to be terminated, and since you have chosen to judge my character so harshly, I think it would be best if I were to leave as soon as possible."

At these words, Mrs. Bingerley sat up, her eyes still brimming with an apparently inexhaustible supply of tears, but her voice was quite steady when she spoke. "But, Mama, Miss Tavener cannot leave yet. We shall have a house full of guests next week for my birthday celebration, and who shall be in charge of the children if Miss Tavener is not? You know they mind her better than anyone else."

The children were thoroughly spoiled by an indulgent mother and grandmother and an indifferent father, and they minded no one. Claudia managed them better than had several predecessors only because she was strong-willed and usually unperturbed by childish vices, but the task was a wearing one and this coupled with the unwanted attentions of her employer had already made her think she would be wise to search for other employment, though it was a pity, for the Bingerleys paid her exceptionally well.

"Susan, the maid who has been helping me in the nursery, is very good with the children, Mrs. Bingerley," she suggested quietly. She felt rather sorry for Emeline Bingerley, who was ruled by her mother and neglected by her husband.

"Pricey will take charge of the nursery, until a suitable governess is found," Mrs. Ramsett said coldly. "At least I know I shall find in her a proper loyalty."

"But, Mama, Pricey cannot handle the children. Miss Tavener—"

"Has tried to seduce your husband under your very nose. When I had the letter from your Aunt Lucretia in London warning me that there was bad blood in the Taveners," Mrs. Ramsett said, spite glittering in her narrowed eyes, "I should have sent her packing at once."

Claudia clamped her teeth together so tightly her jaw ached with the effort to hold back the furious response, but her temper got the better of her. "At least the Taveners do not smell of the shop," she said acidly. "There were Taveners at Hastings and at Agincourt who acquitted themselves honorably while your ancestors were picking dustheaps. But that is why you hired me sight unseen at so exorbitant a salary, is it not? You cannot claim gentility, but you may buy it." She cast another contemptuous glance at Bingerley, who looked almost as aghast as his mother-in-law. Even in her rage, Claudia was a little ashamed of her words, which she knew brought her down to Mrs. Ramsett's level, but she was too furious to listen to any inner caution.

Mrs. Ramsett was so outraged that she nearly sputtered when she spoke. "How dare you, you wicked jade," she said, her cheeks vermilion with indignation. "You will leave this house today—at once. Have your things packed by the time the cart arrives, or I shall order them to be thrown out onto the lawn."

A belated calm was restored to Claudia. "That won't prove necessary," she said with a return to quiet dignity, and left them, oblivious to Mrs. Ramsett calling shrilly after her. She nearly ran into Miss Pricey, who was in the hall suspiciously near to the door. Claudia quite deliberately gave the sour-faced dresser her sunniest smile and proceeded up the stairs to her bedchamber to pack. It would not be difficult to comply with Mrs. Ramsett's demand; she had not brought a great many things with her and since had acquired nothing more than a pair of gloves purchased in the village.

When she reached her room, Claudia rang for a footman to bring her portmanteau from the lumber room, and inside a half-hour she had packed the last of her personal belongings into it. She heard a scratching on the door and assumed it was the footman again to inform her that the cart was ready. But when she opened the door, George Bingerley came into the room.

Claudia fixed him with a cold stare. "Have you come to apologize? I shall save you the breath. I am frankly glad to be leaving, and today's farce only has hastened what I had already planned to do."

"I couldn't tell them, you know," he admitted unhappily. "I might have made it all right again with Emmy, but her mother—that damned she-dragon—would have made my life a misery forever.''

Claudia gave him an arid smile. "You are mistaken if you think Mrs. Ramsett doesn't know the truth, Mr. Bingerley; there is little that escapes her in this household. She has no more wish to acknowledge it than you do. Is the cart ready? I know there is a stage that arrives at the Red Doe just before dinnertime, and I cannot afford to miss it.''

"I have come to ask you to stay the night at least, Miss Tavener, and take the morning mail going north. It isn't proper for you to be going off in this hurly-burly manner. What would your family think of me for allowing it?''

"No doubt the same as I think of you, Mr. Bingerley,'' Claudia said deliberately, and felt considerable gratification when he winced at her words.

"I deserve that, I suppose,'' he said, ''but the milk is spilt now, isn't it? I know you received your quarterly wages only a fortnight ago, but if you need anything further . . .''

"I have ample funds, thank you,'' Claudia said, turning back to the bed to close the portmanteau.

But, in fact, a quick tally of the coins in her purse when she had returned to her room proved that she had little more than was necessary to make the journey north by stage. It was always her custom to send the principal part of her wages to her stepfather to help in the support of their numerous family, keeping only what sum she thought she might need until next quarter. If she had guessed she would be leaving Bingerley within a fortnight of receiving her wages, she would have been more generous with her own allotment.

Bingerley nodded, taking her at her word, and Claudia felt a faint twinge of regret that her pride had caused her to refuse his assistance. It would not be a comfortable journey on the stage, which was much slower than the mail, and her slender purse would not allow her many amenities beyond the price of her ticket. She pushed the thought away as predictable anxiety for the uncertainties of her immediate future and refused to give it countenance again.

"If you wish to do something for me, Mr. Bingerley,'' she said briskly as she tied the strings of her brown merino cloak and slightly adjusted the set of her bonnet in the mirror, "you may ring for the footman to carry my portmanteau down to the cart. I am sure it must be ready by now to take me to the Red Doe." But as she spoke, the footman arrived of his own volition, and so there was nothing for Bingerley to do but reiterate his request that Claudia remain the night at least.

"No. You must see I could not." She held the gaze of her reflection for a moment longer, willing herself to feel no anxiety. "After what has been said this afternoon, I would not know a moment's rest under this roof." She turned and held out her hand to him, which he took mechanically. "I think it would be best if I simply took my leave of you here. Say whatever you think proper to Mrs. Bingerley and Mrs. Ramsett."

With characteristic ineffectualness, Bingerley merely nodded, and Claudia left the room and, a few moments later, Bingerley Court. In spite of concerns for her immediate and more distant future, she felt a sense of relief as the cart, driven by a silent groom, passed the gates and turned into the road that led to the village of Whickham and the Red Doe.

Except for the fact that the cart was so ill-sprung that she felt her teeth would be shaken loose before she reached the inn, the drive into Whickham was unremarkable, and Claudia was let down from the cart in the courtyard of the Red Doe. Her portmanteau was brought into the common room by a smiling, freckle-faced ostler whom Claudia tipped more generously than her limited funds could truly allow because his sunny countenance gave her sagging spirits a much-needed lift.

As she came inside from the bright sunlit courtyard, the interior of the Red Doe seemed very dark at first, but as her eyes adjusted, Claudia saw that it was a large, comfortable-looking room with a number of scattered tables and chairs and a large hearth on which a cheerful fire spit and snapped against the slight chill of an early April afternoon.

There were several occupants in the room: two women and a man at the table nearest the door, a man sitting alone near the entrance to the tap, staring moodily into a large nearly untouched tankard of ale, and four elegantly attired gentlemen at the largest table by the hearth, their loud, ready laughter indicating that they were perhaps not entirely sober despite the early hour.

Surveying this company, Claudia directed the ostler to place her portmanteau at a small table under the window that was a little apart from the others. The ostler promised to send the landlord to her, and it was only after he was gone that Claudia realized she had forgotten to ask him at what time she might expect the stage. It was nearly four, and she knew it must be due soon, but she hoped she would at least have time for lemonade and biscuits before she left, for she had had no luncheon and she scarcely knew when she would again have the opportunity—or the means—to stop for another meal.

Claudia was pulling off her gloves and once again allowing her gaze to wander about the room when a matronly woman of about medium height with grizzled graying hair and a crisp white apron covering her dress came out of the tap and approached her. She introduced herself as Mrs. Braggs, the landlady, and said, none too amiably, "You expectin' someone, miss?"

Claudia was surprised at her tone of voice. "No."

"Then you'd best be gettin' on, miss," Mrs. Braggs said coldly. "This is a respectable house and we don't hold with serving females what racket about unattended. Your sort finds a better welcome at the Anchor a mile or so down the road."

Claudia, still stinging from Mrs. Ramsett's baseless accusations, had had quite enough of being mistaken for a wanton. She composed her features in an expression of hauteur befitting the granddaughter of an earl. It was a trick she had learned from her mother, who despite a life led constantly outrunning the bailiff, had the ability to depress pretension in a duchess. "Indeed?" she said frigidly. "But then you know nothing of me or my 'sort' and cannot presume to judge what will or will not suit me."

The landlady looked less sure of herself. "I beg your pardon if I've given offense, miss," she said uncertainly, "but there's been a boxing match hereabouts near Horsham, and with so many gentlemen in the neighborhood, one has to have a care to see that there's no goin's-on." She folded her arms and a bit of challenge returned to her voice. "I don't hold with goin's-on, miss."

Claudia inclined her head regally. "Neither do I." She noticed that the young man sitting alone was openly watching her, and he smiled faintly and with a distinct air of approval as their eyes met. Claudia could not prevent herself from smiling back. There was something about him, perhaps the good-natured amusement in his dark-brown eyes, that compelled her to respond.

Knowing full well that her unattended position made her vulnerable to unsolicited advances, she looked quickly away. "I shan't be here very long, in any case," she said. "Kindly fetch me a glass of lemonade and a plate of biscuits and then you may tell me how I can purchase a ticket for the north-bound stage."

"That'll be comin' tomorrow morning some time after breakfast," the landlady said, still eyeing her suspiciously. "Were you wantin' a room for the night, then?"

Claudia was so stunned by this news that it showed plainly in her expression. "But surely there is a stage that arrives at dinnertime? I distinctly recall one of the maids at Bingerley Court returning to her home in Buckinghamshire on a stage that left here at that time."

"Oh, aye, miss," Mrs. Braggs said nodding, "but that were discontinued more'n a month ago. The last stage to pass through this courtyard did so today a bit after one, and it were London-bound."

Claudia had read in romantic novels of the more lurid sort how the heroine, having been faced with some shocking information, felt the ground heave beneath her, and she had always thought the description overwritten as well as overused, yet this was exactly what she experienced now. If she had been standing, she was sure she would have swayed.

She knew to a penny the amount in her purse, and no amount of mathematical cleverness would convince her that there was any way her means could be stretched to cover both the cost of her ticket to Oxford on the stage and that of a night spent at the inn. The landlady still regarded her without any degree of friendliness, and the last thing Claudia wanted was for her to suspect that she was incapable of paying her shot. "I shall decide later whether or not I require a room," she said in a tone of dismissal, and Mrs. Braggs, momentarily routed, left to return to the tap.

Claudia had been dealt as punishing a leveler as had any of the contestants at a boxing match. She silently cursed herself for having underestimated her needs when she had sent her wages to her stepfather, and even more bitterly did she castigate herself for her empty pride, which had made her refuse assistance from George Bingerley, which would have been no more than her due since she had worked nearly a fortnight into the present quarter.

Claudia had all of her life prided herself on her resourcefulness. When her father, Charles Tavener, a dashing but compulsive gamester, had run himself and his family into River Tick, it was she who had taken her younger brother into another part of the house and made up games to keep him occupied while her parents fought bitterly over Mr. Tavener's constantly mounting debts; and when Mr. Tavener had finally met a fitting end during the execution of a particularly risky wager, it was Claudia who had comforted her distraught mother and reassured her frightened sibling.

Still in the schoolroom, Claudia had served as her mother's confidante and had encouraged Mrs. Tavener, who was terrified half out of her wits at the prospect of raising two children alone on a pittance. She had also heartily endorsed Mrs. Tavener's remarriage to the Reverend Mr. John Maverly, a gentle, scholarly cleric who doted on the pretty young widow and who was possessed of a private competence as well as being the incumbent of an excellent living. Several years later, when the Maverlys' comfortable circumstances were becoming strained to provide for the futures of a family that had grown by four more children, Claudia had ignored all of her mother's protestations and had hired herself out as a governess to do her part to assure that her brother, William, would go to Oxford and that her parents would not have to scrape to provide for their other children as well. It was for this reason that she took only a portion of her salary for herself and sent the remainder to Oxfordshire.

Though Mrs. Maverly spoke often of the balls and routs she had enjoyed so much while still living a fashionable life in town, and declared that one day Claudia would have her own come-out and perhaps even make an excellent match and repair the fortunes of them all, Claudia knew it was no more than a fanciful dream. Though her uncle was the Earl of Strawbridge, he had made it clear that he had no interest in providing for his niece and nephew in any manner, and a dowerless girl, however well-connected, did not enjoy a brilliant Season and certainly was not likely to make an excellent match, unless, of course, one were quite beautiful, which, Claudia acknowledged ruefully, she was not.

Claudia was not a great beauty, but she had pleasing, even features that were saved from the ordinary by a pair of expressive dark-blue eyes and a pleasant temperament that was clearly displayed in her open countenance. Her hair was dark brown and lustrous and her complexion fashionably fair, but it was her unstudied laughter and a lively intelligence that were more likely to attract. To some, this was beauty of a sort, but not the sort likely to lead a man of birth and fortune to cast all other consideration aside to choose her as his wife.

As Mr. Maverly could not afford to replace the dowry that her father's debts had dissipated, and Claudia felt a Season in town with her Aunt Strawbridge would be a waste of money that could ill be spared, she had made up her mind to seek suitable employment and could not be shaken from her decision. But now, as she sat in the common room of the Red Doe, feeling rather frightened and very alone, she was regretting that decision made five years earlier. She knew it was foolish to be lamenting at this late date, but in spite of her excellent temperament and unquestionable learning, success in her chosen profession had eluded her, and as she sat in a brown study pondering her present uneviable circumstances, she felt quite ready to give it up altogether.

A waiter brought her lemonade and biscuits, but Claudia's appetite had deserted her. She looked at the food without interest, but in the end she ate, for she knew that this was all she was likely to have for her dinner.

The shock at having her plans to travel immediately to Oxfordshire so rudely overset was sufficiently upsetting to cause her usual inventiveness to forsake her. Her mind felt quite dull and the only two solutions to her present difficulty she could imagine were equally unpalatable. The first was to return to Bingerley and beg for a bed for the night; the second to find a barn or cowshed somewhere in the neighborhood where she might take shelter. She did not even entertain the idea of seeking charitable shelter with some householder in the village, for she knew she would likely be judged by any good housewife exactly as Mrs. Braggs had judged her.

She was not the sort of female given readily to weeping, but a brief wave of panic made tears start into her eyes. Claudia recognized this as self-pity, which was an indulgence she knew she could not afford. She quickly wiped her tears away and searched through her reticule for her handkerchief. She was surprised to look up and see that one of the young men from the table near the hearth was approaching her.

"Why does beauty weep?" he said silkily.

"I beg your pardon?" Claudia said, startled. He stood very near to her and there was a strong smell of spirits on his breath.

He made her a little bow and sat himself beside her without invitation. "You are a damsel in distress and I am your knight-errant come to slay whatever dragon it is that afflicts you."

Claudia saw by his expression that he expected a favorable response to his impertinence. He clearly shared the landlady's suspicions concerning her character and had decided to put his assumptions to the test. Claudia's sense of the ridiculous was kindled at the thought of herself in drab governess brown and gray as a *femme fatale*, but she bit back a smile lest he mistake it for encouragement. "I don't believe we are acquainted, sir," she said with ice in her voice.

"I am Francis Benson," he said, unabashed, "and I could not but notice that you seemed upset. Perhaps there is some way in which I could be of assistance?"

"Not unless you can contrive to make another stage traveling to Oxford stop here this evening," Claudia said with a sardonic lift of her brows at his presumption. "Can you?"

He leaned a little nearer to her. "I have a curricle and my own cattle here to take you wherever you wish, Beauty."

"What I wish, Mr. Benson, is that you would leave me in peace," she said, her voice becoming quite rigid. "I have no need or wish for your assistance."

He made no move to leave her, and the smile he gave her was so plainly insulting that Claudia wished she might slap it from his face, but feared a scene that she did not think the landlady would judge in her favor. "You look as if you could ill afford to be so high and mighty, Beauty," he said in a patronizing way. "My friends and I are generous men who know how to treat a lady with proper respect."

Claudia certainly would have struck him at these words, but the gentleman who had been sitting alone sipping his ale rose and came over to her table. Claudia regarded his approach warily, uncertain if she was to find in him a savior or another tormentor.

"I shouldn't think you do," the newcomer said to Benson in a pleasant, light baritone. "But then perhaps neither you nor your friends have much opportunity to meet many proper ladies," he added sweetly.

Claudia met his eyes for a brief moment, and although he leveled a cool gaze on Benson, for a moment a smile flashed through his dark-brown eyes that was for her alone. He appeared to be setting himself up as her champion, but she trusted his motive no more than she did Mr. Benson's.

Benson understood the insult of the other man's words and flushed. His brows snapped together and he said angrily, "Who the devil are you?" He expertly gaged his opponent and saw that he was a bit shorter and slighter than he was himself. He stood up and took a deliberately intimidating step toward the other man. "Interference can be a hazardous enterprise."

The man gave him a winning smile, appearing in no way disquieted by the other man's minacity. "I quite agree. My name is Alistair, Lindsay Alistair."

To Claudia's astonishment, Benson blanched as recognition dawned in his countenance. In response, Alistair made him a faint mocking bow.

"I beg you pardon, my lord," Benson said stiffly. "I had no idea you were acquainted with this lady. It was only a bit of fun, no offense meant." He made a brief bow of his own, mumbled a barely intelligible apology to Claudia, and returned to his companions. As he sat down, he said something to his fellows and the others turned and looked at Alistair, who smiled at them amiably while Claudia stared at him in wonder.

He was an attractive man in a quiet way, fashionably and elegantly attired in a dark-brown coat and buckskin breeches suitable for the country. He had pleasant features, with a faint patrician cast, brown hair with warm chestnut highlights, and his eyes were alight with an inner amusement. In stature he was of above average height and his slim frame was clearly athletic, but Claudia saw nothing about him to inspire the awe that Benson had displayed.

"Well, that was rather remarkable," she said, bemused.

He gave her his charming smile. "Yes, it was, wasn't it? It doesn't always work, mind, but in general I can count on it putting the wind up bullies of that sort who fancy themselves sporting men. They're all cowards at heart, I believe." He motioned toward the chair vacated by Benson. "May I? I don't wish to be guilty of an equal impertinence."

"It would be unkind of me to refuse you, though I probably should," Claudia said candidly. "Who *are* you?"

"Lindsay Alistair," he repeated. "And that gives you the advantage of me."

"Claudia Tavener," she said mechanically. "I meant, who are you that you should have such an effect on that abominable man?"

He laughed softly. "My name is somewhat legendary in sporting circles, I fear."

"But not your modesty," Claudia said dryly.

This time his laughter was outright and his eyes fairly danced. "No. Never that. I have a reputation, you see, that would make most any man think twice about finding himself in a situation where I might call him out or he might find himself forced to call me out. I am a crack shot."

Claudia was not sure what to think of this man. On the one hand, he freely admitted to a reputation that made him feared even by men, but on the other, there was something so engaging about him that instinctively she felt comfortable with him. But she was too conscious of her vulnerability to allow herself any familiarity with him, and when she spoke, her voice was distinctly cooler. "I must thank you, sir, or is it 'my lord'? I am afraid I don't know your title."

"I haven't any title. I am the brother of the Marquess of Lovewell and lord only in courtesy," he replied, adding, "Is this thank you and good-bye? I hope not. Since we both seem destined to spend the night under this roof, we might bear each other company at least through dinner. It is better, surely, than dining alone."

Claudia's suspicion grew. "I have reason for being grateful to you, Lord Lindsay, but in the circumstances I think it would be best if we were to dine apart."

"What circumstances?"

"I am alone and unattended, my lord," she said severely, "as you are well aware."

"And also unprotected. If you are at table with me, you needn't fear any further insult."

Instead of being outraged at his audacity, Claudia could not suppress a small laugh. "Except from you."

He shook his head and smiled. "I'm offering nothing more than dinner. I'm a harmless fellow, you know. Give you my word on it."

"You have just told me your reputation is otherwise," she reminded him.

"Yes, but then I'm not likely to meet with you at Finchley Common at dawn with pistols ready." He saw that she still regarded him dubiously and added more seriously, "I am a gentleman, Miss Tavener. There are those of us who still believe that counts for something."

Her instinct and sense warred fiercely inside of her, and instinct was emerging the stronger. "My stepfather is such a man," Claudia conceded.

"So was your father, Miss Tavener."

"You knew my father?" she said with surprise.

"Charles Tavener, was he not? He was a friend of my father's and frequently visited Lovewell House, and both your mother and father were guests on occasion at Land-grove, my family's estate in Suffolk. You are very like him, you know. We might even claim a connection. Your great-aunt was married to my great-uncle, or something of the sort."

Claudia felt her suspicions being lulled, even though her common sense urged her to caution. "That's a rather tenuous claim to a connection, my lord," she said dubiously but with a faint smile.

"Are you afraid I shall be one of those dirty dishes forever hanging on your sleeve?" he asked, quizzing her. "Not a bit of it." He broke into a full smile, which was seldom far from his lips or eyes and which enhanced his physical attraction considerably in Claudia's eyes. "In fact, if you will permit me to give you dinner, I promise not to play the fool any more than I need to keep you amused."

Claudia smiled in response, but said, "Thank you, my lord. But I cannot. You know it would be quite improper for me to do so."

"To have dinner with your cousin? You have very strict notions of propriety, Miss Tavener," he said severely.

"The landlady would believe we are cousins even less than I do," she said. "She already thinks that I am a . . . a . . . ."

"Light-skirt," he supplied daringly. "Are you still afraid that that is what I shall think? I don't, I promise you." He saw the hesitation in her eyes. "After dinner you may send me to the devil if you please and I shall go willingly at your request."

Claudia knew she should not allow him to persuade her,

but the lemonade and biscuits made a poor dinner and she had had nothing since consuming a light breakfast many hours ago. She could not help liking Lord Lindsay, and this made her decide to ignore the voice of prudence within her. She accepted his invitation and he went at once to the tap to call for the landlord.

As he was doing this, the men at the table near the hearth at last rose to leave. Mr. Benson, as he passed her, caught Claudia's eye and it was all too clear what he thought of her encouragement of Lord Lindsay. Claudia knew she should not regard the opinion of such a man, but she flushed in spite of herself. Her misgivings returned and were increased to full measure by the sounds of a verbal altercation emanating from the kitchen with Mrs. Braggs' voice rising high in vociferous protest.

As Lindsay returned to her she said, "I think perhaps I should not dine with you, after all." She picked up her reticule from the table and drew it closed.

Lindsay put his hand on hers to arrest her. "Please stay. If we know there is nothing improper in our conduct, we would be foolish to allow the judgment of others to affect us."

"If the landlady has her way, I doubt we shall even be served," Claudia said dryly.

Lindsay grinned. "Oh, I have little doubt of that. Her loving spouse has doubtless reminded her that, with the company from the boxing match dispersed, they can no longer afford to pick and choose their custom."

"That does not precisely allay my concerns, my lord."

But with the easy address that had both attracted her and fed her earlier suspicions, he teased her into such a comfortable state that by the time their meal was brought to them by the waiter, they were on very easy terms. Their conversation during dinner was light, inconsequential, and exploratory—the conversation of strangers. With a bit of skillful, inobvious coaxing, Claudia was persuaded to speak of herself at greater length than she had done with anyone for quite some time.

By the time the covers were at last removed, the man and

two women who had sat at the table near the door had departed and the common room was empty save for them. The evening was becoming chill and Lindsay suggested that they remove to a table nearer the hearth.

Claudia removed from her portmanteau a nightcap she was embroidering for her sister, Kate, and Lindsay, who had declined the waiter's offer of port, settled at the table with the remains of a bottle of very passable claret he had ordered for dinner. "Do you enjoy being a governess?" he asked with what appeared to be genuine curiosity.

Claudia was so surprised by the question that she halted her needle in midstroke. "Yes," she said slowly. "I suppose I do. At least I don't dislike it."

"I should if I had had the situations you have described to me tonight," he said baldly. "Of the three posts you have held, even the best of them was far from being to your advantage, and the Bingerley household sounded the worst of the lot. Bingerley made a pest of himself something like that Benson fellow, I suppose."

Claudia had deliberately censored the cause of the altercation that had led to her precipitate dismissal from Bingerley Court, but since he had guessed the truth, she did not hesitate to acknowledge it. "Yes. Something of the sort," she admitted. "At the moment I am not particularly enamored of my chosen career, but it really does have its rewards, you know. The children aren't all ill-behaved and unwilling to learn and the other two families I was with were really quite kind in their way."

"Rubbish," Lindsay said without rancor. "By what you have told me, at the first they sacked you without a thought for your feelings to engage a 'proper' tutor, and at the next you were more a housemaid than a governess."

Claudia laughed ruefully. "No, no, my lord. Did I make it seem so intolerable to you. I swear it was not."

But Lord Lindsay ignored her protest. "Then there was the charming Bingerley to contend with. Not precisely an illustrious career."

His animadversions were rather dampening, for in her heart she knew they were quite true. "What balm you give to my spirits, my lord," she said brightly. "I must thank you, I suppose, for pointing out to me what a shambles I have made of my life."

The smile faded from his lips but still lingered in his eyes. He shook his head. "That wasn't my intention. I merely wish to point out that perhaps governessing is not a career best suited to an attractive, clever, well-bred, and spirited young woman, which I think you are."

There was nothing amorous or insinuating in his tone, but Claudia accepted his ecomiums cautiously as her suspicions rekindled. "I must thank you, again, my lord, though I don't acquit you of flattery."

"Not flattery, merely honest appraisal."

Claudia's eyes narrowed slightly. "And exactly what career would you suggest to suit these qualifications?" she said dulcetly.

He slouched comfortably in his chair and smiled lazily. "If you were of another class of female I might suggest what you are thinking," he said outrageously. "But you may stop looking daggers at me, for that isn't what I meant."

"What do you mean, then?"

He didn't answer her question. He got up from his chair and went over to stand by the large, open hearth. "I am going to insult you, Miss Tavener, and I apologize before the fact. Have you the means of paying your shot for the night?"

Claudia's back was nearly to the fire and she had to twist in her chair to look up at him. She was aghast at this further audacity and dismayed by his easy perception of her circumstances. "That is hardly your affair, my lord," she said frigidly.

He nodded slightly. "True. But like the offensive Mr. Benson, I could not but notice that you became quite pale when informed by Mrs. Braggs that there would be no stages north until morning. Did the Bingerleys see fit to provide you with sufficient funds to return to Woodstock?"

The memory that she herself had refused George Bingerley's offer of assistance made her incapable of righteous indignation at his impertinence. "It is only a fortnight since the quarter," she said evasively.

"And you have just told me at dinner that you always send the bulk of your wages to your family," he said. "Will you allow me to make you a loan sufficient to pay your shot and see you comfortably returned home? I give you my word as a gentleman that it is without any expectations on my part other than repayment of the sum whenever you again have the means to do so."

His pleasant companionship and the excellent dinner had made it all too easy for her to put her dilemma temporarily from her mind, but she knew she could not afford to spend the night at the Red Doe, she had no other shelter, and the evening was rapidly growing darker and cooler. The entice-ment of his offer was powerful, but in spite of the growing affinity between them, she could not quite convince herself to trust him completely. Wondering if she was being a fool, she said, "Thank you, my lord, but I shall manage well enough on what I have."

"How?"

Claudia wished he would accept her evasion, but it was clear that he did not intend to do so. She made a quick decision because she had no other choice. "I shall spend the night here and in the morning return to Bingerley and ask for my fortnight's wages. It will be enough for the journey to Oxfordshire. I was quite well-paid, you know."

"If La Ramsett will permit you in the house. Even if the door is not barred to you, the interview should be difficult and quite humiliating, I imagine."

"So do I," Claudia said shortly, devoutly wishing he would cease acquainting her with every negative likelihood. "I appreciate your offer, but I can't take money from a man I have only just met, however great my need, so I really have no other choice."

Lord Lindsay was a young man who was not without difficulties and concerns of his own, but Claudia's vulnerable plight had made him forget these for a time. Now his facile mind conjured a solution that might benefit them both, though it was sufficiently outrageous and might well cause Claudia to rebuff him completely if he was careless in his presentation of it. He regarded her searchingly for a long moment and then returned to the table. "Your father was renowned as a gamester who never refused any reasonable wager. Are you a gamester, too, Miss Tavener?" he asked with a quizzing lift to his brow.

Claudia regarded him with mild bewilderment, wondering if he were simply changing the subject again or if this were in some way pertinent to her situation. "My father's idea of what was a reasonable wager was regrettably broad, my lord," she said with initial asperity. "If a wager appealed to him sufficiently, he would accept it whatever the consequences to himself or to his family. In that respect, no, I am not a gamester. I know too well the evils of gaming to be drawn to it."

"Is there no game of chance at which you would be willing to pit your skill against mine?"

His words only deepened her puzzlement. "To what purpose?"

From an inner pocket in his coat he withdrew a purse and cast it onto the table. "The usual one. If there is any game at which you think you might be able to best me, name it and we shall play it. If I win, you permit me to frank your return home; if you win, why, then you won't need my assistance, will you?"

"That would hardly be a fair wager," she said. "Either way it would be your money you risked."

He shrugged. "Then wager whatever funds you have against my purse, if you like. If you think you can win."

She read the challenge as clear in his eyes as in his voice. What she had said was true, the fear of the disastrous results of gaming was far more potent for her than the promise of its rewards, but she was not immune to the lure of the chance. Her father had taught her to play whist and piquet, and her stepfather was fond enough of the latter game to give her frequent practice whenever she was at home. She knew herself to be a first-rate player, for not even Mr. Maverly, who was held to be an excellent player himself, could best her three games out of five. Claudia knew that if she agreed it was a tacit acceptance of his help, but temptation already had cracked her armor.

Lindsay calmly sipped his wine and allowed her to make up her mind without further persuasion. He was too clever to push her, knowing full well it would only put up her hackles. He had a greater stake in her decision than she knew, and a positive response to his challenge was the most propitious means to his purpose.

"How do I know your skill is not much greater than mine?" she said at last.

"You don't. That is why it is a game of chance."

As when she had accepted his invitation to dinner, Claudia again threw prudence to the wind. "Very well. But if I win, I win because I am the better player. Is that understood, my lord?"

He sat up straight and his tone took on a new, business-like inflection. "Oh, perfectly. What is it to be, then, Miss Tavener?"

"Piquet."

Lindsay raised his brows. "That isn't everyone's game. You must be rather sure of your skill."

Claudia nodded with a decisiveness she was far from feeling, remembering her father's instructions that a show of confidence and the ability to carry a bluff were as important as any other skills in gaming. "Fairly."

Lindsay went to the door of the tap and called for the landlord. In a few minutes that worthy brought another bottle of claret and two decks of cards. Lindsay inspected both and nodded his approval.

Claudia, sensitive of her delicate position, thought that the landlord gave her a sidelong glance as he placed the decanter and glasses on the table, but she could not be certain of it. After Claudia refused Lindsay's offer to pour her a glass of the wine for fear it would cloud her judgment of the cards, they settled down to play. Lindsay drew a nine for the deal but lost it to Claudia when she drew a six. She viewed this as a positive omen and felt a surge of genuine confidence. She reshuffled the cards of the first deck and dealt.

They began the declarations with a minimum of conversation. Piquet is far more a game of skill than of chance, and Claudia gave it her entire concentration. She won the first two deals rather easily, but not because Lindsay deliberately misplayed his cards, of that she was all but certain. He won the third and fourth, which further allayed any concern that he was deliberately underplaying his hands. And when the final hand was dealt, it was so to her advantage that she felt a surge of excitement that she had to choke down for fear of becoming overconfident.

Analyzing the play as best she could, she saw that while Lindsay was also a superb player, he was too inclined to take broad risks that played against him more often than for him. Lindsay took the final trick, but the outcome was no longer in doubt.

"Damn near rubiconned," he said with self-disgust and some exaggeration. He said as he totaled the score, "Will you give me my revenge, Miss Tavener?"

Caudia had truly enjoyed the play, but she had won a sufficient amount to pay for her room for the night, and her sense told her it was time to rise from the table and bid Lord Lindsay good night. "I would be a fool to risk my stake again. I think if you had not taken so many chances trying to best me in the last hand tomake up for your losses, I would not have won by very much."

"But you still would have won," he said. "Actually I was thinking that we might play for something other than money this time."

His eyes met hers and held them. Claudia had become so relaxed in his company that she felt quite shocked by the suggestion she read into his words. Without lowering her gaze from his, she said coldly, "There is only one thing I can think of that I might have to risk besides money." She pushed back her chair and prepared to rise. "You may keep what I have already won, my lord. I have decided to do as I originally planned."

"I wish you would rid yourself of the notion that I have designs on your virtue, Miss Tavener," he said wearily. "You are a very attractive woman, but my intentions are not amorous. I have in my life sufficient female companionship that I need not attempt to ravish every unprotected female I meet."

"Are you married?" Claudia asked suspiciously.

"No, Miss Tavener, I am, for the present at least, quite unattached. But if your response to my proposal is positive, that may change very soon."

Claudia heard what he said to her, but the implication was so incredible that she discounted it. "What stakes are you suggesting we play for?" she demanded. "I have nothing at all of any value."

He poured out a glass of wine and gently pushed it toward her, ignoring her protest that she did not want it. He was silent for a long moment, carefully selecting the words he would use to make her his proposition. He picked up his glass and drank rather deeply from it.

"I, too, find myself in something of a dilemma, Miss Tavener," he said, watching her over the rim of his glass. "It's a common-enough one for a second son. When my father died several years ago and my brother came into the title and the entail, I was left with an income that may charitably be described as a competence. I am too lazy to be a politician, too blunt to be a diplomat, too fastidious to be a soldier, insufficiently pious to be a cleric, and every heiress I know has spots or a squint, or an incessant giggle that sets my teeth on edge."

"And too cynical to leave your fortune to chance, I suppose," she commented.

He shook his head, smiling faintly, and slouched comfortably in his chair, his long legs stretched out before him. "Not at all. I did think it was only lethargy that prevented me from leaving for London immediately after luncheon today, but now I believe it was luck." He raised his glass to her. "The same luck that brought you here and decreed that our paths should cross."

"I shouldn't have described that as luck," she said caustically.

"Perhaps you will before the night is out." He saw that at the least she was intrigued and was encouraged to continue. "I have an aunt who is also my godmother and who is somewhat eccentric and managing and insists upon arranging all things to her liking. Fortunately for her, she is rich enough to call her own tunes. My own mother died when I was still an infant, and it was my godmother, who is childless, who took her place in my life. In fact, I spent far more time with her and my uncle at their home in Bath than I did at Lovewell House or Landgrove, particularly after my father remarried. I did not get on very well with my stepmother.''

He said this in a very matter-of-fact way, but Claudia was well aware that she was very fortunate to have a stepfather like Mr. Maverly, who was gentle and kind, for she knew there were often resentments between stepparents and the children of a previous marriage.

"Have you any half-brothers or -sisters?" she asked, thinking of her own half-brother and three half-sisters, of whom she was very fond.

Lindsay nodded. "A half-brother who is with the occupying army in Vienna and a half-sister who was just married this past October, but we were so seldom together when they were growing up that we are more as cousins than siblings. My brother, who is a dozen years older than I, is treated by them like an uncle." He gave a quick wry smile. "We are an odd-sorted family, I fear."

Claudia could feel sympathy for him but not empathy, for her own experience was far happier. "So are we in our way. My eldest half-sister, Corrinna, was born when I was nearly seventeen. But my stepfather, Mr. Maverly, has been very much a father to me since he and my mother married.''

"You were fortunate," he said, echoing her own thought. "I hold no grudge against Alicia. When she married my father, she was just eighteen, very pretty, very fashionable, very spoiled, and certainly not prepared to find herself the mother of a man who was already a year older than she and a seven-year-old who, I fear, did not show her a proper respect." A mischievous light danced in his eyes and Claudia could well imagine him as a boy inclined to tease and not take his new young stepmother very seriously.

"David was already at Oxford," he continued, "and everyone was really quite relieved when Aunt Jane proposed that I live with her and Uncle Henry until it was time for me to go off to Eton. I've more or less been there ever since.''

He sat upright. "There is a point to this, Miss Tavener. My uncle died the year before my father, leaving my aunt virtually all his considerable fortune with a vague provision in his will that she should see to it that I was provided for. No doubt he deemed more unnecessary, for it has always been told to me quite plainly that I was to be my aunt's heir, since she has no issue of her own. But it is a legacy of affection, for there is no legal binder and my aunt may leave her blunt to whomever she pleases.''

A faint caustic note crept into his voice, and Claudia's quick mind leapt to an inevitable conclusion. "You mean she is threatening to leave her money to someone else?'' she asked. "How unjust.''

"Perhaps, but as I have said, I have no real claim on her fortune. My mother was her youngest sister, but she has another sister and two brothers, and hence other nieces and nephews.''

"Is it one of these who is cutting you out?''

He was pleased at her quick perception. "In a manner of speaking. My cousin Andrew Stonor, who is Earl of Strait, is quite well heeled and has no need of our aunt's fortune, but he may be recipient of it by default. My godmother has decided that two-and-thirty is too old to still be racketing about town and that it is time for me to choose a bride and be married, and more, I am commanded to fall in love with her as well. Nothing less will please her, she claims.'' He flashed her a quick, ironic smile. "Not unnaturally, I balked at having my life so ordered for me, and so now I live under the threat of disinheritance.''

"But why would she leave her fortune to your cousin if he has no need of it?''

A sardonic light came into his eyes. "Because she knew that I would find that most intolerable. Drew and I are, I trust, both reasonable men of amiable temperament, but together we are oil and water. It has been so since we were boys; Aunt Jane declares that we glared at each other in our cradles. My memory is not that complete, but I am willing to accept the truth of it.''

Claudia was caught up in his history and had all but forgotten her suspicions of him. ''That is infamous,'' she said, outraged. ''It is manipulation and emotional blackmail of the worst sort.''

''I quite agree. That is why I have made no push to comply with her demands, but now it is become exceedingly likely that if I do not do so, I shall indeed lose what, I regretfully admit, I have become arrogant enough to regard as all but mine. I am distressed to discover it, but I seem to possess sufficient avarice to want to do what I can to prevent any of my relatives from cutting me out. Drew, it appears, is on the verge of contracting an eligible alliance, and Aunt Jane has declared that when the banns have been called, she will make them a present of a settlement and secure her fortune to their issue if I do not come to heel by then. If she really does so, she likely will stand by it, even if she feels cause to regret it later. She has a dislike of admitting error.''

Claudia picked up her wineglass and absently sipped at the claret. Her brow was creased as she tried to imagine what any of this, interesting as she found it, could possibly have to do with her. ''But how can you be expected to fall in love with someone simply because you have been ordered to do so?''

Lindsay laughed. ''How, indeed? To speak with perfect frankness, Miss Tavener, I fear I am something of a cold fish, at least in terms of the gentler emotions. I have never been in love, to my knowledge, or at least I have never been laid low by the thunderbolt the poets speak of. And frankly, at two-and-thirty, I have come to doubt I ever shall be. The proposal I am about to make you is one of a purely business nature.'' Lindsay finished the wine in his glass, refilled it, and topped Claudia's glass. This time she made no objection. He knew her curiosity was rampant and he performed his actions with slow deliberation to draw out suspense as far as possible.

His words leant themselves to an obvious interpretation, but it was so incredible to Claudia that she still could not credit it. "What is your proposal, my lord?" she asked, unable to curb her impatience.

He reached across the table and took one of her hands in his. His eyes sparkled with an inner amusement. "Will you do me the honor of becoming my wife, Miss Tavener?"

Not even hearing the words from his mouth caused her to completely believe them. "You are absurd—or castaway," she said with a darkling glance at the level of wine in the bottle.

Lindsay shook his head. "Neither. I am making you a perfectly reasonable, honorable offer."

"Reasonable? We have only just met." She pulled her hand free of his. "Even if I were to listen to you, you would never be able to convince your aunt that ours was a love match."

He shrugged slightly. "I think between us we are clever enough to overcome that difficulty. I see you are not persuaded. Then let us play again, Miss Tavener, for a far greater stake."

Claudia's brows shot up. "Marriage? You cannot be serious."

"Perfectly serious." He took out his purse again and counted out ten hundred-pound notes and spread them on the table between them. "I made an excellent wager on the outcome of yesterday's boxing match. If you best me again at piquet, my winnings shall be yours. If I win, you marry me."

"You are mad," she said with an unsteady laugh.

He shook his head. He was pleased that at the least she had not rejected him out of hand. "It isn't really a mad idea if you look at it logically. We both find ourselves in difficulties that might readily be solved if we were to marry."

"Your difficulties might be solved. My only immediate problem was resolved when I won thirty-five pounds from you at piquet."

"But what about your greatest difficulty? You are still young, Miss Tavener. Do you mean to waste the next thirty or so years of your life fending off the Bingerleys you will work for and being subservient to vulgar cats like La

Ramsett? I know I'm not a grand match or anything like it, but even without my aunt's fortune I am far from a pauper, and I'm a decent-enough sort of fellow, ask anyone who knows me.''

In a way his suggestion was as outrageous as if he were offering her carte blanche, but she was surprised to discover that she was not ready to dismiss it without consideration. A thousand pounds was a great deal of money, more than she would make as a governess over several years of probably thankless labor, and it would be sufficient to ease all of the most pressing of her family's financial difficulties.

He was a good-enough player that she could not be entirely assured of winning, but she did not doubt the odds were in her favor. The consequence of losing, though, was an equally high stake. Lindsay Alistair seemed an amiable, even-tempered, well-bred man with considerable address and a ready humor, but she had known him for only a few hours and knew she could not really gauge his character from what she had observed in so short a time. It was unthinkable that she might find herself pledged to marry a man who was a virtual stranger.

He saw plainly in her expression that a battle waged within her. ''If you win, you have a thousand pounds, Miss Tavener,'' he said, pressing his point. ''With that you may assist your family and have the leisure to remain with them for a time while you secure another position more to your advantage. If you do not win, I still think you could not be said to lose completely. My godmother will certainly settle a generous amount on us and I will make you a handsome allowance, which you may use as you please for your family or yourself. Either way, your circumstances must certainly improve.''

Claudia knew she should reject his offer, but she found she could not bring herself to do it. She had proven herself the better player, and even if he were more cautious in his bidding this time, she felt she still had a better-than-even chance of winning. Her father had taught her always to play the odds.

''Come, Miss Tavener,'' he said, a coaxing note in his

voice. "You bested me the first time, but now I have more at stake, as do you. Let us see who is truly the better player."

Once again the blood of Charles Tavener stirred within his daughter's veins. She could almost hear her father's voice telling her that chance begat opportunity. She had faith in her skill and confidence that she had an excellent chance to best him again.

Lindsay resumed his slouching position and returned his attention to his wine, as if, having stated his offer, he regarded her acceptance or rejection of it with indifference. But there were depths to this man that were barely hinted at in the easy, open manner he affected, which intrigued Claudia in spite of her suspicions and fixed resolve to keep him at a proper distance.

She found she very much wanted to match her skill and wit against his, and she shut out the voice of sense that informed her she had already behaved imprudently enough for one day. "Very well," she said, accepting his challenge. "But I have conditions of my own that must be met if I agree to play for the stakes you suggest."

He showed no visible sign of pleasure at her capitulation. He nodded with uncharacteristic graveness and invited her to continue.

"If I lose—and I don't expect I shall—I shall marry you, but it will be a marriage in name only. If you wish for heirs, my lord, you had best find someone else to make your offer to. Do you agree?"

He bit at his lower lip, carefully considering his answer. He had meant what he said about having no designs on her virtue. He had a comfortable liaison with an obliging matron in Bath, and Claudia, in any case, was not in his usual style. Yet there was something about her that had piqued his interest in a way that was, he was aware, not entirely platonic. "If we are married, I promise not to make love to you unless you wish me to do so," he said, amending her condition.

Claudia's brows rose. "Do you imagine I shall come to wish it?"

He sat up and picked up one of the decks to reshuffle it. His smile was sleepy and his voice unconcerned. "Possibly not. Since you do not intend to lose, it hardly matters.''

His tone was perfectly bland and his eyes held no hint of the mockery she was sure was behind his words. If anything it made her eager to win his money and put him in his place. ''We would have to think up some plausible tale to tell my family as well as yours. I would die of mortification if my mother or stepfather even guessed at what I had done.''

''How do you intend to explain the thousand pounds if you win?''

''I don't know, but I trust I shall think of something.''

''So shall we if I win. Let the play begin, Miss Tavener,'' he said, and handed her the first deck.

Once again she won the cut for the deal and she did not bother to conceal her satisfaction. This, though, proved short-lived. A change—subtle at first and then more pronounced—became apparent in her opponent from the moment the declarations began. Even the now-familiar quality of his voice was altered as his habitual fashionable drawl gave way to a more clipped pronunciation. He won the first hand, not with ease, but by a safe margin, and Claudia taxed her skill to the utmost to win the second and third, but these were the last of her victories.

His bidding was still bold, but this time there were no errors in judgment; nearly every card he played was true. As his skill became manifest, Claudia, disliking to take unnecessary risks, turned instead to greater caution, and this in the end proved her undoing. More than once she saw that his choice of cards was merely bluff and that if she had only allowed herself to be a bit more daring, she might have taken the trick. The game seemed endless to her, and when the score was tallied, she had gained only ninety-six points. Rubiconned.

She met his eyes as he informed her of this. There was no teasing smile there, and no hint of triumph in his countenance. He regarded her almost without expression as he idly reshuffled the cards. He was waiting to see what she would say or do next.

Women were not held to the bonds of honor as men were; she knew that if she manifested her anger and dismay at her loss and refused to make good on the wager, it would probably neither astonish nor disgust him. Yet, even in the shock of realizing that she had indeed lost the wager and the enormity of what that meant to her, she knew she could not go back on her promise. Along with teaching her the skill she possessed at cards, Charles Tavener had inculcated in his daughter the belief that gaming debts were the most sacred of all and were never to be forfeited. Pay or play: those were his bywords.

She swallowed uncomfortably, her mouth suddenly gone dry, and said quietly, "Did you do this on purpose?"

"Win, do you mean?" he asked, his voice once again slipping into a drawl. "Yes. Of course I did."

"I meant did you let me win the first time so that I would underestimate you and believe I could do it again?"

A faint smile reappeared in his eyes. "No. Not really. Let us say rather that I didn't play with as much care at first, but I warned you I had a greater stake this time."

"But when you suggested that we play again for . . . for the wager you suggested," she said, not quite able to verbally acknowledge that she had promised to marry him, "you knew you would be able to win this time, didn't you?"

"I believed it was possible but not certain. You really are exceptionally good, you know. But perhaps in your circumstances you don't often have the opportunity to have your skill really tested. That tends to make one a little complacent, I think."

"I was certainly that if I didn't recognize a Captain Sharp when I met one," Claudia said hotly.

"Do you mean me?" he said, laughing. "Not a bit of it. I've been fleeced myself in my salad days and I assure you I'm no match for the ivory turners."

"You deliberately set me up," she insisted. "Did you plan it the moment you realized I was unprotected?"

He put down the cards and looked directly at her. "No," he said, "I did not. I didn't even know you played piquet then. My first suggestion to play was impulse, Miss Tavener, to assist you if I could, since you wouldn't take my help in a more straightforward way. The second offer was certainly by design, but I have won aided by luck not deception. As the daughter of a gamester, there should be nothing at all anyone could tell you about the vagaries of luck. Do you pay or not?''

It was several moments before Claudia could trust herself to answer him with a clear controlled voice. "I pay," she said, spitting out the words at him.

He more than half-expected her to refuse and felt confirmed that his decision to make her his offer was not as ill-judged as even he had begun to fear it. "Then tomorrow we shall journey to London to procure a special license," he said, unperturbed by her anger and accusations. "I'm afraid we haven't the leisure for a protracted betrothal."

Claudia had had no idea he meant to collect on the debt so quickly and would have protested heatedly, but the discussion was able to go no further. Mrs. Braggs came into the common room, at last interrupting their *tête-à-tête*. She cast Claudia a look that left Claudia in no doubt the landlady felt certain that her first judgment of her had been correct. Proper young women did not racket about the countryside unescorted, and they certainly didn't spend the evening dining and playing cards with strange gentlemen in the common room of an inn. Claudia wondered ironically to what depths Mrs. Braggs would consign her character if she knew what manner of stakes they had been playing for.

"It's well past midnight, my lord. We'll be closin' up the public rooms and goin' to bed now, if you don't mind." She turned another baleful gaze on Claudia and added, "I've made so bold as to prepare a bedchamber for you, miss. You'll be wantin' it, I suppose."

There was something in her voice that suggested to Claudia the landlady suspected that Claudia and Lindsay had intended to spend the night together. Claudia felt herself flush at the implication, however unjust. "Of course," she said coldly. "Please have my portmanteau taken up, and I shall join you there shortly."

"I could show you the way now, miss, if you please," the landlady said implacably.

Claudia had a great many things she would have liked to

have said to Lindsay, but saw that she would have to swallow her bile at least temporarily. She favored the landlady with a curt nod and rose from the table.

"Sleep well, Miss Tavener," Lindsay said with irritating sweetness. "Until tomorrow, then."

"Good night, my lord," Claudia replied between nearly clenched teeth, and followed Mrs. Braggs to a small bed-chamber at the back of the house, well away, she suspected, from wherever Lindsay's room was situated.

# 2

The room in which Claudia spent the night was somewhat small, but quite comfortable, a far cry from the cowshed in which she had imagined she might be forced to sleep. But she found little rest despite the comfort of her bed. In her mind she replayed over and over again all that had passed between her and Lord Lindsay Alistair since their meeting, sometimes merely savoring the events of the evening to feed her anger and at other times editing them to what she might have said or done to avoid the predicament she was now in.

In the end she gained a sort of resignation. Whatever her suspicions concerning Lindsay's duplicity, he had not forced her to accept the wager—for that she could blame no one but herself and her greed for his thousand pounds.

Once she had accepted her situation, her thoughts turned to making it more palatable. She could not disagree with Lindsay's brutal summary of her career as a governess, nor his predictions for her future in that occupation. It was a bleakness that she rarely acknowledged to herself, but she was not unaware of it. There were so few occupations open to a wellborn female who did not marry that it was a choice of evils for most, not a picking and choosing of circumstances.

Not that Claudia had never had any hope of marriage. She had had two offers to be exact, but the first was from a neighbor, a widower twenty years her senior who wore corsets that creaked and whose ample breast was always liberally dusted with flakes of snuff. The other was from the eldest son of Squire Bandworthy, a very respectable match except that he stammered and had no conversation except dogs and horses. Mrs. Maverly had been upset when Claudia had rebuffed his suit, but there was little doubt that the Bandworthys were considerably relieved that their son had not chosen a dowerless girl for his bride despite her highborn connections.

Claudia really had no great concern about concocting a story her mother would not find suspicious. Mrs. Maverly's chief ambition in life was to see all of her children settled as befitted their station in life, and she had never truly accepted Claudia's decision to become a governess. Not only her mother but her stepfather as well would probably be so relieved that she was respectably settled that they would question nothing she told them too closely.

By the time she finally fell into a fitful sleep, Claudia felt almost philosophical. She had no reason to believe that Lindsay was an ogre beneath his amiable exterior, and there was no doubt that, materially at least, her life would be far more comfortable. She was prepared to take him at his word that he did not possess strong emotions, and his acceptance of her conditions made her feel that it would be agreeable and safe to be married to a man who would make no demands on her.

Though there was much still for them to discuss, she would enact him no scenes at breakfast. Since she meant to pay, she would do so with a good grace and make it as comfortable for them both as she could.

Lindsay, too, was subject to his own ruminations, though he saved his for the morning and slept well and rose early. He had not had an undue amount to drink the previous night, but in the light of day he questioned the effect on him of what he had drunk. He could not satisfactorily explain to himself why he had done what he had. His aunt's threats to disinherit him were certainly cause for concern, but surely not desperation. Yet he had made an offer of marriage to a young woman he had known only a few hours. He would not have described himself as being in the petticoat line and was not given much to practiced gallantry, but there was something about Claudia's vulnerability that had touched him and made him wish to rescue her. His offer had done just that, and the double duty of solving his predicament as well.

He did not precisely regret it nor wish to cancel Claudia's debt to him, but he would not have been human not to have had doubts. He hoped that these would be allayed when they met again in the cold, sober light of day. He was conscious of an empathic attraction between them and doubted that the promise he had made to Claudia would need to be kept indefinitely. His act had been purely impulsive, but he did not think he was sorry for the consequences of it; he might have done considerably worse choosing from the more usual display of eligible females in the Marriage Mart.

When Claudia was shown into the private parlor he had engaged for their breakfast, she saw there was a guardedness, an expectancy in his tone and expression that told her that he still wondered if she would keep her word. Seen by daylight instead of candlelight, Lindsay seemed even more of a stranger to her. He was as elegantly attired as he had been the night before making Claudia painfully aware of the dowdiness of her plain dark gray cotton governess dress. But he bid her good morning with a friendly smile and a warmth in his eyes and voice that calmed at least some of her anxiety.

While the waiter was hovering over them, seeing that they were properly served with all they desired, their conversation was general and impersonal. As soon as he was gone, Lindsay asked her plainly, "Do you still come with me to London this morning, Miss Tavener?"

"I said I would pay, my lord," Claudia replied, but mildly and, in contrast to her response the previous night, ungrudgingly.

"I'm glad of it," he said, surprised himself that he truly meant it.

Conversation lagged for a bit as they applied themselves to their breakfast, and Claudia, who was beginning to feel the silence between them lengthening, was glad when Lindsay brought it to an end by saying, "It is to Lovewell House that we are going, by the way."

"To your family?" she said, feeling daunted at the prospect.

"To my brother. I have lodgings in town, but I can't take you there and we need somewhere to stay until we tie the knot. Do you dislike the notion?" Lindsay asked, hearing her dismay. "David can be a bit of a turnip-sucker at times, but on the whole he's a decent-enough sort of fellow."

"He is a what?" asked Claudia, unfamiliar with the cant expression.

Lindsay grinned. "Turnip-sucker. He's a bit prosy and starched up and rather impressed at being the eighth Marquess of Lovewell, but whenever he gets too high in the instep, Vivian brings him down a peg or two and keeps him in line."

"And who is Vivian?"

"His wife. She's my cousin as well as my sister-in-law, and a right 'un. I was in love with her myself once and nearly called David out when he offered for her. It was Viv who pointed out to me that it wasn't at all the thing to go about putting holes in one's own brother. You'll like Vivian."

"Shall I?" Claudia said without noticeable enthusiasm.

"Are you thinking that there might be something havey-cavey going on between us?" he asked, smiling. "There isn't. It was no more than calf love. I was introduced to a delightful little opera dancer about that time and made a cake of myself over her instead."

"I thought you weren't in the petticoat line," Claudia said.

"I'm not. At least, not like some fellows. I quite enjoy the company of women, but my worst enemy wouldn't call me a rake."

"What *do* your friends call you?" she asked waspishly.

Devils danced behind his eyes. "Impulsive," he said, deadpan. Claudia could not help laughing and he smiled again. "That's better. If we arrive at Lovewell House with Friday faces, no one will believe that we have fallen victim to a grand passion."

"Is that what we've done?"

"Well, we shall have to tell them something of the sort," he replied over the rim of his coffeecup. "If we are not to land in the suds with my aunt, we shall have to be consistent."

"I am not convinced we shall deceive your aunt at all," Claudia retorted. "She will never believe our match is not contrived if we marry at once. Who would be fool enough to marry someone one had known for no more than the space of an evening?" she added with dry self-mockery.

"My dear girl," he said as if shocked. "Of course we shan't tell anyone that. We shall say that we had met sometime ago and have had a private understanding. We shall stick to the truth whenever possible. We met when I paid a visit to my good friend—what was the name of that excrescence who tried to seduce you?"

"Your good friend Mr. Bingerley."

"Yes. Dear old Fred."

"George."

He cast her a quick quelling frown. "Bingerley is known as Fred to his intimates. I first set eyes on you when you brought the children to the drawing room to be admired after dinner and I was bowled over at once."

"Nonsense," she exclaimed. "No one will ever believe that. I am not the sort of female who bowls men over."

"But then you are not acquainted with my tastes," he said severely. "Besides, you do yourself an injustice. If you didn't wear your hair like my mother's dresser and wear gowns better suited to a housemaid, I daresay you'd be quite presentable."

"Thankin' you, kindly, m'lord," she said in the accents of a housemaid. "Your lordship is too kind, I'm sure."

He gave her a dazzling smile. "Not a bit of it. That's another reason for staying with David and Vivian for a bit. Viv will take you to her mantua maker and you'll look fine as a five-pence in a sennight. Do you think our story will fadge with your family? I really do think we need to be consistent."

"It will have to answer, I suppose," Claudia replied after a reflective moment.

"Very well, heart of my hearts," Lindsay said, pushing his chair back from the table, "I'll order my horses put to. If we leave now, we'll make London in good time for dinner." He got up to ring for the waiter and turned again to Claudia. "By the by, I think we had better begin the habit of addressing each other by our Christian names. We shall certainly fool no one if you 'my lord' me with every sentence."

Claudia agreed, though the intimacy made her a little uncomfortable. But she realized that it was the first and mildest of many she would have to endure now that the payment of her debt had begun, and she resigned herself to it.

Claudia had assumed that they would travel to London in a private chaise, but when she stepped out of the inn into the courtyard some twenty minutes later, it was a curricule, light and of racing design, with a pair of matched chestnuts attached that awaited her. Lindsay had donned a drab driving coat with a moderate number of capes, and as he stood beside his curricle waiting for her, she thought he looked like an engraving from one of the publications on fashionable life to which Mrs. Bingerley assiduously subscribed. She felt a brief wave of panic at the prospect of finding herself thrust into Lindsay's fashionable world.

He handed her into the carriage with a quick reassuring smile, as if he had read her thoughts, and climbed in beside her, calling to the ostler to stand away from the leader's head. It was apparent to Claudia at once that Lindsay had every right to wear the attire affected by first-rate whips, his driving skill was obviously considerable. As they came to a long, straight stretch, Lindsay expertly flicked the leader on the ear and caught the point on the upward swing of the whip, which even Claudia was aware was a skill reserved only to those that her brother, William, would have called a top sawyer.

Most of their journey was accomplished at a quick pace. Conversation was desultory, Lindsay being preoccupied with his driving and Claudia with her thoughts, and they reached the great metropolis in excellent time. She had not been to London since she and her mother had left to live with Mr.

Maverly in Woodstock, and she could not help being fascinated by the myriad sights and sounds in spite of her nervousness at meeting Lindsay's brother and his wife. Yet all too soon she found herself in front of the portal of Lovewell House, the adventure she had embarked upon very much a reality.

Claudia did like Vivian. Lady Lovewell was an attractive blonde with enormous blue eyes and an amiable disposition not unlike Lindsay's. She had heard their arrival and came running down the stairs as her butler ushered them into the house.

As soon as Lindsay made Claudia known to her, Vivian impulsively hugged her and heartily welcomed her to the family. "I do love a surprise, particularly such a delightful one," she said, unwittingly nonplussing Claudia by her unquestioning acceptance of a complete stranger as her brother-in-law's intended wife. "What a wretched creature you are, Lindsay, to keep her secret even from me. I won't pester you now when you are probably vaporish about meeting Lindsay's family for the first time," she added, linking her arm in Claudia's, "but later we shall have a comfortable cose and you shall tell me every delicious detail of your meeting and courtship. It is so wonderfully romantic. My own history is quite mundane, though I love David dearly. We are cousins and we have known each other all our lives."

Claudia cast a beseeching glance at Lindsay, who was standing a little aside from them. He grinned in response, understanding her fear of being questioned by Vivian about their nonexistent history, and gallantly came to her rescue. "Handsomely over the bricks, Viv," he said to his cousin. "We'll both be happy to satisfy your taste for the romantic, but you're not to overwhelm Claud with a lot of silly questions. She's not used to dealing with rattles like you and will probably cry off before the wedding if she thinks she's going to have to put up with a scatterhead for a sister-in-law."

Vivian took predictable exception to this and delivered an equally unflattering opinion of his character before she realized they were standing in the middle of the hall in the earshot of her butler and two footmen. She laughed at herself for being so easily drawn and informed Lindsay that he was an odious man. Then she gave instructions to have the house-keeper prepare rooms for Lindsay and Claudia and drew them into a spacious saloon to wait while her orders were carried out.

"It is too bad that David is from home," Vivian said as she poured glasses of restorative sherry for Claudia and heself and Madeira for her brother-in-law. "He will be as surprised and delighted as I am. We have both quite despaired of Lindsay ever settling down to an ordered life. May I call you Claudia? I see no point in getting used to Miss Tavener when soon it won't even be your name any longer."

"Sooner than you may think," Lindsay informed her as he folded his tall frame into a comfortable wing chair near the hearth. "I'm going to procure a special license and we shall be wed before the end of the week, if I can contrive it."

Vivian's large eyes became quite round. "But such haste! It is unseemly, Lindsay. People will think that . . ." She broke off, her fair complexion becoming rosy. "Oh, I beg your pardon. I did not mean . . ."

Claudia did not understand Vivian's obvious embarrass-ment at first, but was enlightened by Lindsay's frankly ribald laughter.

"Save your blushes, Viv," he advised her, flashing Claudia a quick, ironic smile. "It is merely impatience, not necessity."

"Thank goodness," Vivian said with a relieved sigh. "No one ever really believes the stories that are made up about vague wedding dates or early births. You should not let Lindsay persuade you also into such a helter-skelter wedding," she advised Claudia. "Men must be taught to curb their impatience from the start, or there is no containing them later. They attempt to have their own way in all things, and it is much harder later to maintain a firm hand."

"Is that what you do with my brother?" Lindsay asked with interest.

"It is what every sensible woman does," Vivian informed him. "I think a wedding in a month or so would be ideal.

You would have time to shop for your bride clothes, Claudia, and perhaps I could even give a small betrothal party for family and a few friends. Would your family come from Oxfordshire, do you think? We have so much room here we could accommodate them easily—''

"Before you start planning the wedding breakfast, Viv," Lindsay interrupted, "you should know that we have quite made up our minds to be married by special license by the end of the week; Claudia wishes it as much as I do," he added, taking Claudia's hand in his and placing a gentle kiss on her palm. "Isn't that so, my love?"

"Yes, it is," Claudia replied obediently, but his sudden loverlike behavior made her uncomfortable.

"I suppose you may choose for yourself," Vivian allowed handsomely. "If you are so set on it, I won't tease you. But if you are to be with us for a sennight, at least we shall have the time to become better acquainted, Claudia. I really do want us to be friends."

"So do I," Claudia responded, thinking that it was the first sincere emotion she had expressed since arriving at Lovewell House.

"What I want you to do, Vivian," Lindsay said, "is to take Claudia to Madame Céleste or whichever modiste you think would suit her best and have a few things made up for her as soon as possible. Offer whatever sum you think necessary for the haste and have the bills sent to me. We'll be going to Aunt Jane when we leave here and I don't want to present Claudia dressed like a dashed governess." He fingered a fold of the gray cotton as he spoke and regarded it with distaste.

"I have been a governess for three years," Claudia reminded him tartly, pulling the material of her skirt more closely around her, "and have had little use for fashionable gowns."

"But now you shall. We shal have such great fun shopping together, Claudia," Vivian said with delight. "And I shall introduce you to all of my friends and you will cut a dash and be the toast of the town. You are so very pretty you are sure to have cicisbei by the dozen."

Claudia laughed, unable to resist Vivian's infectious enthusiasm. "I thank you for the pretty compliment, but I confess you terrify me. I have always lived very quietly, you know."

"Which is why we are going to spend the Season at Bath instead of in town," Lindsay put in. "Bath is rather thin of company at this time of year, but enough of the polite world is in residence for Claudia to get a taste of society before she is thrust into the rigors of the *ton* in London or Brighton."

"One member who is in residence in Bath is my illustrious brother," Vivian said, and when Lindsay raised an inquiring brow, she continued, "He is nursing a bruised heart, he claims. The exquisite Miss Merrifield has finally tossed her cap over the windmill, but not in his direction. She is to wed the Marquess of Hartleigh at the end of June."

"Really?" said Lindsay in apparent surprise. "Aunt Jane led me to believe that it was all but a settled thing between Drew and Miss Merrifield."

"Very likely she did," agreed Vivian, laughter in her eyes. "But you know how she is forever pestering you to find a wife and give up your unsettled bachelor existence; she probably thought it would be a spur to you to do so as well. How delighted our aunt will be with you, Claudia."

"I hope she may be," Claudia said.

She and Lindsay exchanged glances. Claudia felt a knot form in her stomach as she realized that they were speaking of Lord Strait and that the impetus for Lindsay to marry immediately had been removed. Now that they had come this far, it would be no easy thing for them to simply abandon their plans, or at least not without making it obvious that their intent had been to deceive from the start.

After a few minutes more a maid arrived to inform them that their rooms were ready, and Vivian walked with Claudia to hers, chattering all the while about modistes and milliners. Claudia scarcely heard her as she turned over in her mind what Lindsay must be thinking since he had heard the news that his cousin was not to be wed, after all. Lindsay mounted the stairs behind them, and when she and Vivian reached the top, she managed to turn and catch his eye before Vivian led her to her bedchamber.

Vivian would have gone into the room with Claudia, but Lindsay caught her arm and moved her aside. "Claudia needs time to recover from your onslaught, chatterbox," he said in a firm voice. "You can exchange confidences tonight after dinner while David and I try to drink each other under the table."

"Thank you, Vivian," Claudia said warmly, holding out her hand to the marchioness. "I admit that I was a little frightened that you might not think our surprise a pleasant one, but you have made me feel very welcome and accepted."

They exchanged a brief hug and Claudia went into the bedchamber.

Lindsay started to follow her and this time he was admonished by Vivian. "You are not married yet," she said sternly.

"Near enough to keep our friends from counting on their fingers," he retorted, and firmly closed the door on her.

"That was a look of appeal you cast me on the stair if ever I have seen one," he said as he went over to Claudia, who stood before the dressing table turning over a small porcelain jar with a crystal stopper.

"What are we to do now, my lord?" she said, putting down the jar and turning to him.

He sighed with exasperation. "I thought we were agreed, my precious, that you would not address me as my lord."

"That hardly matters if we are not to be married, after all," Claudia said impatiently.

He was nonplussed into a momentary silence. "Why are we not to be married, after all?"

"Where is the need if your cousin's suit has failed? Now you may take your time and perhaps find someone with whom you need not dissemble a love match."

"Are you reneging, Miss Tavener?" he said with deliberate formality after another brief silence.

Claudia was uncertain of her own motives. Perhaps she was grasping at an opportunity to back out of her promise to him, but she wouldn't admit it. "I thought you would wish it, now that the urgency for you to marry is at an end."

His expression was grave, but the smile crept back into his eyes. "A wager is a wager, Miss Tavener. I hold you to it."

Claudia felt a slight stab of disappointment, but perversely she also had a conflicting sense of relief. "I shall honor my debt, my lord," she said stiffly.

"Lindsay," he said with a quick smile, and left her.

The bedchamber that Vivian had had prepared for Claudia was quite beautiful, decorated in shades of blue and cream, and was certainly far grander than any Claudia had called her own before. A few minutes later a young serving girl arrived and informed her that her name was Mary and that she was to be her maid if she gave satisfaction, and Claudia also enjoyed the luxury of a personal servant for the first time in her life.

She found the additional luxuries of a hot bath brought to her room, having her hair dressed for her, and not having to struggle with the tiny buttons at the back of her dress quite delightful, and rebuked herself for the easy way she was prepared to fall into such comforts as if she had enjoyed them all of her life. This was doubtless why she had not been as anxious as she had thought she would be for an opportunity to cry off from her marriage to Lindsay; payment, it would seem, was not to be all on her side.

Vivian had been dressed in an exquisite spotted muslin, obviously made by the hands of an expert seamstress, and Claudia was more acutely aware than ever of her own dowdy wardrobe. She knew without Lindsay to tell her that the plain gowns she had worn as a governess would never be presentable in the circles in which she would likely move as Lady Lindsay Alistair. She was not entirely comfortable with the notion that she would be beholden to Lindsay even for her dresses, but there was no help for it if she was not to appear in public looking like a dowd.

After her bath she allowed Mary to assist her into her best gown, a pale-lilac silk trimmed with delicate embroidery at the neckline and hem—pretty, but woefully out of style. Mary also modified Claudia's usual severe style of dressing her hair by framing her face with a few softly curling tendrils, and Claudia's mirror told her she was presentable, even pretty, but she knew she still could not compare to the fashionable marchioness.

Vivian came to her bedchamber to take Claudia down to dinner, and as they approached the small saloon where the family gathered before dinner, voices were heard emanating clearly from the open door. One was soft, an indistinct murmur, but the other carried and was quite clear.

"Well, if it isn't all a hum, Lin," said that voice, "then why such haste? You tell me she's not up the spout, so the only other thing it could be is that you're finally giving Aunt Jane what she wants to secure your inheritance. I can't say I blame you, but you might have done a great deal better for yourself if you'd picked one of the pretty young things that Vivian has been casting in your way the past couple of Seasons. You have an obligation to the bloodlines as much as I do. Her breeding is good enough, I suppose, but Tavener was a bit of a loose screw, you know. He left his family all to pieces and some said . . ." The voice broke off abruptly, interrupted again by Lindsay's more modulated tones.

There was no pretending they hadn't heard, and Vivian, with great aplomb, gave Claudia a smile that managed to be both apologetic and encouraging. "You must not mind David," she said sotto voce. "He suffers quite a bit from gout, poor dear, and it has sadly affected his temper."

Claudia doubted the insults Lord Lovewell had leveled at her father had anything to do with his gout, but she returned Vivian's smile to show that she did not mean to be offended. They went into the room. Claudia's color was becomingly high as Lindsay presented her to Lord Lovewell. There was a distinct resemblance between Lindsay and his brother, but David Lovewell was obviously quite a few years older than both his wife and Lindsay.

Any guilt she felt for deceiving his family vanished under the cool, speculative stare of the marquess, whose brief smile as he bowed over her hand never reached his eyes. "Miss Tavener," Lovewell said formally, his resonant voice only slightly clearer than it had been when it had carried into the hall. "Lindsay has told me that you are soon to be one of us. As head of the Alistair family, permit me to welcome you."

"I am so pleased that you approve, my lord," Claudia said with more than a trace of irony.

Lovewell's eyes remained expressionless and she couldn't tell if he understood her intent, for the smile he gave her was as cool as his tone had been, but she saw an amused gleam in Lindsay's expressive eyes and felt encouraged.

"*I* could not be more pleased with your choice, dear Lindsay," Vivian said with considerable heartiness. "Claudia and I already deal famously together. I have always wanted a sister, but unkind fate has given me only a brother. The Alistairs have run only to boys for generations, and alas, David and I continue the tradition."

Vivian went on in a light vein to speak of her three sons and her hope that Claudia would soon be able to meet the young Alistairs, who remained at their estate, Landgrove, to continue their lessons while their parents were in town for the Season, and in this way any possible unpleasantness or awkwardness was averted.

Vivian took Lindsay's arm when they went into dinner, and Claudia was left with the marquess for support.

"You are quite a surprise to us, Miss Tavener," he said with a sidelong glance and another chilly smile. "I had no idea my brother possessed such a romantic nature."

"No. Why should you?" she said with a guileless smile as she accepted her place at the table.

The marquess gave her a sharp look, but he only said, "Of course you would know best," and took his own seat.

Dinner was surprisingly pleasant, with Vivian and Lindsay making the effort to keep Claudia involved in their family conversation and in the process giving her a deal of information about members she had yet to meet. The evening might have passed with unimpaired agreeableness if the talk in this vein had not inevitably led to discussion of the Earl of Strait.

"Did Vivian tell you that Drew wears the willow for Miss

Merrifield,'' David asked his brother. "It's a great pity she didn't make up her mind in a more timely fashion," he added in a pointed way.

Claudia kept her eyes on her plate, but she felt a faint warmth steal into her cheeks. David no doubt knew of Lady Ellacott's threats to disinherit Lindsay if Lord Strait were to marry before him.

Whether or not Vivian understood him as well as Claudia did, she made matters smooth by saying, "Certainly it would have prevented Andrew from making a cake of himself over the girl. Do you know, Lin, he actually went to Lady Treves' masquerade dressed up as a shepherd because Miss Merrifield told him she was going as a shepherdess? Drew looked the most shocking quiz imaginable."

"I wouldn't waste too much sympathy on Strait," Lindsay said dryly. "He's imagined himself in love with a half-dozen chits in as many years, but somehow he's always managed to avoid parson's mousetrap. One wonders if it is not, after all, by design."

"Oh, I shouldn't think so, at least not this time," David said, pouring himself another liberal glass of claret. "I am sure he was as anxious for his suit with Miss Merrifield to prosper as you were yours with Claudia. It is a matter of incentive, is it not?"

There was such a mocking quality in his voice that not even Vivian could appear to misunderstand him this time. A silence fell over the table that lasted no more than a few moments, but it hung as heavy as if the moments were minutes. Claudia glanced at Lindsay, who was regarding his brother with a cold glitter in his eyes. Claudia had not imagined that the usually affable Lindsay could look so steely.

"It is a private matter altogether," Lindsay said with a barren smile that in no way mitigated the set-down.

"I do hope your mother and stepfather are pleased with the marriage, Claudia," Vivian said quickly before her husband could speak again.

It was not the most felicitous comment, for Claudia suddenly realized that she had not thought even to write to her mother and that her family no doubt believed her still at Bingerley Court. With her attention so given to the contention between Lindsay and his brother, her wits were not to the fore and she could not think what to say to Vivian in reply.

Lindsay came to her rescue. "We have every hope of it. We shall make a detour to Oxfordshire on our way to Bath and spend a night perhaps with the Maverlys to receive their blessing."

It was the first Claudia had heard of this, and she had no doubt that Lindsay had simply uttered the first reply that came into his head, but she hoped that they would go to Woodstock. It would be the logical thing for them to do—to go to her family as well as his.

Vivian then asked Claudia several questions about her brothers and sisters, and all dissension was put aside, if not entirely forgotten. Soon afterward the ladies retired from the table, and whatever occurred between the brothers after they had left them, Lindsay and David entered the drawing room about a half-hour later in perfect accord.

Lindsay was extremely attentive to Claudia for the remainder of the evening, even sitting so near to her on the sofa that she was made uncomfortable by it. Since she could scarcely move away from him without giving them the lie, she endured the intimacy, though she wondered if there were any point to their dissembling, since it was obvious that Lovewell didn't believe their story of a love match and she suspected that Vivian too had her doubts about them, despite seeming to accept their account at face value.

Encouraged by his brother—a bit caustically—to elaborate on the details of their history, Lindsay did so, improving with alarming glibness on the story he and Claudia had concocted at the Red Doe. Claudia listened to him as fascinated as Vivian, though she sincerely doubted she would remember half of Lindsay's fabrications if put to the test.

It was a tiring and uneasy evening for Claudia, and she was grateful when, shortly after they had drunk their tea, Vivian suggested that Claudia might be weary from journeying most of the day and wish to seek her bed. Claudia was only too happy to agree with her.

Vivian offered to walk with her to her bedchamber, and as Claudia rose, Lindsay stood with her and, to her astonishment, lightly embraced her and bestowed upon her a swift kiss that nevertheless managed to be quite intimate. It was the kiss of a lover, not of a friend. She felt an unexpected shock go through her that was not entirely due to surprise. Her eyes met his with unconcealed outrage; if they had been alone, Claudia would certainly have boxed his ears.

When they reached Claudia's bedchamber, Vivian said, "You must be well-rested tonight, Claudia. Tomorrow we shall visit Madame Céleste and a dozen other shops, and we shall have a great deal of fun spending Lindsay's money while we become better acquainted."

Claudia was not certain there would be any shopping expedition on the next day, but she wished Vivian a good night without further comment. Her weariness was consumed by her anger and she did not ring for Mary because she had no intention of undressing or going to bed until she had spoken with Lindsay however late the hour.

It was a considerable time before she heard the sounds of voices in the hall and then one set of steps continue on and a door across the hall open and close. Claudia knew that Lindsay had been given the room across from hers, and she went at once to tap lightly on the door, heedless of the impropriety of seeking him out in his bedchamber.

Lindsay opened it at once. He was still dressed, but he had removed his watch and fob and the pin from his cravat. He regarded her with mild surprise but stepped back to allow her to enter. "Is this wise, beloved?" he asked with spurious concern. "We've only a few more nights to pass before bliss is ours."

Claudia slipped into the room and then quietly but firmly shut the door behind her. "This may be a humorous matter to you, but to me it is offensive," Claudia said frigidly.

"Oh, surely I'm not as distasteful as all that," he protested.

"I think, my lord, that this farce has gone quite far

enough,'' she said, her voice rigid. "In the morning we will find some excuse to give Lord and Lady Lovewell and then I shall book a seat on the stage to take me to Oxfordshire.'' She at last had the satisfaction of claiming his full attention and all hint of humor was absent from his expression. She had not meant to speak so drastically, but his teasing fueled her rage and made her imprudent.

"If you did not mean to go through with this, you should have made that choice before we came here,'' he said levelly. "I wrote a letter before dinner to my godmother telling her of our impending marriage. If you back out now, you will be the ruin of me.''

"If you did not mean to keep your word to me,'' she retorted, "you should not be surprised that I consider our agreement null and void.''

His brow creased for a moment in puzzlement. "Do you mean because I kissed you good night in the drawing room?'' he asked with genuine surprise. "What of it? We are betrothed. A simple good-night kiss is hardly the prelude to a ravishment.''

"It was not a simple good-night kiss.''

In spite of the gravity of the situation, he could not help smiling. "Well, perhaps not,'' he admitted, "but as David and Vivian were both there to protect you from any onslaught I might have been tempted to make to your virtue, I think your concern is a bit overstated.''

Claudia was both annoyed and amused at his ready acknowledgment of his guilt, but she was far from appeased. "If this is how you keep your word to me on the first night we are together, and in front of your family, what may I expect when we are married and alone?''

He laughed with genuine amusement. "My dear girl, though I have no wish to deny your many attractions, I kissed you good night for the benefit of my brother, who is determined to disbelieve that there is any romantic attachment between us. It was a harmless embrace.''

"It was a liberty you had not my permission to take. It is clear you are not to be trusted, my lord.''

"Oh, come, Claudia,'' he said with an edge of exasperation

in his tone. "You *are* making much of nothing. I'm far from being an innocent, but I have never in my life forced myself on a woman. I prefer a willing partner."

"Then I have nothing to fear."

He smiled in a slow, infuriating manner. "Have a care, my love. I have a taste for challenge. But I don't go back on my word. I intend to be a pattern-card husband."

"You can't want to marry me any more than I want to marry you."

"Well, that depends," Lindsay said reasonably. "I don't know how much you don't want to marry me."

"It is the last thing on earth I wish to do," she replied, but her anger was dissipating and she knew she would not go back on her word either.

"Then you are mistaken," he said. "I can think of a number of other things that I would rather not do than marry you. Don't tease yourself, Claudia," he said, taking her hands in his. "It is only premarital vapors. Our marriage will greatly benefit us both and is an event to be looked forward to, not dreaded."

Claudia's ambivalence was still unresolved but she said reluctantly, "I suppose I must agree, my lord, but I have not your gift for philosophy."

"But at least you manage resignation. That is something." He bent his head and kissed her again, but in such a brotherly fashion that this time she could not object. "Good night, Miss Tavener. I promise you I won't allow you to regret it."

Claudia remained unconvinced of this, but she signified her agreement by a faint nod and then bid him good night. Contrary to her expectations, she fell asleep almost the moment she lay her head on the pillow, and she slept soundly and well until at last the chambermaid who brought her a morning cup of chocolate drew the bedcurtains to let in the bright April sun.

# 3

Claudia and Lindsay had arrived at Lovewell House on a Wednesday, and by Tuesday of the following week all the preparations for a quiet wedding by special license to take place in the chapel of St. George's were complete. Vivian had used whatever means of cajolery or bribery necessary to persuade Madame Céleste to make up three day dresses and two evening gowns, one of which would serve for the wedding, to carry Claudia over until she could visit Bath modistes with Lady Ellacott. Vivian insisted, though in the nicest way to give no offense, that Claudia give the dresses she had arrived with to the maids. Claudia was so far from offended that she very nearly voiced a doubt that any maid in a fashionable household would wish to be gifted with such drab garments.

Claudia felt she had never owned such beautiful things in all of her life. Even her cotton underwear and stockings were replaced with the finest silk and linen, making her feel quite decadent. Vivian's own dresser, Miss Stapley, who was very adept at dressing hair, cut and shaped Claudia's thick tresses into a more fashionable style, and by the eve of her wedding day, Claudia at last felt she looked like the intended bride of a man of fashion.

Lindsay expressed his admiration plainly and even Lord Lovewell's manner seemed warmer to her when he bowed over her hand as she entered the saloon with Vivian. Claudia and Lindsay had dealt together quite pleasantly since their argument on their first night in London, and in this congenial atmosphere Claudia found she had no great difficulty keeping her fears for her future at bay.

If Claudia had been of a romantic turn of mind, she might have felt the cheerful sunshine that seemed to spill into every window of Lovewell House on the morning of her wedding a positive omen. Instead, she was only glad that there was no rain to stain her new gown getting in and out of the carriage at the church. She found it was really best for her not to think thoughts any deeper than that, for there was an uneasiness growing inside of her that she was afraid to give in to lest she cry off from her promise at the very last moment.

But she did not. They were married quite uneventfully by the rector of St. George's with only David and Vivian for witnesses, and a week to the day they had met, Claudia Tavener became Lady Lindsay Alistair.

Lindsay proved quite agreeable to visiting her family before going on to Bath, and it had been decided that they would leave for Oxfordshire the morning following the wedding. Claudia had written to her mother and stepfather detailing the false history of her and Lindsay's courtship and informing them of their planned arrival, which she had deliberately not posted until Saturday. Vivian had again suggested that Claudia might wish to invite her parents to the wedding, but Claudia declined to do so, preferring to present them with a *fait accompli*.

After a toast in their honor was drunk in the rector's study, the entire party returned to Grosvernor Square. There was no formal wedding breakfast, only a light family repast, and when it was done, Claudia felt a strong sense of anticlimax. It was as if she had expected some immediately discernible changes as the result of her wedding, and the only one presently manifest was the change of her name from Tavener to Alistair.

As soon as they had eaten, the marquess and marchioness made excuses to leave Lindsay and Claudia alone to enjoy the privacy coveted by most newlyweds. Lindsay sat slouched in his chair staring into the middle distance while he sipped his coffee. Claudia, too, was preoccupied with her thoughts and was a bit startled when he addressed her.

"Well, it is done," he said without expression.

Claudia could not gauge his humor. "Are you repenting?"

"No," he replied, and lapsed into silence again for a minute or so before saying in a matter-of-fact way, "We shall have to retire early tonight to either your bedchamber or mine." He saw the alarm come into Claudia's expression and laughed. "Not to fear, dear wife. I am suggesting nothing you would regard as improper. But we must at least give the pretense of being lovers, or we shall fool no one. We'll play piquet if you like."

Claudia all but shuddered at the prospect. "I think not. Vivian told me that neither she nor David would be at home tonight, so there is no need for feigning spending the night together."

"Do governesses live in such a netherworld between upstairs and downstairs that they know nothing of servants' gossip?" he asked with an incredulous lift to his brows. "If we do not at least play the part of lovers, the entire household will know of it by morning, and likely half of the polite world by noon."

"Must we waste an entire evening in idle pretense?" Claudia asked imploringly.

He gave a bark of laughter. "I think marriage to you, my dear Claud, will prove most beneficial. At the very least it will keep my vanity in line. We shall read at opposite ends of the room if you cannot support my conversation for a few hours."

But, in fact, their first evening as husband and wife passed quite comfortably. After the Lovewells had left, Claudia did read while Lindsay played the pianoforte, and when it could be put off no longer, they retired to her bedchamber, which she chose, feeling that she would be more comfortable in her own room than in his.

The first few minutes they were alone together were not easy for her. She was suddenly extremely conscious of

Lindsay as a man, and the bed seemed to her far larger and more inviting than she had remembered it from only a few hours earlier when she had last visited the room. But Lindsay made some light comment that made her laugh, and her uneasiness was quickly dissipated. In the end, they did play piquet with mixed results: she lost one game and won the other.

Vivian gave them her own chaise for the journey to Oxfordshire and they traveled in well-sprung comfort, arriving in Woodstock by late afternoon of the following day. They avoided any expectation of their spending the night at the rectory by stopping first at the Crown Inn and taking rooms there.

At the sound of the approach of their carriage, Claudia's young stepbrothers and -sisters came tumbling out of the house to see who was arriving in such style. Following the children more sedately down the front steps was her mother, whose curiosity got the better of her sense of dignity and beckoned her out of doors to greet the fashionably accoutred chaise with the unfamiliar crest. When the steps were let down and Claudia emerged, she was at once surrounded by a circle of bobbing young faces. In the hubbub, Lindsay descended from the carriage without ceremony and stood a little behind Claudia, calmly waiting for the chatter and questions to subside so that he could be presented in due form to Mrs. Maverly.

Claudia at last extricated herself from the babble and hugged her mother, who returned the embrace briefly and then pulled back to say, ''My dearest Claudia, what a sly puss you have been to keep such a thing from your own mother.'' She turned to Lindsay with a bright welcoming smile. ''You must be Lindsay. Mr. Maverly is from home and will be so disappointed not to have been here to greet you himself. We were both so pleased by Claudia's letter telling us of your plans to marry, though of course we deplored your impatience. We would both have wished to give you a proper wedding from our own parish, but at the least you must amend your plans and remain at least a fortnight so that we can have all of our friends to a party to celebrate.''

Mrs. Maverly paused for breath and Claudia said quickly, "Yes, Mama, we shall discuss it all, but not in the street, if you please. Is Papa visiting with old Mr. Crawford again?" she asked by way of diversion as she took her mother's arm and guided her back into the rectory. She cast a quick look behind her at Lindsay as they mounted the outside stairs, and he gave her a brief, bemused smile in return.

The time before dinner was spent in answering endless questions from Mrs. Maverly and her inquisitive brood, who seemed to regard Lindsay as some rare exotic creature to be minutely examined with covert looks and giggles, which he bore with manful equanimity. When Mr. Maverly returned, he added his might with jovial heartiness and finally rescued Lindsay by bearing him off to his study for a bit of sherry before dinner was served.

Mrs. Maverly then shooed her younger children from the room and demanded to know from her eldest daughter why she had given her no inkling of her attachment to Lord Lindsay.

"Because I believed it would never come to anything," Claudia said, thinking ruefully that it was becoming easier with each recital to have answers already fabricated for questions about her and Lindsay. "You know if I had told you about her and Lindsay. "You know if I had told you about him you would have been in alt hoping that he would ask me to marry him, and I did not think that he would. After all, I was a mere governess and he is the son of a marquess."

Mrs. Maverly bristled. "You are the granddaughter of an earl, the cousin of several viscounts and barons, and can even claim a connection to a duke. You have nothing to blush for in your breeding, Claudia."

"Of course not, Mama," Claudia said appeasingly, but added with a dimpling smile. "But governesses, you know, are expected to blend into the furniture when attractive gentlemen of noble lineage come to visit."

"I wonder that that dreadful harridan Mrs. Ramsett, whom you wrote to me about, even permitted you in the same room," Mrs. Maverly exclaimed, her indignation kindling. "How on earth did a man of Lord Lindsay's breeding come to know such a shocking set of shabby genteels and mush-rooms?''

Claudia laughed. "It was not as bad as that, Mama. I will allow you that Mrs. Ramsett is not a very well-bred person, but George Bingerley's principal fault is greed. He married poor Miss Ramsett for her exceptional dowry. I doubt he had any idea that her mother came along with it.''

"Then he was well-served for his avarice, since that woman has made herself virtual mistress of his household," her mother said righteously. "I confess, Claudia, I supposed you would soon be returning to us, for I knew from your letters that you were unhappy, though you did not precisely say so. In fact, I had already begun to look about for another post for you, since I knew you would not listen to either Mr. Maverly or me and remain at home with us. Lady Cosgrove told me only the day before I received your letter from Lovewell House that she is thinking of letting go the young woman who is instructing her three girls and though I know you do not like Elsa Cosgrove overmuch, it would have answered perfectly.''

Claudia did not agree with her at all—in fact, her opinion of Mrs. Ramsett was considerably higher than the one she had of Lady Cosgrove, and she offered silent gratitude that she had been spared that fate, whatever her odd marriage to Lindsay might hold.

"Well, my dear," Mrs. Maverly said, patting her hand as she rose to take Claudia upstairs to refresh herself before dinner, "all is well that ends well. I could not be more pleased with the match you have made. Did you know that Jane Ellacott and I were presented in the same Season? We were quite bosom bows for a time, though we did not keep in touch with much regularity after your papa died." She sighed wistfully for the fashionable life she had left behind with her second marriage. But it was only a momentary melancholy, for she was really very happy as Mrs. Maverly. "I do believe I shall give you a letter to take to Jane along with my love and good wishes.''

"Of course, Mama. It will be the very thing to make Lady

Ellacott smile upon me as Lindsay's wife," she said with a smile.

"As if you needed anything but yourself," Mrs. Maverly said indignantly. "Even if you did not have a grand dowry, Lord Lindsay is a lucky man to have won you." She stopped and hugged Claudia. "I am so happy, Claud. I never thought to see you so respectably settled," she said, oblivious to the backhandedness of the compliment.

Mrs. Maverly did protest at their decision to spend the night at the Crown Inn and their unwillingness to put off their plans to journey at once to Bath, but an invitation by Lindsay on behalf of his unknowing brother for all of the Maverlys and Claudia's brother, William Tavener, who was visiting with friends in Leicester, to visit Landgrove at the end of the summer did much to still her objections.

"It wasn't as harrowing as you feared, was it?" Lindsay said into her ear as they went into the dining room, and Claudia had to admit that her expectations of awkwardness or even outright disbelief on the part of her family had proven entirely unfounded.

Dinner was a pleasant, lively meal as the older members of the nursery were allowed to eat with the adults for this special occasion. Claudia, observing how well Lindsay conducted himself with her brothers and sisters, answering absurd questions seriously and listening with unfeigned interest to childish accounts of adventures, had the thought that he would make an excellent father. Realizing the implication of this, she banished the thought at once, though not before she felt a warmth come over her that she chastised herself for as missish.

After dinner Lindsay firmly cemented his position within the Maverly family by making the very popular suggestion of a game of lottery tickets. Claudia begged to be excused from the game on the grounds that she was tired after a day of travel, but willingly went to sit in the chair beside her stepfather when he beckoned her to his side.

Claudia knew Mr. Maverly's gentle nature too well to suppose he meant to question her closely or in any way rebuke her for her hasty marriage, but she was still relieved when he informed her at once that he quite approved of Lord Lindsay as a husband for her. "He seems an unexceptional young man, my dear, who thinks just as he ought on most matters. I have long thought that you would make an excellent wife for some good man, and I trust that in Lord Lindsay my prayer for your happiness has been favorably answered."

Claudia's gaze traveled across the room to observe Lindsay partaking in the noisy game with gusto. "He is a good man, I think," Claudia said, speaking her thought aloud.

Mr. Maverly's brow knit. "You think?"

Claudia reddened but answered glibbly, "I meant that I have never witnessed in him an inconsideration for others. In truth, Papa," she added honestly, "even though we are now man and wife, we have not really known each other for very long."

The rector of Tauton Green was silent for a moment. "My dear," he began at length, "I would not for the world put you to the blush, but I hope you will feel comfortable enough to be candid with me. I have never thought you of an impulsive nature and I find myself concerned at the suddenness of your marriage to Lord Lindsay."

There was a question in his tone, though he did not precisely ask it openly, and his gentle blue eyes were plainly troubled. Claudia knew that he suspected, as had Vivian had, that their connection had been more venal than romantic and that their hasty marriage was a necessary consequence. It was doubtless what most people would think until time gave their suspicions the lie.

"If you are thinking that there was anything that constrained us to be married, Papa, I can assure you there was not," she said, happy to be able to reassure him on that head.

The rector, pleased, nodded and smiled. "It is not that I doubted your adherence to the values your mama and I have attempted to instill in you, Claudia, but we all of us, at times, fall victim to passions we frequently do not understand yet have great difficulty resisting."

Claudia had formed the usual schoolgirl *tendres* for local youths, but she never had any difficulty keeping a firm control of her emotions. The thought of being swept away by passion for Lindsay—or for that matter, any other man she had known—made her smile a little at the unlikeliness of it, but she agreed gravely with her stepfather that the flesh was indeed at times weak.

Mr. Maverly patted her hand. "You are content in your choice, my child, are you not?" he asked, clearly not yet completely convinced, despite her assurances.

Claudia was a bit dismayed by his acuity and his question distressed her, but she realized with some amazement that she was not discontented with her marriage. Claudia could not help liking Lindsay, for his mind was quick, his sense of humor droll, he was always excellent company, and they thought alike on many subjects. She knew she might have done considerably worse in her choice of a husband even if she had gone about it in a more conventional manner.

She was also more pleased with her life than she had been for some time. It was a relief to know she would never again be in what Lindsay had rightly called the netherworld between upstairs and downstairs that was the lot of governesses who were neither servant nor family. And she had already come to the reluctant conclusion even before she had left Bingerley Court that she did not really have a calling to educate the young. Being a governess for her had simply been a means of supporting herself in a respectable manner.

She felt some reluctance to admitting it, but Claudia knew that she was looking forward to her new life as Lady Lindsay Alistair. She enjoyed owning lovely fashionable dresses, having a maid of her own, and being addressed as "my lady," and she was really quite excited at the prospect that she would soon be gracing balls and parties where she would be meeting persons of the first consideration. These ambitions, which she did not hesitate to castigate as shallow, made her a little uncomfortable, but she was amused with herself as well. So much for the nobility of poverty. If she had had the choice of going back to that fateful afternoon at the Red Doe to undo all that had occurred since, for the first time she was reasonably sure she would not take it.

"Yes, Papa," she said, and knew that she meant it. "I am content."

The next morning found Claudia and Lindsay travelers once again as they began their journey to Bath. Claudia's realization of her acceptance of her marriage benefited their relationship considerably, for it removed any lingering hesitation she felt at being on intimate terms with Lindsay and they arrived in Bath in perfect good humor with each other.

Claudia had visited Bath a number of times in the company of her parents before her father's death, for Mr. Tavener had been convinced that the famous waters were beneficial to his gout, which had flared up from time to time and caused him to retire from his usual amusements. Claudia had always liked Bath and thought it a beautiful city with its perfectly laid-out crescents and terraces.

Lady Ellacott's house was situated in Laura Place, and though it might not have been described as a mansion, it was certainly impressive and clearly the property of someone of considerable means.

They received no spontaneous greeting such as they had at Lovewell House. A butler went to apprise Lady Ellacott of their arrival and they were presently bowed into a sitting room on the first floor in a manner more befitting a presence chamber.

The royal analogy continued, for Lady Ellacott sat in a large high-backed chair at the far end of the room near windows overlooking the garden. Lindsay had never described his godmother physically to Claudia, and she had somehow managed to form an image of a sour-faced and somewhat hagged old woman despite the fact that her mother had told her that she and Lady Ellacott were of an age, but this picture was dashed the moment they entered the room.

Lady Ellacott was neither old nor sour-faced and haggish. Claudia judged she was not yet fifty years of age, and her frame, while not in any way obese, was robust. She was a pretty woman as well, and might have been a beauty in her youth. She remained seated as Claudia and Lindsay approached, regarding them in a searching but uncritical fashion. Standing beside her chair, in the image of a courtier, was a young man of about Lindsay's age. He was tall and well-formed, with soft, curling silver-blond hair, surprisingly dark-brown eyes, and features that were almost femininely pretty.

Claudia did not note him when she first entered the room, all her attention then being given to Lady Ellacott, but the moment she did look up and her eyes met his across the room, she felt a sudden wave of inexplicable emotion pass through her; she felt at first cold and then hot.

Without realizing it, she must have stopped, for she felt the pressure of Lindsay's hand under her elbow, pushing her forward, and she forced her fascinated gaze away from the exquisite stranger.

Lady Ellacott extended her hand to her godson in an appropriately regal gesture and Claudia half-expected him to drop to one knee in a gesture of allegiance.

But Lindsay simply bowed over Lady Ellacott's hand in the usual manner, leaning forward to add a kiss to her cheek. He turned to Claudia with an encouraging smile and said, "This is Claudia, Aunt Jane. I hope you will come to love her as much as I do."

Claudia was more aware of the gentleman beside Lady Ellacott than she was of Lady Ellacott herself, and more conscious of the impression she must make on him. Feeling absurdly missish and aware that her color was high, she murmured a greeting to Lady Ellacott that sounded insipid in her own ears.

But the older woman seemed rather pleased by her diffidence. "I am not a dragon, my dear," she said, laughing, "whatever this sad rattle nephew of mine may have told you. I am very pleased to welcome you to our family. I remember your mother and father quite well. Your mother and I were confidantes in our youth and your father was a friend of my late husband. They were always so gay, so ready to kick up a lark in those days. How sad to think they are both gone now.'' She glanced up with a smile at the young man beside her. ''You must allow me to make known to you Lord Strait, who is also my nephew. He has been eager to meet you since we had news of your wedding from Lindsay. His sister, Lady Lovewell, I must tell you, has also written much in your praise.''

The Earl of Strait not only bowed over Claudia's hand but brought it lightly against his lips with old-fashioned but charming courtliness. His eyes, unnervingly, never left hers. ''So much in your praise that I wondered at such a paragon giving her heart to Lindsay. He's a pleasant fellow, I'll allow, but hardly worthy of such perfection.''

''As you imagine you are, Drew?'' Lady Ellacott said quizzingly.

Andrew Strait's laughter was a rich, delightful baritone. ''Of course not. I am not such a coxcomb, I hope.''

''I am very pleased with my choice, my lord,'' Claudia replied to Andrew, feeling the need to abort any likelihood of flirtation between them. ''It is I who wonder at Lindsay's choosing to love me.''

Mild surprise flickered in Lindsay's eyes, Lady Ellacott beamed at her in approval, and the earl smiled faintly, accepting the set-down with good grace.

It was Lady Ellacott who spoke. ''I cannot tell you how happy I am made by your marriage, my dear. Lindsay is to me the son I never bore, and his happiness is very important to me. If you will love him and be a good wife to him, you shall have not only my love but my gratitude as well.''

''I hope that I shall be worthy of it,'' Claudia murmured, feeling as if she were reciting lines in a play. As she stood before Lady Ellacott, the weight of her deception seemed much greater to her than it had when it was merely in abstract.

''Perhaps you do not know, but Andrew has just suffered a grave misfortune in his affairs of the heart,'' Lady Ellacott said. ''So it gives me even greater satisfaction to see that Lindsay at least has been blessed in his choice of a bride.''

"And so timely," Drew said blandly.

Lindsay flashed Andrew a quick smile. "Kind fate has certainly smiled upon me. I regret I cannot felicitate you as well, Cousin."

Andrew returned an enigmatic smile of his own. "Perhaps my next foray into the affairs of the heart will be more successful."

"Of course it shall be," Lady Ellacott said bracingly. "Any young woman should be honored by your attention, Andrew. Do you not think that Andrew is an exceptionally handsome fellow, Claudia?"

Not for the first time, Claudia regretted her fair complexion and the ease with which her color gave away her thoughts. "Lord Strait is indeed blessed with countenance," she managed to say in a voice that thankfully did not also betray her inner turmoil.

They had left her parents early and made excellent time from Woodstock and it still wanted some time before dinner. Lady Ellacott belatedly recalled that they had been traveling most of the day and suggested that they might wish to rest and refresh themselves. "Perhaps even a hot bath would not come amiss," she said as she turned to Andrew to ask him to ring for Storry, her butler. "I have given you and Claudia the large bedchamber at the back of the house, Lindsay. It is not only the most comfortable of the guest bedchambers, but it has windows that overlook the garden."

Claudia realized that Lady Ellacott meant for them to share a bedchamber, and she looked to Lindsay, her eyes quite round. Lindsay said promptly, "That is very thoughtful of you, Aunt Jane, but it is our custom to keep separate but adjoining bedchambers. The pair opposite that room will do for us nicely."

"But you are only just wed," Lady Ellacott said, quite clearly shocked at the notion that they might wish to sleep apart. "That is a deplorable custom. In my day a married couple behaved like one and shared one bed as God intended. 'And the two shall be as one,' " she quoted piously. "I do not wonder that there are so many unhappy marriages these days when husband and wife are afraid of a bit of intimacy.

It seems wonderful to me that a young man and woman in love would wish to be parted from each other even for the span of a night.''

"Nevertheless, Aunt Jane, it is what we prefer," Lindsay said, standing his ground.

"Nonsense," Lady Ellacott said as Andrew, after listening to this exchange with interest, obediently went to the bellpull and gave it a firm tug. "I have already given orders that the room be prepared for you and your baggage taken there. By the end of the week you shall both be thanking me for refusing to allow such foolish modern notions."

Storry entered with an alacrity that suggested he had been hovering in the hall, perhaps near to the door, and he was instructed to show Lord and Lady Lindsay to their bedchamber.

Claudia kept her composure, though she scarcely knew how. She wanted to protest, but knew she dared not. If Lady Ellacott were to suspect that theirs was a mere business arrangement, she might well take umbrage and refuse to make Lindsay the settlement she had promised; then all would be for nothing.

She felt rather than saw Andrew's gaze upon her, and her complexion, which had become quite pale when she realized she would be expected to share a bedchamber with Lindsay, darkened again. She did not understand what it was about Andrew that made her feel so oddly unsettled and made her blush like a gauche schoolgirl, but it seriously discomfited her.

As if bent on unnerving Claudia, Andrew insisted on accompanying them to the first floor. Lindsay moved a little ahead, speaking with Storry, and the earl fell in step beside Claudia.

"I suppose you think my aunt's notion of marriage quite gothic, Lady Lindsay. May I call you Claudia since we are cousins now?" Claudia murmured assent, keeping her eyes down as she lifted her skirt slightly to climb the stairs. "Even newlyweds need a bit of distance to make intimacy more piquant."

His tone was perfectly bland, but Claudia felt rather than

heard his sarcasm. She had an unaccountable and very disturbing desire to reassure him that her marriage was only in name. She could not help her attraction to the earl, but she did not mean to encourage it. "Lindsay snores," she said flatly, and won a peal of laughter from her companion.

Lindsay, who reached the top of the stair just ahead of them, demanded to know the reason for his cousin's mirth. Andrew repeated it with relish, adding, "You are fortunate your bride was unacquainted with your habits beforehand, Lin, or perhaps we would not now be wishing you happy."

Lindsay cast Claudia a darkling look. "Claudia has said she finds my many fine qualities far exceed any minor imperfections, have you not, my love?"

"Repeatedly," Claudia said dryly, and allowed Storry to bow her into the bedchamber she would share with Lindsay.

Lindsay followed her and turned abruptly, almost colliding with his cousin on the threshold. "Be a good fellow, Drew, and have Storry tell my man not to come up until I ring." With that he virtually closed the door in Andrew's face. He turned back to the room to find Claudia regarding him, a stormy expression creasing her brow.

"I do not snore," he said indignantly.

"And I have no wish to prove the truth of it," she replied, displaying some heat. "This will not do, Lindsay. You will have to find some excuse to convince Lady Ellacott to give you another room."

"Such as? I did try, you know."

"But not very hard."

Lindsay sighed. "If I'd pushed too hard, I would have made her suspicious. Aunt Jane is an eccentric, but she's no fool. She'd never accept our marriage if she thought I had married merely for the sake of the inheritance."

"Which is exactly what you have done."

"What *we* have done," Lindsay said, adding tartly, "The time for regret and recriminations is past, my love. We are married and the game is afoot. Having to share this room is a nuisance, but hardly worthy of making a fuss that could overset everything."

"It is more than a nuisance," Claudia insisted. "It is a

violation of the specific conditions of our agreement.''

"I pledge to keep command over my baser passions,"
Lindsay said with a wry smile.

Claudia, who was looking about the room as if for a means
of escape, focused on an interior door a few feet to the left
of the bed. She crossed the room and opened it, entering
another bedchamber. She turned and said triumphantly,
"You may sleep in here tonight. There is no need to say
anything of it to your aunt."

"I won't need to. I have told you how quickly the minutest
details of our personal lives are spread throughout the
household. The maid who makes up that room will tell her
best friend the kitchen maid, who will tell the footman she
has been flirting with for the past month, who will just
mention it while he is helping Storry clean the silver, and
so on. We have no secrets from those we pay to serve us,
I fear."

Claudia knew the truth of what he said, but she hesitated
to acknowledge it lest he read too much into her concession.
In spite of his assurances that he would not take advantage
of their intimate circumstances, she could still remember the
feel of his lips against hers, and it made her uncomfortable
to think of spending an entire night lying beside him barely
clothed. "If you will not sleep in here, then I shall," she
said, refusing to give up the idea completely.

"There will be talk no matter which of us spends the night
in there." He went over to her, d rew her out of the room
without resistance, and firmly closed the door. "Very well,
Claudia. I shall speak to Aunt Jane after breakfast tomorrow
and convince her that she must accept our preference for
separate bedchambers, but for tonight I think we must
comply. If we are so set against it for even one night, it will
certainly make her suspicious. Be reasonable! We have been
married less than a sennight; anyone would wonder at it."

Claudia did not want to give ground, but she finally bowed
to the force of his argument. "But," she admonished as she
capitulated, "you will not cozen me into agreeing to spend
a second night together. Either you or I shall have to move
to the other room tomorrow."

Lindsay agreed and then tactfully left her so that she could send for Mary to help her change from her traveling clothes. Somewhat mollified by his consideration, Claudia was able to appear quite in charity with Lindsay at dinner without having to feign it in any way. They dined *en famille* and Lindsay kept both ladies amused with a constant flow of humorous chatter and slightly scandalous gossip that even Claudia enjoyed, though she was unfamiliar with virtually all of the people they discussed.

All too soon the evening was ended and it was time for them to seek their beds. Claudia had hoped that Lindsay's consideration would extend to allowing her to retire first so that she could change and be in bed and asleep before him, but shorly after tea had been served in the withdrawing room, he rose and offered his hand to Claudia.

"We have had a long day, my love," he said, ignoring the dagger look that crossed her features. "Will you forgive us for leaving you so early in the evening, Aunt Jane? Being rattled about in a carriage—even in a well-sprung one like Vivian's—is wearing."

"Of course," Lady Ellacott said, beaming at them. "And you must not worry about coming down for breakfast in the morning. Newlyweds must keep their own hours."

Lindsay agreed gravely that this was so and then looked expectantly at Claudia, who had not yet taken his hand or risen. He read murder in her heart, but he gave her his sweetest smile and reached down to take her hand, since she had made no effort to rise.

Claudia had no choice. She wished Lady Ellacott a good night and allowed him to escort her out of the room, but as soon as they were out of sight of the door, she shook off his arm and cast him a furious glare. "You at least might have allowed me to go up first to change and fall asleep before you," she said accusingly.

"I should have made a very unconvincing newlywed if I had. As it was, we stayed longer than we should have if we were really the eager lovers we are pretending to be." They reached the bedchamber and he opened the door and went in before her to light a lamp from the bed candle.

Claudia started toward the bellpull but he caught her arm and stopped her. "You can undress yourself tonight. We would scarcely wish for the intrusion."

Claudia gave him a smoldering look and swept past him to the armoire where Mary had placed her nightdresses. She pulled out the first one that came to hand, tossed it on the nearest chair, and with her back turned rigidly against him, began to undo the small buttons at the back of her dress. After a few moments she felt his hands push hers away and he completed the task for her. She turned and looked up at him, anger and suspicion setting her features.

With one finger he traced her brow as if to wipe away her frown. "It is merely friendly assistance, Claud," he said, and turned and went into the adjoining room, gently closing the door.

When she had undressed, Claudia quite deliberately put out the lamp before getting into bed, and Lindsay, when he returned to the room a short while later, did not relight it but undressed by the faint flicker of the single bed candle.

Claudia was huddled at the edge of the bed, her back irresolutely turned against him. When he finally got into bed beside her, she stiffened, but he made not the smallest effort to touch her. He adjusted his pillows to his satisfaction, sought a comfortable position, and then was still.

In spite of his assurances, Claudia lay as far from him as the width of the bed would allow, as if guarding against the most accidental touch. But Lindsay seemed content with the space allotted to him, and in a relatively short time his even breathing told her he had fallen asleep.

Though she could scarcely credit it, Claudia was obliged to own that she was annoyed. She would have been righteously indignant if he had so much as attempted to kiss her good night, but despite his promise, she had expected him to make at least a token attempt at her virtue, and perversely, she was piqued that he had not. To add to the insult, his peace was so little disturbed that he had fallen asleep within minutes of getting into bed.

Her well-developed sense of the ridiculous made her laugh

at herself, but a vague feeling of letdown lingered however much she chided herself for absurdity. When she at last fell asleep, though, it was not of Lindsay she dreamed but of a man with silver-blond hair and a dazzling smile who beckoned her to she knew not what forbidden delights.

# 4

Claudia did not awaken from her dreams until the sun was well risen. Her fears that there would be awkwardness between her and Lindsay in the morning proved groundless. He had risen before her, dressed, and by now very likely had taken his breakfast as well. She dressed in a crisp spotted muslin that Vivian had bestowed on her from her own wardrobe, and went downstairs to the breakfast room, finding only Lady Ellacott, who was sipping coffee and reading the latest London papers, which she had delivered to her every morning.

Claudia quickly learned that no apologies were expected for her lateness. "I told Lindsay that you both might have had breakfast brought to you on a tray," Lady Ellacott said as she poured out a steaming cup of coffee for Claudia, "but I should have guessed that nothing would keep Lin from his morning ride. You must not mind, my dear, if not even you can persuade him against it. It has been his custom since he was in short coats and first came to live with us. Ellacott was still alive then and we would all go out for the exercise, but I had a fall a few years ago and injured my back, so I am not as steady in the saddle as once I was. Do you ride? No?" she said with some surprise. "Then you should exert yourself to learn. It would be very nice if you could accompany Lindsay every morning, and you may take it from one who had an excellent marriage that it is these small, companionable things that strengthen the bond between you. Now, tell me, my dear, all about your dear mother and Mr. Maverly and all the little ones. I enjoyed the letter you brought to me from her prodigiously, but I have a thousand questions and you must be proxy for your mama.''

Claudia was only too happy to oblige, for while she was kept busy answering questions about her family, Lady Ellacott could not quiz her about her meeting or courtship with Lindsay. She found the information that it was Lindsay's practice to ride every morning a bit disturbing, for it brought home to her just how much they were all but strangers to each other. She knew nothing at all of his personal habits or pleasures and still less of his friends and interests.

"Mrs. Maverly also expressed the hope that I would sponsor you in society," the dowager said when she had finally exhausted her queries, "which of course I shall, for as Lindsay's aunt it is my clear duty even if I did not like you for yourself. But you must realize, Claudia, that society here is not at the level that you will find in London.''

"Good," Claudia said, laughing. "I think I should be terrified to find myself thrust willy-nilly into the *ton*. Mama has done her best to instill in all of us a proper address and decorum, but I am not at all sure I would know how to go on in the fashionable world, and I hope that you will be my mentor.''

Lady Ellacott patted her hand fondly. "It will be my great pleasure, my dear. But you shall go on splendidly, I haven't a doubt of it, and perhaps by the Little Season you will wish to go to London and permit Vivian to introduce you to her own circles there." She cocked her head and gave Claudia a long critical look. "You are not only very pretty, but you have a lively, clever mind. Insipidness may be the fashion for young girls fresh from the schoolroom, but it is wit and style that are truly admired. I believe you will take very well, and that you will be a credit to your husband.''

Claudia was a little discomfited by these ecomiums as a twinge of guilt for her deception assailed her again. "I hope

Lindsay's friends will not be disappointed in me," she replied.

"How should they be?" Lady Ellacott said with a reassuring smile. "He will be quite envied, at least among his own sex. If you are still not too tired from your journey, we shall go to the Pump Room today. One meets all of Bath there. Then afterward we may take sedan chairs to Madame Torquay's establishment in Milsom Street. Vivian wrote that you would wish to have a few more dresses made up for you, and Madame Torquay is quite the best modiste that Bath has to offer. I hope you don't dislike walking or taking chairs. The streets are so steep that we only use town carriages for inclement weather and special occasions."

Claudia made no objection to any of these plans. She was quite eager to embark on her new life and trusted Lady Ellacott to show her the best way to go on. Lady Ellacott had a few household duties to occupy her before they left, and Claudia used the time to wirte to Vivian, detailing their visit to her parents in Oxfordshire and telling Vivian of her pleasurable impression of Bath and of her hostess.

When they started out, they decided instead to visit the shops on Milsom Street first, for Lady Ellacott felt they would then have the opportunity to rest themselves for a bit when they went to the Pump Room. Their shopping expedition was a complete success. Claudia found any number of patterns and bolts of material to please her and she discovered the pleasure of being able to purchase whatever took her fancy without having to count the cost.

Since her knowledge of current fashion was limited, mostly she bowed to the advice of Lady Ellacott and the modiste, merely approving or disapproving their suggestions as her personal taste dictated, and she frankly lost track of the number of dresses she agreed to purchase. At the miliner's it was much the same and at every shop they visited thereafter. On occasion, Claudia's innate sense of economy demurred at a selection she thought likely to be costly, questioning whether the item was truly necessary, but Lady Ellacott needed only to insist that it was indispensable for a lady of fashion for her conscience to be assuaged. In this manner, by the time they reached the Pump Room, Claudia had ordered and purchased more finery than she could have imagined she would possess the whole of her life.

Claudia had no difficulty believing Lady Ellacott's remark that all of Bath came to the Pump Room. Though the Season in Bath did not truly begin until autumn and Lady Ellacott declared that Bath was woefully thin of company, the room was quite filled with both ladies and gentlemen, some sitting in chairs circling the perimeter of the room, many others standing in small groups conversing or strolling about arm in arm, carefully weaving in and out of the crowd.

Claudia dutifully drank the water handed to her by the attendant, though she privately thought it had the taste and smell of warm metal. Lady Ellacott pressed her to take another, declaring it excellent for the digestion, but Claudia declined, certain that a second glass would be more likely to overset her digestion than aid it.

It seemed to Claudia that Lady Ellacott was acquainted with everyone in the room. Claudia's hand was bowed over many times, by Lord Carlow and Mr. Ledgerton and Sir Francis Kirkby and a number of others, as each man assured her of the pleasure it gave him to make her acquaintance. Claudia curtsied to the Duchess of Borodon and was made known to the Countess of Dunne, and as each introduction followed the next, Claudia felt increasingly at her ease. It was very disconcerting, though, to meet so many new people at once, and she was glad when Lady Ellacott led her over to a corner of the room where a woman of about the dowager's age sat with a younger woman beside her.

There were fortunately a few empty chairs next to them and two of these were claimed by Lady Ellacott as she made Claudia known to her particular friend, Mrs. Maye, and her daughter, Mrs. Conniff. After greetings were exchanged, the older women fell into conversation, but Mrs. Conniff offered Claudia only a chilly smile before returning to a study of the room.

Claudia might have ignored Mrs. Conniff's rudeness and made an effort to converse with her, but she was as eager as her new companion to look about her, examining faces that were not yet known to her and firmly planting in her memory every article of fashionable attire with which the ladies adorned themselves. What she saw reassured her that she and Lady Ellacott had selected for her a wardrobe that would place her second to none of the elegant young women who graced the Pump Room.

Glancing toward the doorway, she saw Lord Strait come into the room, stand a little away from the door, and carefully scan the company. Though she told herself not to refine too much upon it, it was flattering when, catching sight of her, he made his way directly to her side, pausing only to exchange a greeting or two with acquaintances as he passed.

No amount of self-recriminations were to any avail; the nearer he approached, the more she felt as if her internal organs had been replaced by a blancmange, and when he bowed over her hand with an admiring, intimate smile and begged permission to take the chair next to hers, her heart was pounding so fiercely in her breast that she feared he must hear it.

Lady Ellacott and Mrs. Maye were so engrossed in their conversation that they scarcely noted his approach, and his greeting to Mrs. Conniff was accorded no greater warmth than she had bestowed on Claudia before returning to her mute observation of the company.

"When I called at Laura Place this morning and was told you were gone out, I guessed this is where my aunt would take you," he said. "She claims the waters keep her in good health, but I think it is the gossip that keeps her spirits in form." He glanced down at the glass in Claudia's hand. "What do you think of our famous waters, Cousin Claudia?"

"Not a great deal, I am afraid."

He laughed. "Your honesty is refreshing, but the fashion is to find it invigorating."

"I am afraid I have no pretentions to fashion, my lord," she said, meeting his smile with a faint one of her own. "I have lived quietly and out of the fashionable world. I know no more of being in fashion than my charges knew of geography when I first arrived as governess."

"Ah, but you taught them, did you not?"

"And who shall teach me? Lindsay?"

He gave a short laugh and shook his head. "Lindsay would never do. He cares more for shooting and horses than for the set of his coat."

"From what I have observed," she said, feeling obligated to come to Lindsay's defense, "my husband is not out of the fashion. In fact, I think he is quite elegant."

"Oh, to be sure," Andrew agreed. "My cousin is always well-turned-out, but not his most ardent admirer would describe him as a pink of the *ton*."

"Mama always told me that such men were coxcombs," she said with a demureness that was belied by the quizzing gleam in her eyes.

"*Touché*, Cousin Claudia," Andrew said, his smile broadening. "I am served out for my effrontery. I acknowledge your husband to be a paragon of all manly virtues. Does that reinstate me in your good graces?"

"You have never been outside of them, my lord," she said, a little amazed at her own boldness in daring to flirt with Lindsay's cousin. She was powerfully attracted to Andrew—she could not deny that to herself—but she knew instinctively that she was flirting also with something potentially dangerous to her peace and possibly her future as well.

Andrew took one of her hands in his and Claudia felt her pulse quicken. Even if she had wanted to pull away from him, she doubted she would have had the will to do so. "Lindsay has had better luck than he deserves, I think," he said enigmatically. "I hope that we are to be friends, Claudia. Very dear friends," he added, dropping his voice so that there was the hint of suggestion in it.

Claudia was both discomposed and exhilarated. "I hope we may become friends, Andrew," she responded with an outward show of calm, steadfastly ignoring the insinuation in his words and behavior. She gently withdrew her hand from his. "Lady Ellacott complains that not a fraction of society is to be found in Bath these days," she added in a more commonplace tone, "but I seem to have met a great many people today." Glancing to her right, she saw a very familiar face and felt a wave of relief though she was not sure why. "There is Lindsay," she said. "He must have just come in. Who is that tall, elegant woman he is speaking with?"

Andrew paused for a moment before answering. "That is Mrs. Hart. She and her husband, who is quite elderly and an invalid, live in Lansdown Crescent."

"Is she a friend of Lindsay's?"

Again there was hesitation. "Yes. In a manner of speaking." Before she could question him further he said, "And that is Kitty Lodder, who has just joined them. She is also Mrs. Maye's daughter and now lives with her mother since her husband, who is with the Foreign Office, was given an assignment in Brazil."

Even as he was speaking, Mrs. Hart walked off and Lindsay and Mrs. Lodder began walking toward them. "Claudia, I must make you known to my best friend when I was in short coats," Lindsay said as they came up to them. "You would never think of it to look at her today, but Kitty was forever getting me into the most shocking scrapes and letting me take the beatings for them as well."

Mrs. Lodder gasped. "What a bouncer! Who was it who was not permitted to go to Lansdown to view the monument because Mama discovered that all the saltcellars were full of sugar at her dinner party the night before. She wouldn't believe a word against you, even though you had had luncheon with us that day and had ample opportunity to commit your crime."

Lindsay smiled and shook his head, refusing to admit his guilt. "It was doubtless an honest mistake made by some luckless housemaid. You mustn't mind her slander, Claud. Kitty is still jealous that I got my own pony for my eighth birthday and she had to wait until she was ten."

Claudia was very happy to meet Mrs. Lodder, who was near to her own age and of a very different temperament from Mrs. Maye's younger daughter. Mrs. Lodder suggested that they stroll about the room to become better-acquainted and Claudia agreed with alacrity. They discovered themselves to be in perfect charity with each other from the start and in the space of a quarter hour were well on the way from being mere acquaintances to becoming friends.

An oblique question from Claudia about Mrs. Lodder's sister brought a laughing response. "Was Honora rude to you? You must not mind her. She is one of those females who never wastes her energy on her own sex. It is only in the company of gentlemen that she becomes truly animated."

Claudia was not unfamiliar with the type, and quite understood, though understanding brought with it mild contempt. "But she gave no more notice to Lord Strait," she said. "He is an exceptionally attractive man, after all."

"Quite exceptionally," Mrs. Lodder agreed. "But, you see, Honora set her cap at him her first Season and he paid no more heed to her than he would to a gnat buzzing about him on a warm summer day. She would have been more forgiving if he had openly rejected her, I think."

Claudia, who as a governess had suffered a great deal of impassive indifference from people who seemed to scarcely regard her as a person at all, knew well that such apathy could sting worse than an open rebuke. But she could not imagine that as personable a man as Andrew had any intention to wound and had very likely been unaware of the interest he had engendered in Honora.

She said something of this nature to Mrs. Lodder, who gave a dry laugh. "Perhaps, but it has always been my experience that exceptionally attractive men are always only too well aware of the sad effect they have on our sex. Andrew Strait has been breaking hearts since his first Season on the town."

"You say that as if he had no heart to break," Claudia chided. "If he has broken hearts, he has recently been paid out, I am told."

"Ellen Merrifield. It is a pity, I suppose. They would have been well-suited if only Andrew had been the highest bidder."

Claudia was shocked at this display of cynicism in Mrs. Lodder, and some of the rosiness of their blooming friendship faded for her. "I collect you are not fond of Lord

Strait,'' she said a bit coolly. "I have only just met him, but I have found in him nothing to dislike.''

Kitty Lodder started to speak but closed her mouth and bit reflectively at her lower lip. "It is not a matter of liking or disliking,'' she said at last. "Lindsay and Andrew and I are all of an age and have been friends since our nursery days. Let us say rather that we have no illusions about each other.''

With these words they were returned to the corner of the room where Lady Ellacott and Mrs. Maye sat. Lindsay was gone, as was Mrs. Conniff, but Andrew was still where they had left him. Claudia took the chair beside him but Kitty declined to join them.

"Do you attend Lady Surcet's rout party tonight?'' Andrew asked Claudia as Mrs. Lodder walked away.

Claudia shook her head. "Lady Ellacott thinks it would be wise if I rested tonight, and I own I am tired after all the shopping we did this morning. We are to go to the card party at the New Assembly Rooms on Monday, and that will be my first evening out, though I have entered my name in both Mr. King's and Mrs. Guynette's subscription books as soon as we arrived. I only hope I shan't disgrace myself by not being able to put half of the right names to the right faces on Monday.''

"Do you play at cards, Cousin?''

Claudia could not prevent her sardonic smile or the rich irony in her tone. "Oh, yes. I play. But I find it a pernicious habit it is best to curb.''

"Your father was well-known for his skill at cards, I believe I have heard.''

"But not his luck at them,'' she said aridly. "I have inherited the latter in full measure.''

He smiled. "Did you find yourself fleeced once? I detect a note of self-recrimination, I think. We play only for chicken stakes at the Assembly Rooms, so you need have no fear of finding yourself at a standstill.''

A sudden thought suggested itself to her and she said, "Does Lindsay play often at cards?''

"As much as any of us do. He is not a gamester, if that is what you are asking."

"Does he play well?"

There must have been something in her tone that alerted Andrew she had a special interest in his answer. He gave her a swift, sharp glance. "My cousin tends to excel at most things that capture his interest," he replied. "It makes him a superb companion at some times, and a tiresome one at others. But I possess skills of my own in compensation," he added with a smile. "Will you excuse me, Claudia? I have a call I must pay before returning to York House, where I am staying, to change for a dinner engagement." He bowed over Claudia's hand, holding her eyes with his as he did so. "I dine at Laura Place tomorrow night, Cousin. Until then, when I may behold your loveliness again."

If any other man had said such a thing to her in a voice so vibrant with promise, she would have been amused, but Andrew made her feel a twinge of pleasurable anticipation she knew she should suppress but could not.

Shortly after Andrew had left, Claudia and Lady Ellacott returned to Laura Place. The dowager declared herself quite exhausted and in need of a rejuvenating rest before dinner. Claudia was tired, but far from sleepy and she made her way instead to the library.

Lady Ellacott's library was not extensive, but her taste was broad and the selection of books rather good. Claudia soon found herself lost in the discovery of old friends and new acquaintances as she familiarized herself with the contents of each well-stocked shelf of books. Her progress was slow and she gave no thought to time until her occupation was interrupted by Lindsay.

"So this is your refuge," he said, coming into the room. "I might have guessed it, I suppose, from your former career. Are you a bluestocking, dear wife?"

Claudia turned and smiled. "No, I have no such pretensions. You have pointed out, you may recall, that I was not a very great success at being a governess."

"Not through a fault of your own," he answered. "Your lack of success was as much due to the fate that sent you to people like the Bingerleys as it is to luck with the turn of a card.''

She paid no heed to his quizzing. His words put her in mind of her conversation with Andrew. To her chagrin she felt her cheeks grow warm yet again as she remembered the flirtation that had passed between them and the effect his smallest touch had on her pulse. She pushed aside any feelings of self-reproach and made herself meet Lindsay's eyes. ''Andrew told me today that you are an excellent player at cards. I think I have been what my brother would call plucked.''

''Would he?'' Lindsay said, laughter in his eyes. ''No. I told you it was not so.'' He reached out his hand to touch her arm, but she moved away from him to avoid the contact and he let his hand drop. There was no change in his voice when he spoke, but the amusement had faded from his expression. ''Are you still so unreconciled to our marriage, Claudia? I thought we have dealt tolerably well so far.''

Claudia did not know how to answer him. She admitted to herself that she was not displeased with the change in her circumstances, but she still disliked the way that this had come about and it gnawed at her peace that it might have been by design instead of by fate. Instead of answering him, she said, ''Have you spoken with your aunt about separate bedchambers?''

Lindsay nodded. ''Yes, and I have convinced her that it is what we prefer. She will allow us to please ourselves, though she doesn't like it above half.'' He broke into a sudden grin. ''It would appear that getting me riveted was only half of her plan. Now she will not be at peace until we have given her a great-nephew or -niece to lavish her affection on. She seems to think it is less likely if we insist on sleeping apart, which has some truth to it.''

''If you do not wish to condemn your aunt to unremitting disappointment,'' she said caustically, ''you had best convince her against that hope as well.''

''Not a bit of it! She would smell a rat in the space of a moment. We'll let her suppose it is the vagary of nature. Or who knows,'' he added provocatively, ''perhaps someday we shall astonish ourselves and decide to oblige her.''

Claudia informed him caustically that this was unlikely, but she did not choose to press the point. It was enough that he had risked Lady Ellacott's suspicion by insisting on separate bedchambers, and Lindsay was making sufficient effort to be agreeable that she did not wish to mar the harmony between them.

But her own peace was severely tested on the following evening when Andrew dined at Laura Place. He said little during dinner, but she frequently looked up from her plate to find his eyes upon her. Invariably, the effect of his regard was the same, though she berated herself for succumbing to a schoolgirl's *tendre* for Lindsay's beautiful cousin, she could not control the surge of emotion she felt whenever their eyes met.

Though he gave no outward sign of it, Lindsay was not unaware of the rise and fall of Claudia's color whenever her attention was given to his cousin. He had no illusions about his own physical attractions compared to those of the earl, but he found Claudia's obvious attraction to Strait disturbing. He also thought he better understood why she had flinched from his touch the day before, and he liked it even less. He discovered that there was, after all, a limit to his complacency.

He believed that Claudia was a woman of principle who would not readily embrace infidelity despite their agreement not to interfere with each other's interests, but he suspected that his cousin was subtly feeding Claudia's attraction to him. Strait would know just how to entice without alarming her conscience unduly so that by gradual insinuation his indirect assault on her virtue would succeed where a direct course would all but certainly fail.

Andrew's design for engaging in dalliance with Claudia he did not wonder at; they knew each other too well. If the earl was successful, he would have the greatest triumph of their lifelong rivalry, and even more to the purpose, he would discredit Claudia and through her Lindsay.

His suspicions were confirmed after the ladies had left him and Andrew to the enjoyment of their wine.

"Allow me to felicitate you, Cousin," Andrew said, lifting his glass in a toast. "You have a delightful wife in Claudia."

Lindsay smiled lazily. "Yes, Claudia is something of a treasure. We shall deal very well, I think."

"Aunt Jane could not be more pleased. She has confided in me the whole of your rather romantic history. It's almost as good as one of Mrs. Radcliffe's books. Very creative."

Lindsay let the shaft go wide of the mark. "It's a pity I can't offer you equal felicitations, Drew," he said sweetly. "The betting at Watier's was four-to-one that Miss Merrifield would have you over Hartleigh."

"Did you win or lose?"

"Win. A monkey."

Andrew laughed. "Your luck is holding true, Coz, but I wouldn't be complacent about it. Luck can turn again overnight. Perhaps this time my luck will be in."

"The stakes, I fear, are closed."

"Are they?" Andrew's voice took on a more serious note. "Aunt Jane has not yet sent for Mr. Jolliet, and even papers that are signed can be rescinded."

Lindsay's eyes narrowed. "Why should they be?"

"Our aunt is sometimes capricious in her fancies. She has taken particularly well to Claudia, but her alt often fades as quickly as it began."

"I've no fear that she will find anything in Claudia to disappoint her."

Andrew pushed back his chair from the table. "I hope you have cause to be sanguine, Lin," he said. His smile was caustic. "I, on the other hand, never place my bets until I am sure my horse can carry the field." He took out his watch to check the time. "I'd best go do the pretty with the ladies. I'm promised to friends at the Pelican."

He waited for a moment for Lindsay to rise, but Lindsay poured himself more wine and sat back at his ease. "I shouldn't dream of casting hurdles in your way, Drew," he said easily. "The field is open if you can stay the course."

Andrew smiled again. "We shall see."

# 5

Though Lady Ellacott assured Claudia that the party they were to attend was just the usual Monday-night card assembly at the New Assembly Rooms, Claudia took as much care with her appearance as if she were attending a grand ball given by one of the royals. She decided on a straw silk gown with a very high-cut bodice that emphasized the shape of her breasts and that fell into soft folds about her hips, flattering her figure with every move. Lady Ellacott's own dresser, Miss Kerry, dressed Claudia's hair into the style known as "the artless." About her throat were gathered strands of pearls and adorning her ears were pearl drops, both pressed upon her by the dowager, who insisted that Claudia must make free use of her jewel box until she was able to acquire jewels of her own.

It still wanted a quarter-hour before she need go down to dinner and Claudia stood before the cheval glass, marveling that the lovely creature who stared back at her was actually herself. Lindsay came into the room through the door that connected their bedchambers and stood surveying her critically. Claudia found she was anxious for his verdict.

"Quite exquisite, Claudia," he said. "I knew you would do me credit when you shed your drab governess feathers. But I am not certain about straw silk with your coloring.

Something with a little less yellow in it would have suited you better, I think."

Claudia was not really surprised at his candid appraisal, but she had wanted unconditional approval to boost her confidence for her first *ton* party, not uncompromising honesty. "I am surprised you attend to what would suit me," she said tartly. "Andrew said you took no notice of fashion."

"Did he?" demanded Lindsay, a lively look coming into his eyes. Lindsay's shirt points were not as high as Andrew's, nor was his neckcloth as intricately tied, but Claudia acknowledged that her husband was elegantly if quietly attired. "I take more notice of the latest kick in female rig than he'd suppose. There's no need for us to draw daggers, Claudia. I told you you look a treat, but I'd stay away from anything with any hint of yellow in it in the future. With those coppery lights in your hair, you'd look like a kitchen candle if the color were more pronounced."

Claudia gave a small gasp of outrage, but then succumbed to laughter. "You are a horrid, provoking man! I think this gown is vastly becoming, and so does Vivian, who helped me to choose it."

"You shall probably have every man in the room at your feet," he said with belated gallantry, and then offered to take her down to dinner before their altercation could escalate.

Walking into the New Assembly Rooms, Claudia was again astonished by the number of elegantly dressed people who filled the rooms. Though some faces were familiar to her now, there were still many more unknown to her. If this was Bath thin of company, she could not imagine what it would be like in London during the Season, when all the world came to town. It was not long after they arrived that they found Mrs. Maye flanked by her two daughters. Claudia was very happy to renew her acquaintance with Kitty Lodder. Both Mrs. Lodder and her mother greeted Claudia with enthusiasm, but once again Mrs. Conniff favored Claudia with no more than a nod of recognition and an arid smile.

"How lovely you look," said Kitty Lodder to Claudia. "You must have had your gown made in town, for even the best of our modistes, who are usually quite good and *à la mode*, have not quite that flair for cut, and the color is so vastly becoming to you.''

Claudia sought Lindsay's eyes and he acknowledged her challenging glance with an engaging smile. "I'm promised to play whist with Charmichael and Stewart,'' he said to Claudia, "but I leave you in good hands. Kitty's up to every rig and row; she'll steer you clear of the sharks.''

"I wish I might have enjoyed her guidance a fortnight ago,'' Claudia said to him in a dulcet tone.

Lindsay's smile broadened, but Mrs. Lodder, not understanding their private jest, said, "Did you have bad luck at cards? You needn't be concerned that you will squander your pin money here. We only play for what most of the men regard as chicken stakes. The gentlemen only come here at all because it is the fashion to do so and so that they may flirt openly with their inamoratas while their wives are occupied at the whist tables.''

"And who do their wives flirt with while they are at play?'' Claudia asked archly.

"Why, their cicisbei, of course,'' Lindsay said promptly. "I believe, my dear, that yours has arrived.'' He made her and Mrs. Lodder a brief bow and left them.

Claudia searched the room with her eyes and saw that Andrew was conversing with another gentleman near the door. She was nonplussed by Lindsay's remark. He spoke quite matter-of-factly and with no disapproval in his tone, but Claudia was disturbed that he had noted her attraction to Andrew. She had not realized that she had so easily given herself away.

But the fact that Lindsay was not blind to the attraction she felt toward his cousin did not prevent her from welcoming Andrew with obvious pleasure when he approached her a few minutes later. If Lindsay had displayed the smallest hint of censure, she might have been more circumspect, but she found herself piqued by his appearance of complete unconcern.

"I wonder that Lindsay can bear to let you out of his sight

tonight," Andrew said as he bowed over her hand. "You have never looked lovelier, dear Cousin. I confess myself quite dazzled."

Claudia accepted his fulsome compliments with a laughing disclaimer, but the admiration in Andrew's eyes was plain to be seen and she could not help contrasting this to Lindsay's critical, almost-detached evaluation of her appearance. She knew it shouldn't have mattered to her what Lindsay thought, since theirs was purely a business arrangement, but it rankled nevertheless.

"Do you play tonight?" Andrew asked. "You must uphold the standard set by your father for superb play."

"Were you acquainted with my father?"

"I hadn't that pleasure," Andrew replied, "but I certainly knew of him by repute." Claudia looked up at him with a swift startled glance and he saw the defensiveness spring into her eyes. "I meant that he was renowned as a top-of-the-trees sportsman," he added gently. "As is your husband. In fact, I confess myself surprised when I learned of your marriage. It would have been more in Lin's style to have returned to town with his friend's best hunter in tow rather than a bride."

"I must thank you for the pretty compliment, my lord," she said with exaggerated civility. "Mr. Bingerley's best hunter threw out a spavin, so Lindsay was obliged to settle for me."

"I meant that Lindsay is ot known to be much in the petticoat line," Andrew said with an appreciative smile. "I always supposed he would pop the question to some female he met on the hunting field while his resistance was low after a long day in the saddle."

Claudia laughingly admonished him, but given Lindsay's flat unromanticism, she privately agreed. Andrew challenged her to a game of piquet, but Claudia, because of the game's association for her, refused, claiming a prior commitment to play whist with Lady Ellacott. She did so for better than half the evening, but after refreshments had been served, when Andrew begged her again to pit her skill against his, she finally agreed.

Andrew played well—not with Lindsay's skill, but with sufficient ability to prevent Claudia from winning too easily. During the play their conversation was limited mostly to declarations, and when the game was over, he ruefully declared himself to be beneath her touch. "I bow to your superior skill, Cousin. You are a more equal match for Lindsay, I fear. If you were to play with him, he would give you a more challenging game."

"I have already had that pleasure," Claudia said with a dry inflection. She agreed to his suggestion that they stroll about the room, and allowed him to take her hand and place it on his arm.

"I hope I did not offend you with my plain speaking about Lindsay, Claudia," he said as they wove their way through the many tables. "Our acquaintance is from the cradle and you will find we are both rather free in our opinions of each other."

"Quite free," Claudia agreed with a smile. "I am put in mind of my two stepbrothers who are separated in age by less than a year. Though there is a deep affection between them, each seems driven by a need to prove himself the equal or superior of the other at most skills."

"Yes, that is how it is between us," Andrew agreed. "Lindsay's latest success has put my nose sadly out of joint." He smiled down at Claudia, who was regarding him in an inquiring way. "In the most important arena of all," he said, "that of the heart, I am utterly routed."

Claudia, thinking he referred to his disappointment with Miss Merrifield, said, "Vivian and Lady Ellacott have told me that you have cause to be unhappy, but you should regard it in a positive way, as not meant to be rather than as a failure."

"It is not my failure I regard so much as Lindsay's success."

Claudia looked at him in surprise. "Surely you would not carry your rivalry to the length of attempting to best each other in an affair of the heart."

He shook his head slowly. "It isn't that." He paused and added, "I'm afraid if I tell you, you will disbelieve me or condemn me for being the most fickle creature alive.''

"Why should I?''

"It is not Lindsay's success in matters of the heart that I envy, it is that *you* are his chosen bride.''

They had left the main assembly room and were strolling the corridor outside, which was nearly empty. Claudia was suddenly aware that they were virtually alone. His meaning was ambiguous and she chose to deliberately misunderstand him. "I am sure you need not envy us. You will meet someone else who will engage your heart.''

They reached the end of the corridor and he stopped and turned to her, taking both her hands in his. "I already have.''

"Please do not,'' Claudia pleaded, not wanting to hear the declaration she knew was coming.

"Tell me that you did not feel the same current of attraction when we met, Claudia,'' he said, his voice low and vibrant, "and look at me as you do so, and I will never speak of my feelings for you again.''

She wanted to say it, but the words denying her attraction to him refused to form on her lips. "You know I cannot,'' she said accusingly. "You should not be speaking to me in such a way, even if it is true.''

"How could I help saying to you what is in my heart?''

His tone was so melodramatic and his words so like something from a play that Claudia's sense of the absurd was kindled and she had to bit her lip to keep from smiling. This was too serious a matter for levity. "I am your cousin's wife,'' she said severely.

"Did you feel the same for Lindsay when you met?'' he demanded. "Do you even feel it for him now?''

There was no doubt of her answer to this, but she could not permit herself to make such an awful admission, which would give Andrew the encouragement that he sought. "I have no intention of betraying my husband with you or anyone else, my lord,'' she said coldly.

"But you would betray your own feelings.'' She attempted to withdraw her hands from his, but he would not release her. "I'm sorry, Claudia. Please, don't run away from me. You are right, I shouldn't be speaking to you in such a way, but I can't be still when my need for you is so strong.''

Claudia scarcely knew how to respond to him. Her heart was pounding and she felt a mixture of excitement and trepidation. It was intoxicating to have a man as attractive as Andrew declare himself captivated, but her values, which were deeply instilled, would not permit her to forget that she was another man's wife, however loveless that marriage might be. The world, she knew, would think as Andrew clearly did: that as long as she did not love Lindsay or he love her, it was perfectly admissible for her to take a lover, but she could not convince herself that it would be other than immoral and utterly reprehensible.

When she remained silent, he said, "Silence denotes consent. I may be precipitate, but I know I am not mistaken. I am not, am I, Claudia?''

"If you are so certain, why do you ask?'' she said evasively.

"Dear Lord, Claudia,'' he said forcefully. "Cast me some crumb. Tell me at the least that you are not indifferent to me.''

Claudia could not ignore his appeal. "I am not indifferent,'' she admitted, though she knew that in doing so, she was ensuring that he would continue to pursue her.

He let out his breath as if he had been holding it and gave a soft, self-mocking laugh. "And with that I shall be content. For now, at least. I'll take you back to my aunt.''

Claudia consented to take his arm and they returned to the principal room.

Lady Ellacott was not at the whist table where Claudia had last seen her but in a corner of the room on a sofa in a grouping of chairs set aside for those who wished a respite from the play. Beside her was Lindsay. Claudia knew she had no reason to reproach herself, but she would have preferred not to have had to face her husband so immediately after her *tête-à-tête* with Andrew. For a moment she imagined there was a speculative look in Lindsay's eyes as they rested briefly on her, but his manner when he greeted them showed no sign of suspicion.

"There you are, dear Claudia,'' said the dowager. "If you

don't mind, I thought we would leave a bit early. The assemblies always end promptly at eleven and it is such a crush to find a sedan chair with everyone leaving at once.''

"I don't mind in the least," Claudia said without hesitation. "I am a little tired, in any case."

Andrew promptly offered to procure their chairs and he and Lindsay went ahead of them to do so. Claudia and Lady Ellacott followed at a more leisurely pace. "Did you enjoy yourself, my dear? I am afraid that our card assemblies are a bit tame for the younger people."

"Oh, I did not find it so," Claudia said with more truth than the dowager could know. "I enjoy playing at cards and I am quite content with quiet affairs until I feel less strange with so many new acquaintances."

"It is good that Andrew is here," Lady Ellacott said, "and that Harriet Maye's daughters happen to be staying with her as well. This way you have a few acquaintances with whom you may feel comfortable right away, and in time your circle will expand in a natural way. I hope you and Lindsay mean to spend a portion of each year in Bath. I know he has always loved the town, I wish you might come to do so as well."

"I am sure I shall," Claudia said politely as they reached the entrance hall.

Lindsay and Andrew were waiting for them with their sedan chairs. Andrew declined an invitation to Laura Place, and as he voiced his regrets, he handed Claudia into her chair, bowing low over her hand with an intimate smile and a speaking look.

When they arrived home, Lady Ellacott insisted that they have tea before retiring. They sat for about an hour discussing the events of the evening before Lady Ellacott at last arose to go up to her bedchamber. "I sent word to my man of business, Mr. Jolliet, yesterday that I wished him to wait on me," she said before she quitted the room. "He is coming at ten, if either of you wish to be part of our discussion. There will be no papers to sign yet, Lindsay, for I want to hear what suggestions Mr. Jolliet may make before I decide on any disposition of property."

"We shall both join you, Aunt Jane," Lindsay said

promptly. "I am sure Mr. Jolliet's suggestions will be valuable."

Claudia knew that this was what Lindsay had been waiting to hear since their arrival in Bath. She herself was more than a little curious to hear what their settlement would be, not so much to know the actual amount that would be decided upon but as the end of the chapter that had begun with her marriage to Lindsay.

Claudia also decided to go up to bed and started to follow Lady Ellacott, but Lindsay caught her arm as she bid him good night and drew her into a swift embrace. Once again he kissed her as he had at Lovewell House, lightly but with an intimacy that set her heart pounding.

When he released her, she looked at him in astonishment. His smile was characteristically bland. "Good night, dear wife," he said softly with an underlying suggestion of deeper meaning in his voice.

"Good night," Claudia said in a voice that was barely steady.

Lady Ellacott was standing by the door waiting for Claudia and gazing upon them fondly. But Claudia was certain that this time Lindsay had kissed for a reason other than to convince his godmother of the affection between them.

Mary found her mistress very untalkative as she undressed and combed out Claudia's hair. Claudia had more than one cause for concern to occupy her. Interpreting Lindsay's behavior as he bid her good night, she was sure that it was his way of informing her that he was not blind to her flirtation with Andrew. It had been an act of possession.

Almost as upsetting to Claudia was her own response to Lindsay's kiss. Once again she had been stirred in spite of herself. Though she felt none of the strong attraction for her husband that she felt for Andrew, Lindsay's embrace had set her pulse beating as rapidly as had Andrew's.

It disturbed her very much that she could be attracted to one man and yet respond to another, and made her wonder if perhaps she had feeling fors Lindsay of whic she was unaware. She found this thought even more alarming. Her relationship with Lindsay was a business transaction entered into for their mutual benefit and mutually agreed upon that it should be nothing more.

Perhaps there was some degree of physical attraction, but she would not allow that there could be more. Claudia was certain on his side there was not. Her experience with the George Bingerleys of the world had taught her that men need not feel more than desire for a woman to approach her; and beyond his kissing her, she had no indication that Lindsay had any feeling for her other than that of friendship.

As little as she wished to form an illicit connection with Andrew did she wish to find herself becoming attracted to a husband who would never feel more for her than a tepid desire. She could not call it more when they had slept together in the same bed so chastely. It was something, perhaps, if he disliked her flirtation with his cousin, but that was likely more owing to pride than any deeper emotion.

Of all the pitfalls that she had imagined she would face marrying a man who was virtually a stranger solely for the sake of convenience, the one that had never occurred to her was that she might be in danger of falling in love with him. Her last thought as she at last fell into sleep was that she would never be so great a fool.

The following morning, promptly at ten, Mr. Jolliet arrived at Laura Place, and Lady Ellacott insisted that Lindsay and Claudia be present from the beginning of their discussion. When they came into the library, where the meeting was to take place, she took the hand of each of them and said, "You make the most delightful pair. I must tell you, Claudia, that I was delighted that Lindsay had chosen the daughter of an old friend for his bride, but now that I have come to know you a little, I am delighted for your own sake. If Lindsay had planned this to please me, he could not have made a better choice."

Claudia dared a quick sardonic glance at Lindsay, which he met with the faintest upturn of his lips. "Thank you, Aunt Jane," he said soberly. He then bent a tender glance on Claudia and added quite untruthfully, "But I confess your approval was not my first consideration."

Lady Ellacott laughed as she settled on a small sofa near

the tall double windows. She motioned Claudia to sit beside her. "Of course, not, dear boy," she said indulgently. "But I never supposed you would forget what you owe your position and contract a *mésalliance*."

"Such choices are always unfortunate," said Mr. Jolliet. He sat at the desk in the window overlooking the street, cleared his throat, and began, "I understand, Lady Ellacott, that you have decided to make an immediate settlement on Lord and Lady Lindsay, conferring on them an annual income in addition to other endowments in your will."

"I am not sure what amount I have in mind in principal," Lady Ellacott said, "but I thought to give Lindsay and Claudia an additional ten thousand a year. With what you already have from your mother, Lindsay, you should be comfortably fixed. Then, of course, when you begin to fill your nursery, I shall make appropriate additions as necessary. You know how I look forward to spoiling your little ones when they come."

Lindsay smiled with obvious gratification. "Unless I discover that Claudia has a penchant for gaming for high stakes, I expect we shall manage quite well."

Claudia was too stunned to respond to his deliberately provocative words. Lindsay had told her that his present income was about six thousand a year—a huge sum in itself to her thinking—but now their income would be more than sixteen thousand a year. She had never imagined it would be such an amount, and realized that Lindsay, at least, had been playing for very high stakes indeed that night at the Red Doe.

"I hope Lady Lindsay may not have a taste for gaming," Jolliet said with a disapproving frown for Lindsay.

"Oh, no," Lady Ellacott replied, patting Claudia's hand. "Claudia is much too sensible. It is a sad thing to see any female go the way of poor Georgiana Devonshire. They say when she died and Devonshire learned the whole of her debt, he was quite horrified, despite the extent of his fortune."

"Claudia has already learned the danger of an incautious wager," Lindsay said audaciously.

"Have you, my dear?" asked Lady Ellacott, her brow creasing with concern. "I hope the stakes were not too high."

"It was a wager of no consequence," Claudia responded, casting a quick warning glance at Lindsay.

Mr. Jolliet cleared his throat again and brought the discussion back to the point. Within half an hour all of the particulars had been considered and debated and Mr. Jolliet began to put the papers on which he had taken notes into his leather satchel. "If you do decide to accept your aunt's offer to purchase you a house here in Bath and make it your principal residence," he said to Lindsay, "get in touch with my assistant and he will go over with you a list my office maintains of properties currently on the market."

"Claudia and I must discuss the matter," Lindsay replied, "but I think it likely that we shall do as Aunt Jane wishes. Bath has always been more my home than London or even Landgrove."

"Going to take up residence, are you, Lin?" asked Andrew coming into the room unannounced. "Aunt Jane will be pleased." With these words he bent and kissed Lady Ellacott dutifully on the cheek and bowed over Claudia's hand with such a smoldering look that it was clear, at least to her, that he wished to kiss her in a very different way.

"I hope Lindsay and Claudia mean to do so," Lady Ellacott confirmed. "I have offered to purchase them a house if they will do so."

Andrew turned, his brows rising as he looked from his aunt to Lindsay. "Oh, is that why Jolliet was here?"

"Yes," said the dowager. "You know I told Lindsay that I would settle an immediate sum on him and his wife if he made a suitable marriage. I think it is always a shame to make one's heirs wait until one is dead to enjoy a good income."

"And Lindsay, as usual, has lived up to expectation," Andrew said with an enigmatic inflection that nevertheless betrayed a hint of acid. "My felicitations, Cousin."

Lindsay, who had seen Claudia's blush when Andrew had bowed over her hand, said softly, "I take no credit for running true to type. It appears to be a family characteristic.

Did you ask Rumbold for me if he means to sell his bays?''

"More horses, Lindsay?" inquired Lady Ellacott. "I hope you do not mean to spend the whole of your income on hay and grain. Your wife may have something to say on that head.''

"I merely replace the chestnuts I sold to Alderley last month. He offered me such an absurdly high price that I could not refuse it, though they were prime goers and I was sorry to lose them.'' Lindsay favored Claudia with a lazy smile. "I shall buy a pretty hack for Claudia as well, and then she won't be able to berate me.''

"I don't ride," Claudia said, aware that such a statement made to a sportsman like Lindsay must sound like sacrilege.

Andrew gave a sharp bark of laughter. "Good Lord, Lin. Didn't you know that? You must be in love if you asked Claudia to marry you before you saw her mounted.''

"I didn't conduct my courtship on the hunting field, Drew. I intend to teach Claudia to ride. She is quite excited at the prospect, are you not, my love?"

"Oh, quite," she said without enthusiasm. Claudia was not afraid of horses, but once, while she was still in the nursery, she had been put up on her father's horse during a visit to the country estate of a friend, and the skittish animal had been restive beneath her, causing her to grab handsful of mane to remain in the saddle. She had not fallen, but she thought it a long way to the ground from atop her father's hunter and had never minded that this aspect of a gentlewoman's education had been neglected in her. She had no reason to believe her sentiments would change on repeating the experience.

Storry entered the room to escort the solicitor to the door, and shortly after, Lindsay remembered an engagement and Claudia had letters to answer from her mother and Vivian. The earl stood to take leave of them, holding Claudia's hand in his for a bit longer than was absolutely necessary.

When he released her, Claudia unconsciously touched her hand where Andrew's fingers had rested. She looke dup to find Lindsay regarding her, but as before, there was nothing in his expression to suggest that he in any way objected to his cousin's attentions to his wife. Claudia was aware of the conflicting sensations of annoyance and relief, and decided that the latter was the more pertinent. She had no intention of allowing her relationship with Lindsay to become anything more than they had agreed upon.

# 6

Claudia had not taken Lindsay's comment about teaching her to ride seriously, but a few days later at dinner he informed her that her lessons could begin as soon as she wished.

Claudia was not at all certain that she wished to learn, but for the dowager's sake she said, "I would like it above all things, but I have no dress suitable for riding. I suppose I may have one made, but it will take some time before it is ready."

"I was saving this surprise for you, Claudia," said Lady Ellacott with the air of someone conferring a great treat. "When I realized that we had not thought to order a habit when we were shopping, I had Kerry alter one of mine to fit you. She is an excellent needlewoman and I think you will be quite pleased with the result. You shall need to have a habit or two made for you, of course, but this should do quite well for your lessons."

Claudia turned her eyes to Lindsay, who was regarding her with the blandness that she was coming to recognize as a sure sign of his guilt. "Did you know of this, Lindsay?" She tapped his hand none too gently with the edge of her fan. "How bad of you to give me no hint of it."

Lindsay nobly refrained from wincing, but he removed his hand from the likelihood of further attack. "I didn't wish to spoil the surprise." He got up. "I'll send word to the mews

to have our horses brought around at seven-thirty tomorrow
so that we can begin before breakfast. You would not wish
to postpone it, I know.''

Claudia would have gladly postponed the riding lesson
indefinitely, and she felt that he knew it. A small knot of
anxiety formed in her stomach, but she concealed her inner
agitation and consented to Lindsay's proposal without demur.

The following morning when Kerry helped her into the
amber-brown riding habit, Claudia had to admit that whatever
manner of figure she would cut on the back of the horse,
the dress at least greatly became her. She allowed her hair
to be coaxed into a tight knot at the nape of her neck and
a jaunty beaver was set on the soft curls that framed her face.

Lindsay was outside, already mounted and awaiting her.
The dun gelding Lady Ellacott's groom, John, held for her
seemed placid enough and not overly large, but still she felt
a tremor of nervousness as he hoisted her into the saddle.

Coming up beside her, Lindsay showed her how to hold
the reins and instructed her in the basic commands she would
need to give her mount. His horse was a rather large-boned
chestnut with a wide blaze and rolling eyes. The chestnut
didn't kick out at her horse, but he had an alarming habit
of raising his near hind leg and bringing it down again with
a discernible thud near enough to her mount to make him
sidle.

''Just keep a short rein on Lancelot until we are out of
the city,'' Lindsay said to her as they started at a sedate walk
down Laura Place, ''and don't let Hotspur trouble you. He
likes to put on a show of bravado but he has no vice.''

Claudia eyed the chestnut more nervously than she did her
own horse, but Lindsay was close enough beside her to take
her reins if she had trouble, and the groom was to her right
and a little behind to make her feel that she was comfortably
surrounded.

''Aunt Jane has a taste for fanciful names,'' he said,
looking over the dun gelding with a critical eye. ''You
needn't fear Lancelot will live up to his brave name. He's
a comfortable ride, if not quite a complete slug.''

Claudia only hoped his idea of comfortable was similar to hers. "Is Hotspur yours?"

Lindsay nodded. "He is *not* a slug."

Claudia still regarded the larger gelding dubiously as it tossed its head to the limit of its martingale and mouthed its bit. "He looks as if it would like to bolt with you."

Lindsay smiled. "I daresay he would. But don't look alarmed, he won't be given the opportunity, and in any case, I doubt Lancelot would be tempted to take his lead. We'll continue until the fields just beyond Sydney Gardens and then we'll have our first lesson. There's nothing I can comfortably show you in the street."

It was not a great distance to ride beyond the pleasure gardens, but Claudia wished they were not to go so far. Yet, by the time they had at last reached the open country, she found, to her astonishment, that she rather liked the feel of the rhythm of the horse beneath her and that she was far more willing to begin her lesson than she had supposed she would be.

Lindsay began by reinforcing the simple commands he had taught her at the start, teaching her to post and how to put her horse on the proper lead for the canter. At first the increased pace frightened Claudia, but in a very short time it exhilarated her. When Lindsay at last informed her that they had covered enough for her first lesson and could return home, she actually felt a pang of disappointment. She bent forward and bestowed a grateful pat on Lancelot's neck as she had seen many horsemen do when their horses performed well.

"He is an excellent creature," she said to Lindsay, who pulled up Hotspur beside her. "I only hope he may forgive you for calling him a slug."

"I didn't quite say that," Lindsay protested as they turned their horses toward Bath again at a walk. "I should find him a bit slow-going, perhaps, but he's first-rate for our purpose. Do you like him so much? Shall I make Aunt Jane an offer for him?"

A sparkle of pleasure came into Claudia's eyes and then

quickly died. "I could not accept so extravagant a gift."

"No?" Lindsay asked with mild surprise. "Not even from your husband?"

"It wasn't part of our agreement that you should buy me horses. I see that it is necessary for me to dress more fashionably if I am to be a credit to you, but it would be unfair of me to expect more than that."

Used to grasping high-flyers and matchmaking mamas who assessed his material worth and prospects before exposing their impressionable daughters to his company, Lindsay was amused. "What a pinchpenny I have taken to wife," he declared as if aghast. "My dear Claudia, what you have had of me are the merest fripperies."

"You have not seen the tradesman's bills yet," she countered.

"That is true," he said gravely. "Am I quite ruined, then?"

"I only hope you may still be laughing at quarter-day," Claudia replied, laughing herself. "I am serious, though, Lindsay. If there is anything you think extravagant, I wish you will deduct it from the portion of the settlement you have promised me."

"Don't be absurd," he said, sounding annoyed. "I should cut a pretty figure keeping such an account for my wife."

"But ours are not the usual circumstances," Claudia insisted.

"No," Lindsay agreed with a wry smile, "they are not. But I think that on the whole we have dealt with them tolerably well. Do you still wish we had never met at the Red Doe?"

Claudia's eyes flickered to his. "I never said that."

"But I'll wager you've thought it." He laughed.

"Occasionally," she admitted. "I am not sorry we met," she added, and knew that she meant it.

Lindsay's eyes stayed on her for a moment and then he simply said, "I'm glad."

Claudia felt suddenly shy. "Will you teach me to hunt as well?" she asked to cover it.

"If you like. In six weeks you should be ready to manage

a few low hurdles. Would you like to learn to drive as well?''

"Yes, I think I would," Claudia said without hesitation. She saw him regarding her quizzically and laughed. "Yes, I know this is a turnabout for me, but I never guessed I should like riding half so well."

''Don't fall into the error of overenthusiasm at the start. If you push yourself too far too soon, you will end up stiff as a ramrod and declaring that only fools let themselves be jostled about on great smelly beasts.''

Claudia protested, but as they approached the entrance to Syndey Gardens, her attention was claimed by the sight of approaching riders. One of these was Andrew, another was Mrs. Hart, and the other two were Mr. Cassalet and his wife, whom Claudia had met at a small soiree she had attended the previous evening.

Andrew detached himself frm the other two and rode up to Lindsay and Claudia. "My dear Claudia! Can my eyes deceive me?" he said, reaching for Claudia's hand to press to his lips. "I thought you didn't ride, and yet I find you looking like Dianna mounted and ready for the hunt.''

As usual, the mere sight of him was enough to raise Claudia's pulse, and even knowing that Lindsay's eyes were on her could not prevent the warmth of the flush that stole over her. "Not quite that," she said, smiling in an attempt to pretend that she felt no confusion. "But Lindsay does not believe me hopeless.''

"Far from it. Claudia has done superbly," Lindsay concurred. "She has light hands and a comfortable seat. The talent is clearly inborn. The rest will be merely technique.''

The Cassalets and Mrs. Hart came up to them at a more sedate pace. After the barest exchange of greetings with Claudia, Mrs. Hart turned to Lindsay and said, "It is really too bad of you, my lord. Did you forget you were promised to ride with us this morning? We waited nearly three-quarters of an hour and only gave up when we met up with Strait, who told us he had not seen you since last night.''

"Did we have an engagement, Sally?" he said in a soft drawl. "I can't recall it.''

"I thought it was understood," she said with a pretty pout.

Claudia thought she saw a flicker of annoyance come into Lindsay's eyes, but he smiled with his usual amiability. "Not to my knowledge," he said in a soft murmur.

"We're going out near Beechen Cliff to look at the view," Mr. Cassalet informed Claudia. "Beg you and Lord Lindsay will join us. Daresay you'd like it excessively, Lady Lindsay, since you've never seen it before."

Claudia would have liked it very much, but she doubted her newfound horsemanship was up to a long excursion. "Thank you, but I fear I am only a novice rider, and frankly, a rather tired one, so I beg you'll excuse me. But that does not mean Lindsay cannot join you if he wishes."

"I too shall beg off today," said Lindsay without hesitation.

"Please don't for my sake, Lindsay," Claudia pleaded, feeling a little guilty that her lesson had kept him from another engagement. "John may escort me back to Laura Place."

"*I* shall escort you, Cousin," said Andrew promptly. "I have another engagement this morning and I'm not going, in any event. Go along with Sally and Fred, Lin. Claudia is in safe hands, I promise you."

"Of course she is," Mrs. Hart said as she maneuvered her horse beside Lindsay's. "Come, Lindsay, you mustn't disappoint us."

Claudia added her voice to the chorus again. "Please go, Lindsay. I shall feel that it is because of me if you do not, and I should dislike that excessively."

Lindsay's eyes met hers in a long look, but the expression in them was so unreadable that she almost felt as though he looked through her. "Very well," he said in a voice that, for him, was so clipped it was almost curt. "Tell Aunt Jane I shan't be back for luncheon."

Mrs. Hart was clearly delighted by his decision and she leaned toward Lindsay to say something to him that dissolved his sober expression and brought back his more usual smile. Claudia, viewing them with their heads together, felt somehow excluded. The parties separated and she and Drew continued on toward Laura Place, but Claudia could not resist turning in the saddle and looking after the others for a moment. Yet again she had an uncomfortable sensation of separateness and wished she might ride after them.

She turned back and glanced at Andrew, who was regarding her with a level gaze. "Did you enjoy your first lesson, Cousin Claudia?"

"Very much," Claudia replied, and launched on a monologue describing all that she had learned that morning. In spite of the presence of the groom a discreet distance behind them, Claudia felt a bit uncomfortable being alone with Andrew, and it was the only thing she could think of to do to prevent him from flirting with her.

Andrew appeared to take her hint and made her no further compliments; instead, he made suggestions about riding that were not precisely contradictory of what Lindsay had taught her that morning, but that managed to convey that better methods might have been employed to make her lesson easier and her advancement quicker.

"But everyone says that Lindsay is a first-rate horseman." Claudia said. "I'm certain I may trust him to instruct me in the best manner."

She did not mean to deliver a set-down to Andrew, she was merely speaking her thought aloud, but his color heightened. "Oh, yes, Lindsay is a top-of-the-trees Corinthian," he agreed. "There is no doubt of that. I did not mean to suggest that he is not, merely that he is being excessively careful in schooling you. You seem so eager to advance that you may soon find yourself chafing at his caution."

Claudia saw that she had offended him. "Perhaps I shall," she said gently, though she did not believe that she would, for she had enjoyed her lesson and Lindsay's method of teaching her excessively.

They rode on in silence for several minutes, and Claudia's thoughts returned to her husband and the party he had joined. "Have Lindsay and Mrs. Hart known each other for some time?" she asked cautiously, uncertain why she did so. It was obvious that Lindsay and Mrs. Hart were on terms of intimacy.

"They have been particular friends for many years," he

said, the insinuation in his tone unmistakable, though his next words sought to deny it. "But you must not make any foolish assumptions. I am certain it is nothing more."

Claudia feelings were mixed. She knew it was not improbable that Lindsay would have a mistress—if not Mrs. Hart, then someone else—but she found the idea of it somehow distasteful and chose to accept Andrew's assurance, though it was tepidly given. She informed him that she was not given to foolish assumptions and then quite deliberately changed the subject.

When she told Lady Ellacott a bit later where Lindsay had gone and with whom, she was further relieved that the dowager gave not the slightest sign of concern or disapproval, which Claudia was certain she would have done if she knew or suspected that Lindsay and Mrs. Hart were lovers. Claudia gratefully put the entire disturbing idea out of her mind.

Over the next sennight, Claudia's riding lessons continued daily, and as her skill in the saddle grew, so did the friendship between her and her husband. She felt at times as if they had known each other far longer than a month, and to her surprise she sometimes found herself confiding her feelings and philosophies to him as she once had with her brother William.

Only two things occurred to mar this comfortable relationship. The first was Andrew's constant attentions to her, which, though she was careful not to actively encourage, she could not quite bring herself to completely discourage. At least there was no hint of reproach from Lindsay; at times she even wondered if he noticed.

The second was the pricking of her own conscience because by pretending to be in love with Lindsay, she was deliberately deceiving Lady Ellacott, of whom she was also growing genuinely fond. Though it was unquestionable that the dowager could be quite autocratic and even manipulative at times, Claudia believed that there was no malice in her, merely a wish to control the lives of those she cared for, for what the dowager perceived as their own good.

Mr. Jolliet returned at the end of the following week with

the settlement papers drawn up and ready for signature, but Lady Ellacott, who was also becoming quite attached to Claudia, decided that she wished to make changes to give Claudia a small income of her own. "So that you will not be quite dependent on Lindsay even for your pin money," she explained. "I have always enjoyed my own income even when Ellacott was alive, and I pitied my friends who hadn't a penny to bless themselves with except by the good grace of their husbands."

She gave no weight to Claudia's assurances that it was unnecessary. "No, my dear, I have quite made up my mind to it," she insisted, "and when you and Lindsay have little ones, I shall see to it that they too have a bit of independence, though you needn't fear I mean to spoil them."

The lovely dresses and gowns that Claudia had ordered began to arrive, so that her transformation from mousy governess to fashionable young matron was virtually complete. Lindsay insisted on giving her an exquisite set of sapphires, which brought out the blue in her eyes, and Lady Ellacott bestowed on her several pair of earrings and a diamond choker despite Claudia's protests that she was being too generous. The dowager continued to urge Claudia to make free use of her own jewels as well.

On the evening of the first private ball that Claudia was to attend at the home of Lord and Lady Welby, Lady Ellacott said, "My dear, it has just occurred to me that the Ellacott diamonds would go famously with your gown. Do please me by wearing them tonight."

Claudia was touched and a little alarmed by the offer, for she knew the diamonds were a family heirloom and virtually priceless. "You are most generous, ma'am, but I think I should be terrified all night that I would loose them or that a stone would somehow come loose from its setting."

Lady Ellacott laughed at her fears. "Nonsense. You must get used to wearing them, my dear, for with the title in abeyance and no other Ellacott to pass them on to, they shall go to Lindsay when I die, and so to you."

Claudia put aside her misgivings and followed Lady Ellacott to her dressing room. Instead of ringing for Kerry, the dowager pulled a small stepping stool to the farthest end of the mirrored cupboard and lifted a leather-covered case from a top shelf. Claudia, fearing for Lady Ellacott's safety, reached to take it from her as the dowager stepped down from the stool.

Lady Ellacott produced a small key from a fine chain pinned to the pocket of her underdress and opened the lock. The case had three velvet-lined drawers and she opened the middle one of these. The diamonds were shaped into fine rosettes of gradually diminishing size from a center rosette the core of which contained a stone of several carats. It ought to have been gaudy, but was so delicately wrought that it was, instead, exquisite.

The many facets of the stones caught the light in the room and spit out small darts of brilliant fire. Claudia, who had no particular fondness for jewels, was mesmerized. "It is the loveliest necklace I have ever seen!"

Lady Ellacott smiled, pleased by her reaction, and helped her to fasten the diamonds about her throat. She then opened the bottom drawer and extracted a pair of diamond rosette earrings that exactly matched the necklace.

Claudia took them and went to the dressing table to remove her pearls and insert the diamonds. She turned to Lady Ellacott and smiled delightedly, her eyes sparkling to match the diamonds. Her simply cut gown of pale green silk, the color of sea froth, was made infinitely more becoming by the wonderful jewels.

"Thank you, Aunt Jane," she said with genuine gratitude. "I promise to take very good care of them, though I know I shall probably be on the fidget all night for fear that an earring will fall out or the clasp come undone."

Lady Ellacott laughed. "I beg you will not be so foolish. As Lady Lindsay you must do your husband credit. And that means always being turned out as finely as you can be."

Perhaps it was the boost of confidence that wearing such magnificent jewels gave her, but Claudia felt that she had never looked lovelier in her life, and with the assurance this gave her she enjoyed Lady Welby's ball more than any other entertainment she had attended since coming to Bath as Lindsay's wife.

Although waltzes were not permitted at any of the public Bath assemblies, no such conservative restrictions were placed on private parties and Claudia permitted both Lindsay and Andrew to lead herinto the exhilarating dance.

Of the two, she decided that Lindsay was the more skilled performer, but it was more exciting to be held in Andrew's embrace without any fear of censure, and she enjoyed the thrill of flirting with him more openly.

When they returned to Laura Place, Claudia followed Lady Ellacott to her dressing room to see the Ellacott diamonds safely returned to their case. Claudia was occupied with undoing the clasp of the necklace and gave only a portion of her attention to Lady Ellacott as she climbed the stepping stool to remove the leather case again from the shelf. She looked up sharply when she heard the other woman gasp and saw a white object come rolling forward off the top of the jewel box. The danger to Lady Ellacott did not register in her mind until she heard that lady give a stifled scream and saw her falling from the stool. The white object hit Lady Ellacott's shoulder squarely and bounced to the floor, shattering. The jewel box teetering on the edge of the shelf started to topple as well and only Claudia's sudden movement to pull Lady Ellacott away from the wardrobe saved her from being struck by that as well.

Miss Kerry came rushing in from her mistress's bedchamber and there was sufficient noise from the accident that a footman who was in the hall came running into the room also, followed by Lindsay and his man, Rush. The scene that greeted Lindsay was sufficient to disturb even his usual sangfroid. Claudia was on the floor nearly prone, with Lady Ellacott stretched out against her. There was blood on Claudia's gown and Kerry was screeching that her mistress had been killed.

Lindsay curtly ordered the footman to remove the hysterical dresser and to see to it that no other curious servants were given admittance to the room. He then knelt beside Claudia and his godmother. He lifted Lady Ellacott gently and carried her into her bedchamber. Claudia, shaken and unsteady herself, allowed Rush to help her to her feet, and she followed them into the other room.

"What has happened?" he asked in a level voice when he had deposited the swooning dowager on the bed.

"I am not sure," Claudia said, her voice trembling a little. "Something fell off the shelf when Aunt Jane moved the jewel box, and fell on her. I don't think it hit her head. She has just fainted." There was a small gash on the dowager's shoulder from which blood was slowly oozing to bear this out.

Lindsay instructed his valet to see to it that his aunt's doctor was sent for immediately, and then said to Claudia, "See if there is any water in the pitcher beside the dressing table. If not, see if you can convince that banshee in the other room to fetch some for you."

Claudia was not driven to such straits, for there was sufficient water in the pitcher for her to soak several fine lawn handkerchiefs that she found in a drawer of the dressing table. Lindsay took one of these from Claudia and placed it on Lady Ellacott's brow; with another he cleansed the blood from the wound on her shoulder.

Lady Ellacott moaned and her eyes fluttered open. "Oh, my goodness. Did it hit me?" She tried to sit up and winced with pain as her question was clearly answered.

Claudia took one of Lady Ellacott's hands, gently chaffing it. "Yes, Aunt Jane, it did, but only on the shoulder. I was terrified that it would strike your head, but you moved back in time."

"Yes, I recall now. I was so stunned that I could not move again, and it was you who pulled me away before the jewel case fell on me as well." She squeezed Claudia's fingers painfully, so strong was her emotion. "You have saved my life, my dear."

Lindsay had walked into the dressing room again and now he returned carrying several pieces of the object that had fallen on his aunt.

"What on earth is it, Lindsay?" asked Lady Ellacott, looking around Claudia to observe her nephew as he fitted the largest pieces together.

He looked up and said with obvious puzzlement. "It is Uncle Tom's head of Cicero." He stood and came toward them, holding the three largest pieces together to make at least two-thirds of the head complete. It was of miniature size of the sort used as a shelf decoration or a paperweight and appropriately weighted with lead for that purpose. It was small, but a solid, heavy object.

"How on earth did that come to be in my dress cupboard?" demanded Lady Ellacott.

Lindsay shook his head, but his expression was grim. He said, "I have sent Rush to fetch Doctor Canby, Aunt Jane. I think your shoulder may be dislocated and it would be foolish to wait until morning when swelling might make resetting the joint even more painful."

Lady Ellacott agreed, though her smile was wan at the prospect of further pain to her shoulder, but she did not protest and dutifully remained on her bed until the doctor arrived.

The doctor came promptly, having been fetched by Rush personally, and concurred that the Lady Ellacott's shoulder was indeed dislocated. He frowned while Lady Ellacott told him the story of her misadventure and asked one or two penetrating questions about how such an object would find its way into a dress cupboard, received no satisfactory answers, and shooed everyone from the room but Lindsay and Miss Kerry, whom he drafted to assist him.

Knowing that Lady Ellacott was in good hands, Claudia gratefully went to her own bedchamber after carefully returning the diamonds to the leather case. It was not long after she had undressed and Mary had brushed out her hair that there was a soft knock on the communicating door to Lindsay's room and he came into her room. He was able to reassure her that the injury to his aunt was slight and that she was mostly shaken by the experience.

"It is a very good thing, though, that you were with her," he remarked. "If the jewel case had struck her as well, I think she would have been seriously hurt."

"You must not make me out to be heroine," Claudia said lightly, conscious of her undress, though their circumstances were far from erotic. "Perhaps I should even take part of the blame, since it was because of me that she was removing the case from the cupboard."

"That's absurd and you know it." He took her hand in both of his. "Not everyone, I assure you, would have had such presence of mind to pull Aunt Jane out of the way."

Once again Claudia felt suddenly shy with him and she pulled her hand from his and moved a little away. "The doctor seemed very curious about how the accident occurred," she said as she unconsciously drew her dressing gown a little more closely about her. "I confess I am puzzled too how that paperweight came to be there. It was not when Aunt Jane removed the case earlier to bring out the diamonds."

Lindsay didn't answer at once. He sat on a corner of the long, wooden blanket chest at the foot of the bed. "I can't but wonder that myself," he said in a voice so pregnant with meaning that Claudia could not mistake him.

"It is odd, certainly, but nothing to make a mystery of," she responded after a moment of consideration. "Perhaps Kerry had some reason for placing it there, not recalling that her mistress would be moving the case again tonight to return the diamonds to it." Lindsay's derisive smile informed her of his opinion of that theory. "You can't suppose it was put there deliberately?" she asked, incredulous. "By whom and for what purpose?"

"The very purpose it served: to injure, perhaps more," he said grimly.

"Who on earth would wish to injure Aunt Jane? And why?"

"Someone who would stand to gain by it, I suppose," he replied almost disinterestedly. "If the paperweight had hit her head or the jewel case fallen on her . . ." He paused as if he could not quite finish the sentence, but Claudia understood him well enough.

Claudia puzzled over this for a moment and at length said, "If she had been killed, who but you would stand to gain from it?" She broke into a smile and said with attempted lightness, "This isn't some sort of backhanded confession, I trust."

He didn't respond in kind as she expected. "I would certainly gain," he concurred, "but not I alone. The settlement papers and Aunt Jane's new will have yet to be signed, you will recall. If I wished my aunt ill, I would have been better advised to bide my time."

His intent was plain, but Claudia refused to give it credence. "Who, then, is the villain of this piece?"

He made no reply, waiting for her to voice the answer that was in both their minds.

"This is absurd," Claudia said with sudden impatience. "It was an accident, and nothing more."

"I don't believe Doctor Canby thought so."

"And neither do you?"

"And neither do I."

A silence fell between them that was palpable. The ticking of the mantel clock was unnaturally loud, and the flickering of the bed candles, which were the only light in the room, seemed suddenly sinister.

Claudia capitulated. "You think Andrew had something to do with it," she said, breaking the silence at last.

"I own it is difficult for me to do so."

"Apparently not impossibly so," she said, faintly jeering. "I am perfectly aware that there is not a great deal of love lost between you and Andrew, but don't you think this is carrying it a bit far? Andrew always treats Aunt Jane with affection, and you told me yourself that he was a rich man."

Lindsay shrugged as if indifferent. He was not entirely certain he believed in his own suspicions. What he found more to his interest was Claudia's championing of the earl. "Drew should be well-fixed," he replied, "but I have no notion how he conducts his financial affairs. Acquisitiveness is quite often a trait of the rich."

Claudia turned away from him and said, her tone clearly distressed, "It is too abominable and completely improbable. I won't listen to you if you intend to say such hateful things."

Lindsay watched her as she walked away from him. Her

response was not entirely unexpected, and it gave him a rather grim satisfaction. He realized that perhaps that was why he had spoken his thoughts aloud. He would have been better pleased to have been mistaken.

Lindsay stood and followed her. "What do you know of Strait's character?" he said without inflection.

"What do I know of your character?" she retorted, genuinely disturbed by his suspicions. "That you are willing to lie and deceive your aunt for the sake of her money. I wish with all my heart I may never be cursed with a great fortune and greedy, grasping relatives."

Lindsay felt an icy anger steal over and claim him. It was a rare occurrence for him to lose his temper, but the threads of restraint were fine and all but broken. "By all means let us agree," he said, his voice dulcet but with an underlying hardness. "I am a reprehensible creature. But what does that make you, dear wife? There could have been no duplicity without your cooperation."

Claudia recognized that she had at last succeeded in pushing Lindsay's equable temperament to its limit, but the events of the evening had shaken her as well. "You forced my hand."

"I forced you to accept the wager I offered you?" he said as if attempting to understand. "Do you know, I quite thought you understood what stakes we were playing for, but perhaps I am mistaken. Am I, Claudia?"

"No," Claudia said, furious that he forced the admission from her.

"I thought not," he said with a singularly sweet smile. "Then this is just a falling-out among thieves, is it not?"

Claudia wheeled to face him, her own eyes blazing with anger, but before she could speak, he took her arm in a strong grip. "However disappointed you may be with our bargain, whatever you may think of my character, you are my wife and I expect you to remember that when my cousin attempts to make love to you." He saw her involuntary start. "I am neither blind nor a fool, Claudia."

Remembering how she had encouraged Andrew's attentions at the ball little more than an hour earlier, she became defensive. "You said we would be free to go our own ways," she reminded him in frigid accents.

He laughed mirthlessly. "You never disappoint me, my love. How unjust of you to fling my own words back in my face. So I did, but acquit me of complacency. If I am guilty of duplicity in our marriage, I am well-paid-out, am I not? Of all the men in Bath it must be Strait who captures your fancy. Merely fortuitous? I think not. What do you imagine Strait's intentions toward you are, Claudia?"

Claudia felt her heartbeat quicken as he put into words what she herself had so far refused to acknowledge. "He has made no improper advances toward me," she said with more vehemence than truth.

"Yet," he said with a sardonic curl of his lips.

"Your suspicions are as insulting as they are iniquitous," she said hotly. "Did it occur to you at all that Andrew might value me as a friend?"

"No. Strait doesn't make friends; he forms useful connections. I've no wish to wound your vanity, my love, but you are not in his usual style. I haven't made up my mind yet if it is simple spite because I have cut him out of Aunt Jane's fortune, or a definite attempt to discredit you with Aunt Jane and through you me, though I fancy the latter theory. Wills can always be changed again and old women are notoriously capricious."

Claudia found his matter-of-fact appraisal of Andrew's attraction to her even more insulting than his deliberate taunts. She was more flattered than she cared to admit that a man as attractive as Andrew Strait should so patently desire her. Even though she did not intend to allow herself to be seduced by Andrew, she didn't want to think that he wanted her, not for herself but to punish Lindsay. "It is you who are spiteful with your ridiculous accusations. Your accusations against Drew are more to your discredit than his."

He made her an ironic bow. "I thank you, Madame Wife. It is plain to see which of us possesses credit with you. I only hope that you don't find to your own discredit that you were mistaken."

Their eyes held in a gaze so intense that the rage between them was bound to ignite. Claudia tried to pull herself free of his grasp, but he held her fast, pushing her against the edge of the dressing table.

His mouth came down on hers; she held herself rigid, refusing to allow herself to respond to him. But against her will and her reason, her body played her false and her lips became pliable beneath his. Her senses were so heightened she could hear the pounding of her own heart and feel the buttons of Lindsay's coat pressing against her breast.

He held her against the dressing table, arching her back until it was painful. She reached behind her to grasp the table for balance and accidentally overturned a bottle of scent, sending its sweet musk fragrance into the air. He caressed her with a gentleness belied by the roughness of the embrace. One hand cupped her breast and teased it even as his tongue forced its way between her teeth. Beneath his skillful caresses and quite against her will, desire awoke and grew within her.

At last he released her and she immediately slipped out of his embrace, putting distance between them emotionally as well as physically. "You gave me your word that you wouldn't force yourself on me," she said unable to keep the breathlessness from her voice.

"I said I wouldn't force you," he said, and his voice was unsteady as well.

"Then my virtue is safe."

"From me at least."

"I might have expected that from you," she said bitingly. "It is plain you cannot abide Andrew and will accuse him of any offense to discredit him. I wish you to leave, my lord."

"Very well," he said in a tone that made it clear his anger had not abated either. "There are other beds where I may spend the night."

Without another word he went out of the room. Listening in spite of herself, she heard him leave the house. A part of her did not really want to understand the conflicting emotions besetting her. It would have been so much more comfortable to be able to crawl between the sheets and pretend that they did not exist, but such a degree of denial was alien to her nature.

Though she was quite alone, she felt the burning in her cheeks and put her hands to her face to cool them. What manner of woman was she who could imagine herself attracted to one man and yet respond with such feeling to the advances of another? It mattered little that Lindsay was her husband; it was certainly not duty that had made her pulse race when she had been in his arms.

At last the events of the evening, combined with her troubled cogitations, made her aware of her weariness. She blew out the candles, removed her dressing gown, and got into the bed, which suddenly seemed very large and empty. It was absurd, but tonight she wished that Lindsay would be lying beside her as he had done on their first night in Laura Place. This time she knew he would not have so easily turned away from her and fallen asleep.

The following morning found Lady Ellacott out of bed and sitting in her favorite button-back chair, taking her breakfast at a small table set up by Kerry, who insisted on waiting on her mistress herself. The alarming pallor had left her face and a very fetching, frilled pink dressing gown hid all sign of the bandages that bound her bruised shoulder.

But the dowager was feeling far from in good frame, for during the night she had developed a sniffle she very much feared would become a full-fledged head cold before the day was out. "It is really too bad," she complained to Lindsay as he sat in the chair beside hers. "But they say that trouble never comes alone. I only hope I may be mistaken, for you know that once I have a cold it always takes me at least a fortnight to be rid of it. Claudia has made some friends, I know, but she may yet be uncomfortable going out without me, and it would be too bad if she were forced to sit at home every night because I have caught a tiresome cold."

"It may be unfashionable for a wife to be escorted everywhere by her husband, but it is hardly unheard of," Lindsay commented dryly. "You may trust me to see that Claudia is well-entertained."

"Yes, but you know that you prefer the card room to the

dance floor, Lindsay, though I have never understood why, since you are a particularly good dancer. It might be better if Harriet Maye took Claudia under her wing until I am able to go about again. I shall send a note to her this morning.''

Lindsay made no comment. Kerry came in to remove Lady Ellacott's breakfast tray, and only when she was gone did he speak again. ''Claudia has taken quite well, I think,'' he remarked. ''I don't believe she sat out a single set last night.''

''Of course she did not. She is really quite lovely, Lindsay.'' She reached for his hand. ''I cannot tell you, dearest boy, how relieved I am that Claudia is your wife. I know I vexed you greatly when I declared that I would disinherit you if you didn't marry and settle down, and I feared that I would force your hand and push you into some quite unsuitable match. I would never have truly disinherited you, whatever I may have said. In fact, I should probably have made you a settlement in another year or two, whether you married or not.''

Lindsay covered her hand with his; there was an absent, almost unfocused look in his eyes that alarmed the dowager. ''Lindsay? Have I said something to upset you?''

''No, of course not,'' he said, patting her hand and then letting it go. He got up and went over to the window. He could not completely controll he sudden inner roiling of emotion. He had married only to please his aunt and secure his inheritance, and now that it was too late, she informed him that he need not have entered into the marriage at all. What had occurred between him and Claudia the previous night was as disturbing to him as it had been to Claudia, and he was suddenly furious that so much unwanted turmoil had come into his life, and all to no purpose.

He had been aware for some time that his attraction to Claudia had grown and that he very much wanted to make love to her, but to keep his promise to her that theirs would be a marriage of convenience, he had maintained a distance between them by affecting complete unconcern. Last night, though, after viewing her encouragement of Andrew at the ball and hearing her hot defense of the earl against his suspicions, it had been beyond his ability to feign indifference. He had never supposed when he had made his odd proposal to Claudia that the day might come when he would find himself falling in love with her. He too had wanted a marriage of convenience and nothing more.

"I have upset you," Lady Ellacott said concerned. "Am I mistaken, Lindsay? Did you marry Claudia merely for the sake of my fortune?"

"If he did, I am sadly deceived," said Claudia, coming into the room. She bent and kissed Lady Ellacott's upturned cheek. "At the very least," she said with a bright smile, "I know he did not marry me for mine." Claudia was uncertain what manner of discussion she had interrupted, but she had felt the tension as soon as she entered the room and sought to dispel it.

She was dressed in her riding habit for their morning ride and Lindsay regarded her with unconcealed surprise. He had not supposed she would wish for her lesson today after their quarrel.

As if there were not the least constraint between them, she went up to him and bestowed a chaste kiss on his cheek. "Am I very late? Did you breakfast yet?"

"Yes. If Aunt Jane will excuse me, I'll send for our horses." He left the room to do so and Claudia sat in the chair beside Lady Ellacott that he had earlier vacated. She inquired after Lady Ellacott's injury and was relieved to know that the doctor's prognosis was positive, though she commiserated with the dowager over her fears that she had taken cold.

Claudia had no idea how or where Lindsay had spent the night or what time he had returned to Laura Place, and she knew she would not ask him. She had dressed for their lesson because she was determined to go on as if the night before had never happened. Nothing else was conducive to her peace.

Lindsay's manner toward her as they began their ride was equally unchanged: amiable, familiar, bantering, and somewhat offhand. There was nothing at all to suggest either the would-be lover or the suspicious husband. Claudia could almost suppose that she had imagined their quarrel of the previous night.

It was a warm day and they were not out very long before the warmth of the sun made their horses begin to lather. As they turned toward Bath again at a slow walk to cool the horses, Lindsay remarked, "I spoke with Aunt Jane about buying Lancelot for you."

"Did you? I told you I would rather you did not."

"My dear girl," he said with an underlying exasperation in his tone, "who shall have the mounting of you if I do not? I am your husband even if it is merely a courtesy title. In any case, Aunt Jane means to give Lancelot to you. I would have preferred to pay her, but she won't hear of it, so there is no need for your sensibilities to be offended."

"Is is just that I would dislike it excessively to feel as if I owed you more than we agreed," Claudia said. His eyes on hers became warm, and she had, unbidden, the memory of his lips on hers, almost as if he had just kissed her again.

"I should dislike it also," he said evenly. "There is little of pleasure in obligation."

"I suppose I must be grateful that you believe so," Claudia said tartly.

He raised his brows. "I thought we were pretending that last night had not occurred. You must tell me the rules, Claudia, if you wish me to play the game properly."

"It isn't a game," she said with sudden annoyance. "Not to me."

"Nor to me," he said quietly, and pulled up his horse, causing Claudia to do the same. He put his hand over hers on the reins. "Let us not come to cuffs, Claudia. Perhaps I did dishonor my word last night when I kissed you. I can't apologize for wanting to kiss you, but I do beg you pardon for offending you. If it is any consolation, I did nnot intend it."

Claudia expected him to mention her own response to him, for she could not deceive herself that he had been unaware of it, but he did not and she was grateful. She accepted the offered truce and hoped that there would be nothing more between them to discomfit her. To please her Lindsay even acknowledged that his suspicions of Andrew were very far-fetched and it was most likely that one of the housemaids had put the paperweight in the closet and it had rolled onto the jewel case accidentally when Lady Ellacott had put it back before going to the ball.

Lady Ellacott's prediction that she was catching cold proved to be correct. She resigned herself to spending the next several days confined to her bedchamber, but this did not prevent her from receiving her closest friends who came to call, and on the third day after the accident, Claudia visited Lady Ellacott after she had changed from her riding habit and found Mrs. Maye visiting the dowager.

"I have asked Harriet if she will include you in her party at the fete at Sydney Gardens tonight, Claudia," Lady Ellacott told Claudia. "I know you said you would stay and bear me company tonight, since Lindsay has another engagement, but it is quite unnecessary for you to make such a sacrifice."

"But it is no sacrifice, Aunt Jane," Claudia assured her. "I take pleasure in your company and there will be other fetes I may attend."

"Your sentiments do you credit, Lady Lindsay," Mrs. Maye said approvingly as she began to gather up her reticule and gloves to take her leave of the ladies, "but Jane is quite right to insist that you go. She is clearly in no need of a nurse, and there is no reason for you not to go out as you planned. You told me yourself how much you were looking forward to the fete and fireworks at Sydney Gardens tonight, and you shall not miss your pleasures. Our carriage shall call for you at eight, if that is convenient. Dine lightly, if you please, for we shall take supper early before the fireworks and leave by midnight, for even here in Bath the public entertainments may turn a bit rowdy as the morning hours progress."

Andrew walked into the room unannounced as this speech was in progress, and after saluting his aunt with a kiss on her cheek, he said, "Wine and high spirits are always a boisterous combination, but Sydney Gardens is no Vauxhall, Cousin, where no woman of virtue may walk in safety without the protection of an escort after a certain hour. Perhaps we shall meet tonight. I've a mind to see the fireworks myself after I've dined with friends.''

It sounded to Claudia an open bid for an invitation to join their party, and Mrs. Maye did not disappoint him. Andrew made a polite show of reluctance and then accepted with characteristic grace.

# 7

Though Claudia had no intention of encouraging Andrew to suppose that there could be more than friendship between them, she could not help being pleased and flattered that he was willing to arrange his plans to be in her company at the fete. A small inner voice counseled prudence, but it was all but quelled by the pleasurable anticipation with which she looked forward to the evening. She might well have spent the day indulging in daydreams about the evening ahead, but shortly before luncheon all thought of flirtation with Andrew was banished temporarily from her head.

In the month since she and Lindsay had been married, Claudia had corresponded faithfully with Lady Lovewell, and when Lady Ellacott had her accident, she had written at once to apprise Vivian of the mishap her aunt had suffered. It was only three days since the accident and Claudia was not yet even expecting a reply to her letter, and so she was completely astonished when a smart chaise and four with the Lovewell crest emblazoned on the doors pulled up before the portals of Laura Place.

Vivian, with her maid to bear her company, came into the entrance hall and immediately embraced Claudia, who had come down the moment she had seen the arrival of the carriage from the window of Lady Ellacott's sitting room.

"My dearest Claudia," Vivian said, favoring her with a

long appraising glance while footmen scurried in the hall about them gathering up her belongings, which were so many that she might have been moving into Laura Place for good instead of merely visiting. "You are an absolute vision. I knew exactly how it would be when you shed your gray chrysalis. You are a beauty, nothing less."

Claudia laughed at the odd compliment. "Well, I won't deny that I do feel rather like a butterfly. Even a caterpillar may attain to beauty when draped in finery."

"You do yourself an injustice, as I am sure Lindsay has told you. Is he at home? But since I am so shockingly ill-mannered as to descend upon you without notice, I do not deserve that anyone should be here to greet me when I arrive. How is Aunt Jane? I resolved to come as soon as I received your letter."

"I won't pretend I am not very glad to see you," Claudia assured her as they began to ascend the stair, "but it was hardly necessary, if that is your only reason for coming. Except for contracting a head cold on the same evening, Aunt Jane is quite well and definitely on the mend."

"I never doubted it," Vivian replied with a dimpling smile. "But it was a splendid excuse to visit, and if matters were more serious than you wrote, then I should be here to help you bear the burden of the housekeeping. I am only come for a few weeks, not until Michaelmas, though you must think so with so much baggage, but I fear I can never travel light." She linked her arm in Claudia's. "I know I should pay my respects to Aunt Jane at once, but I have been looking forward to seeing you and talking to you since I left town. Letters are all very well, but not the same as being together, don't you agree?"

Claudia did agree and they went at once to her sitting room. Though Claudia had written much of her experiences since she had come to Bath, Vivian insisted on hearing it all again. With skillful questioning, Vivian helped her to remember little anecdotes that she herself had all but forgotten, and the two women were laughing and exchanging opinions and confidences about their mutual acquaintances as if they were friends from their cradle days rather than connections by marriage of little more than a month. Though completely at her ease with Vivian, Claudia was circumspect when mentioning Andrew, for though she trusted Vivian's discretion, she could not forget that Vivian was Andrew's sister and Lindsay's cousin.

They were still talking and Vivian had not even retired to her room to refresh herself after her journey when Lady Ellacott, leaning on Kerry's arm for support, came into the room and remonstrated with her niece for her neglect.

Vivian jumped up at once and embraced her aunt enthusiastically. "Forgive me, dearest Aunt Jane," she said with a winning smile. "I feared you might be resting after luncheon and did not wish to bother you, but mostly I was just so eager to hear all of Claudia's news that I could not resist enjoying a comfortable coze with her at once."

"Of course I forgive you, Vivian, my love. Who can not?" she said, receiving her niece's ardent embrace. "Why didn't you tell me you would be coming? Has Storry ordered a bed-chamber prepared for you?"

"I came because Claudia wrote to me about your accident. But though I was deeply concerned, I confess it is not my only reason," she said, adding in a confidential tone. "David has been a perfect beast of late about a few silly bills from my modiste. He cannot comprehend why I cannot patronize Mrs. Rielly like his friend Lord Tilly's wife does, and must go to Madame Céleste instead. Céleste is ruinous, of course, but, dear Aunt Jane, have you ever actually seen Lady Tilly?"

Lady Ellacott laughed at her nonsense, and conversation became general, concerning Vivian's journey and the husband and children she had left behind in London, and gossip about mutual friends who were in town for the Season. But at last Vivian acknowledged that she would like to rest a bit and refresh herself from her journey before dressing for dinner.

"There shall only be the three of us for dinner tonight," Lady Ellacott said. "Lindsay is dining with friends and Claudia will be leaving us shortly afterward to attend the fete at Sydney Gardens tonight."

"Oh, not now," said Claudia at once. "I shall send word to Mrs. Maye and we may enjoy the whole of the evening together."

But Lady Ellacott would not hear of her making such an unnecessary sacrifice. "I thought we were agreed that you were to enjoy your evening as we originally intended. Now I shall have Vivian to keep me company and we shall doubtless spend the whole of the evening in long boring discussions of the children and a great many people whom you have yet to even meet. I insist that you go to the fete. If Vivian means to make a long stay, we shall have many evenings together."

"Please, Claudia," Vivian said prettily, "don't change your plans for my sake. I should feel dreadfully guilty."

It did not take a great deal to persuade Claudia, for in her heart it was what she most wanted to do, though her conscience told her she should use any excuse to avoid a meeting with Andrew that was certain to further the flirtation between them. But even Lindsay, when he returned home and learned of Vivian's arrival, agreed that neither he nor Claudia should give up their engagements, and so Claudia found herself at a quarter-past eight in Mrs. Maye's carriage on her way to Sydney Gardens.

Claudia had been to Sydney Gardens before, on afternoon strolls with Lady Ellacott and once at a private breakfast given by Lady Stourbridge, but this was the first time she had been there at night and she was enchanted by the multicolored lanterns strung out above the paths and in great profusion in the area where refreshments were served for the many revelers. Both Mrs. Lodder and Mrs. Conniff were part of their party, and the latter declared in languid accents that she vowed it was nothing to Vauxhall, but since Claudia had never seen the famous pleasure gardens of London, Sydney Gardens did not suffer in the comparison for her.

An orchestra played all the most popular airs and reels for their entertainment, the food was excellent and plentiful, the conversation at their table lively, but Claudia never forgot that Andrew had promised to join them, and she found herself looking up expectantly whenever anyone passed or approached their table. She felt a tiny stab of disappointment each time it proved to be a stranger rather than Andrew.

When he arrived at last, he took the empty chair next to hers, smiling at her in an intimate way. Claudia was determined not to respond to him in any extraordinary manner, but the warmth in his eyes as they rested on her affected her whether she wished it or not.

"We had almost given you up, my lord," Mrs. Conniff said coolly. "Confess, sir, you nearly forgot us."

Andrew laughed. "No, no. How could that be? I am made welcome by no less than four of the loveliest women in Bath. By the number of dagger looks cast my way as I approached your table, I would say I am the envy of every buck and tulip present."

"Oh, fie, my lord," Mrs. Maye said with a rippling laugh. "Do you imagine you turn our heads with your pretty speeches? You had best stay close to me, girls, or Lord Strait may attempt to lead one of you down an unlit path."

The others appeared to find her words amusing, but Andrew's eyes met Claudia's and the teasing expression there told her plainly that that was exactly what he wished to do with her. Her sense of virtue, and no less her common sense, told her that she should avoid such an occasion at all costs, but when they left the refreshment area and the fireworks began, Andrew stayed close to her side and it was all too easy for him to see that they became separated from Mrs. Maye and her party in the large crowd of revelers that surged together all seeking the best vantage point from which to view the display.

"It will be best if we stay back a bit," Andrew said, laying his hand over hers and pulling her a little farther away from the others. "We'll see most of the fireworks as well as anyone and we won't be pelted with cinders like most of the others when they set off the grand finale."

Claudia agreed, steadfastly ignoring the whispered warnings of her conscience. Nor did she object when he brought her closer to him, one hand slipping familiarly about her waist. She knew that if she allowed him to draw her farther into the shadowed lanes behind them, he would attempt to make love to her, but she permitted this as well. Her pulse quickened at her own temerity, yet a feeling of impending excitement enveloped her and seemed to negate her will to keep him at a proper distance.

He did not disappoint her. "I almost feared that I would find you had changed your mind and remained at home tonight," he said when they were well into the shadows but still commanding a view of the spark-laden sky.

"I nearly did. I still think it was rude of me to come here when Vivian has only just arrived from town, but both she and Aunt Jane would not hear of my missing the fete." She kept her voice as light and noncommittal as she could. She would not for the world have told him that she had been eager to come for his sake alone.

"I flattered myself you would have another reason for avoiding a meeting tonight," he said ruefully. "But now you make me fear that it is all vanity." He paused as if hesitant to go on. "I *have* flattered myself, but perhaps I am altogether mistaken. Since the night of the card assembly I have thought of nothing but being with you again. I supposed it was only our unique circumstances keeping us apart."

His words excited her, but they frightened her as well. He spoke softly, but there were people all around them, and Claudia felt cold anxiety that they might be overheard. "I think it is better if we are not much together," she said, and would have moved a little away from him, but he drew her nearer to him.

"Do you know why I was so late arriving tonight?" he asked, dropping his voice lower in pitch and speaking so near to her that she could feel his breath on her cheek. "I don't forget that you are my cousin's wife; I, too, have reservations about our being together. But I couldn't stay away, not if there was the least chance that you would be here tonight and we could be together without either Lindsay or my aunt to make us fearful of giving our feelings away."

Claudia would not admit her feelings to him, but she didn't deny them either. "I shouldn't have come, either," she said a little breathlessly.

"But you did, and with the same anticipation, I think."

His voice had a silky quality that was almost a caress. It thrilled Claudia, but at the same time discomfited her. She couldn't deny his words and she had the feeling of tumbling headlong into something she feared she would not be able to control. "I am the one who forgets my husband," she said unsteadily. "We should find Mrs. Maye."

"You forget your husband because you aren't in love with him," he said boldly, making no move to release her from the half-embrace in which he held her. She began to protest but he silenced her by placing a finger to her lips. "You know it is true."

Claudia had no idea whether it was so or not. In spite of her attraction to Andrew, neither was she indifferent to Lindsay. Before she had met either man, she had always been tolerably well-acquainted with her emotions, but now her feelings were troublesomely elusive. "Lindsay has been very kind and a good husband to me," she said as a compromise to the understanding that eluded her. "I owe him loyalty and more."

"That isn't love, it's duty."

The noise of the fireworks, which had been tremendous, quietened at last and she became aware of voices as people returned to the refreshment area, passing fairly near to them. They were still out of sight of the main pathways, but anyone venturing from these could stumble on them at any moment, and her pleasurable anticipation receded as her discomfort grew.

As if he sensed her withdrawal, he brought her even closer to him. "It isn't duty that brings you to me," he said again in a caressing way that was tantalizingly seductive.

"You do flatter yourself, my lord," Claudia said with outward coolness, but her pulse was beating faster again.

"Oh, I know you aren't in love with me either," he said softly, his lips very close to hers. "Not yet." He brought his lips down on hers gently, but in a moment the embrace became one of passion.

Claudia's heart was hammering in her chest, but she knew it was as much from fear that they would be discovered together by some acquaintance as from his skill as a lover.

She brought the kiss to an end by turning her face away from him, and when his lips began to trace a path from her throat to her breasts, she finally forced herself to push him away. "Everyone is returning from the display," she said in a hurried whisper. "Mrs. Maye must be missing us by now."

He took her hand in his to pull her back to him, but Claudia had expected this and managed to elude his efforts. Shivering a little from the force of waging emotions of excitement and anxiety, she pushed past him and out once again into the light of the lanterns.

He was close behind her and caught her up just as she stepped onto the main pathway. He grasped her upper arm none too gently and she turned toward him again but was arrested by the sight of Mrs. Conniff standing a few feet farther along the path, staring at them with shocked surprise. Claudia could well imagine how her plunge out of the darkness and Andrew's pursuit must look to any observer, and her anxieties were realized. Yet it was not she who blushed, but Mrs. Conniff, who looked quickly away and continued on toward the refreshment area as if she had not seen them.

Andrew saw Claudia's stricken look and said bracingly, "Don't refine too much on Honora Conniff's reaction to seeing us together, Claudia. It is only surprise. She is a woman of the world and understands these things."

"But I am not, Andrew, and I fear I don't understand at all," she said levelly, her eyes searching his as if seeking the answer that escaped her. "I can't play Lindsay false, however much I find myself attracted to you."

"Do you imagine he accords you the same loyalty?" Andrew said, his lips turning up in a faint sneer.

"I have no idea," she said in a tone that made it clear that she wished to hear no more, and turned away again.

But yet once more he stayed her. "Claudia, I'm falling in love with you."

His words were not entirely unexpected, but still disturbing to her. "You scarcely know me," she said with a flatness that should have discouraged him.

"Don't imagine me a fool, Claudia. Your marriage to

Lindsay is purely convenience. You married to escape the drudgery of a governess's life, and he married you to secure his inheritance. Don't tell me otherwise, I shan't believe you.''

All Claudia's pleasure in the evening was at an end, and she wished she had never given in to her impulse and come when in her heart she knew what would be the outcome. The prospect of flirtation with him was exciting, that of becoming his mistress frightening, and she knew that this was what he wanted from her. ''Whatever our reasons for marrying, I could never play Lindsay false.''

''And how does he use you?'' Andrew asked bitterly. ''He wants you for his personal gain. I love you, Claudia.''

''You must not say so,'' she said with real distress. They still stood to the side of the lane, and people passing near to them sensed, if not heard, the intensity of their conversation and eyed them with ill-concealed curiosity. It was only a matter of time before someone else who knew them both saw them, and in a town like Bath, renowned for its quizzes and gossips, they would be the *on-dit* of all polite society by breakfasttime the following morning.

With more concern for her reputation than Andrew's sensibilities she said, ''I must find Mrs. Maye now. We shall have to speak of this another time.'' She withdrew her hand from his and saw that his expression was startled and displeased; no doubt he was used to a very different response when he made a declaration of love to a woman, and though Claudia was far from indifferent to him, she felt it was the only response she dared to make.

They met up again with Mrs. Maye and her daughters and Claudia's heart nearly stopped as she saw Lindsay beside Mrs. Conniff in earnest conversation. She thought that Mrs. Conniff looked away from her rather quickly, and her guilt at having permitted Andrew to make love to her made her fear that Mrs. Conniff had told Lindsay that she had seen them together.

Lindsay looked up at her and smiled. He said something to Mrs. Conniff and left her to attach himself to Claudia's side. ''Are you enjoying the fete?'' he asked.

Claudia pushed down her anxiety and said with creditable steadiness, "Very much."

"The fireworks were particularly good tonight. I hope you saw them well from your vantage point."

She looked up at him sharply but found no overt suspicion in his eyes. "Yes," she replied, not trusting herself to say more.

Her unaccustomed reticence at last elicited a remark from him. "Is there something the matter, Claudia? Would you rather I hadn't come? I only did so because Robeson and the others wanted to go on to the Pelican and I didn't care to."

Claudia realized that if she did not get herself in hand Lindsay would be certain to guess the truth. She forced herself to breathe evenly and calmed her racing pulse. "No. I am glad you have come. I am just a bit tired."

"Shall we leave, then?"

Claudia nearly agreed but, knowing the hour was still early, decided against it, for it was likely taht Lady Ellacott and Vivian would still be up and wanting to hear the details of her evening. "Perhaps in a bit. I would not wish to be rude to Mrs. Maye, who has ordered punch to be made for us."

Lindsay was asked to join their party and readily agreed, but Andrew excused himself from returning to their table and left shortly afterward. Though his civility toward Claudia was unimpaired and his manner as easy as before, Claudia knew she had offended him by treating his declaration of love with such a sad want of feeling. She supposed it was for the best, but her spirits might have been lowered by this if Lindsay, with his gift for caustic but nonabrasive humor, had not been present to tease her into good humor.

The punch was excellent, and though Claudia knew it was strongly laced with spirits, she accepted a second cup of it from Lindsay, rather liking the warm feeling it gave her inside. As the effects of the punch were felt by all, their party became increasingly convivial and even Mrs. Conniff thawed a bit to join in the banter among Lindsay, Claudia, and Kitty.

"You are very lucky, Lady Lindsay," said Mrs. Maye,

"to have the company of your husband when you are out of an evening. Poor Kitty seldom enjoys the escort of Roger, for his duties as secretary to Lord Monkshurst often cause him to be occupied in the evenings."

"Actually I count myself lucky to have the company of my wife tonight," Lindsay said, turning to Claudia with a smile as he placed his cup on the table. "It has been a while since I was here last, but I seem to recall there are a number of lanes and pathways to enjoy an idle stroll." If he saw the sudden anxious look that came into Claudia's eyes at his words, he gave no sign of it. "Shall we see how many we may find, my love?"

Claudia felt her knees turn rubbery. She was not yet certain if there was more to his words than on the surface, but she feared it. She forced a smile and fell back on her earlier excuse. "Perhaps another night. I am rather tired."

"A walk in the evening air is held to be invigorating," Lindsay said, and their eyes held for a moment, hers searching his and his telling her nothing at all.

Claudia obediently stood and took his arm. He further alarmed her by bidding Mrs. Maye and her daughters good night, informing them that he would see his wife home. Claudia's heart began to pound, and after a minute or so she had to laugh at her absurdity. It was not as if she suspected he meant to take her into a secluded part of the gardens to throttle her. At the very worst, they would quarrel, and though unpleasant, it was hardly something to fear.

They walked in silence, for Lindsay was also preoccupied with his thoughts. Though Mrs. Conniff had told him that she had seen Claudia and Andrew together in a potentially compromising situation, he had no idea what exactly had occurred between his wife and his cousin and his pride would never allow him to question Claudia. His imagination, however, was equal to the truth. He had no doubt of the attraction existing between Claudia and Andrew, but he was reasonably certain that however violently Andrew had made love to her, Claudia had not succumbed to him. But he had lived in the world too long not to know that it corrupts, and the strictest of values could be undone by a honeyed word

in the right season. He could not say why, but the all-but-
certain knowledge that another man had been making love
to his wife made him suddenly aware of the intensity of his
desire to possess her.

He led her to a grotto that led to a waterfall cleverly lit
by lanterns from behind to make the water sparkle as it fell,
and after they had dutifully admired it, he led her down a
different path than the one they had come. "It is a beautiful
night tonight," he remarked, "but Bath can become unpleasantly hot as the summer progresses. We should think
about going to Brighton or Cheltenham. Or we could go to
Lovewell. Vivian suggested that we might want to spend
some time there before going to town for the Little Season.
I have to remain for a bit to look at houses with Jolliet, but
you might prefer to go before me and I'll join you when I
can."

Claudia's earlier anxiety began to return. "But why would
I wish to do that? I would be quite uncomfortable in a strange
place without you."

"Almost you unman me, my love," he said with a brief
laugh. "I haven't had much cause to suppose you found my
company necessary. I am flattered, of course, but you may
change your mind by the end of June, when the heat becomes
unbearable at times."

The mocking, amused mask Lindsay habitually wore to
face the world so seldom slipped that Claudia was never
certain what thoughts really lay behind it. Yet she sensed
that her anxieties were not unfounded. "I shouldn't think
so. I would rather wait until you would be free as well."

"Which is it to be? Brighton, Cheltenham, or Lovewell?"

"Brighton," Claudia said without hesitation. She was
thoroughly enjoying her venture into society and was not at
all eager to find herself returned to the quiet life of the country
again so quickly.

"A popular choice," he remarked. "Vivian and David
will be there, and for that matter so will Strait."

Claudia felt that they were at last coming to the point. "I
shall enjoy having friends there from the start," she said
cautiously. "It is always more comfortable."

"Especially when they are particular friends," he said entirely without inflection.

"Honora Conniff told you what she saw, I gather," Claudia said flatly, not seeing any point in maintaining a pretense at misunderstanding him.

Something in her tone told Lindsay what he had already guessed was true. "She told me that she saw the two of you together in a way that might have been construed as compromising. She said you seemed agitated. He was making love to you, I suppose."

He spoke so nonchalantly that Claudia might once again have beenpiqued at his lack of concern, but she chanced to look up at him and there was just sufficient light for her to read the expression in his eyes, which made her feel as if a cold hand clutched her inside.

He halted and so did she, turning to face him. "Are you in love with Drew?" he asked, a steeliness in his tone that she had never heard there before.

She had not been able to openly deny loving Lindsay to Andrew, but to her own surprise, she had no difficulty assuring Lindsay that it was not love she felt toward Andrew. "No," she said, awkwardness making her speak with hesitation. "He is . . . very attractive. I know I should not have encouraged him, but . . ."

"But you could not resist," Lindsay said without rancor. "I have often wondered why Drew finds so much in me to envy."

If Claudia had been merely listening to the sound of his voice, she might have continued to be deceived into supposing him indifferent, but looking directly into his eyes, she recognized for the first time that much of the outward amiable care-for-nobody manner that her husband assumed was his defense against the world. She was suddenly very aware of him as a man so near to her.

"I have told you there is nothing between Andrew and me," she said, looking away from him.

He put his hand under her chin and raised her face to him again. "Not yet?"

"Not at all." Though she could not have said why, Claudia

knew he was going to kiss her and she knew that she wanted him to. She expected his kiss to be light and teasing, the way it had been before, but the moment his lips touched hers, she felt the unexpected intensity of his desire and the awakening of her own.

His tongue parted her teeth as his hands caressed her, leaving molten trails of desire wherever he touched her. Instinctively she returned his caresses, astonished at her own boldness yet exalting in it as well. She was nearly breathless and her heart pounded in her ears; she withdrew from him a little, not resisting him but trying to regain some control of her rioting emotions.

He understood and held her close to him without attempting to kiss her again at once. He was as shaken as she; though he had found her physically attractive and even desirable since the day they had met, he too was unprepared for the strength of suddenness of his arousal. He wanted her more than he could ever recall wanting any other woman before.

"I think we should go home, Claudia," he said very, very softly.

Claudia understood him. When they reached Laura Place tonight, they would not go to their separate rooms. Her desire for him, so unexpected, confused her, but she had no doubt of it. She wanted him to make love to her. "Yes, I think we should," she said, and boldly kissed him, lightly but with promise. Feeling suddenly shy, she turned to go back the way they had come.

When they arrived at the house, she accepted a bed candle from the footman and started up the stairs, acutely aware of Lindsay behind her. At the door of the bedchamber they had shared their first night in the house, she turned and in the flickering light of the bed candle saw the questioning look in his eyes. Claudia knew he would keep his word to her; the decision was hers. She hesitated, but there was never any real doubt in her mind what her decision would be. She put her hand to the back of his head and drew his lips to hers. She then turned and went into the room and Lindsay followed her, quietly shutting the door behind them.

Claudia awoke the next morning much later than her usual

hour and feeling languorously content, like a cat stretched out in the sun. The bed beside her was empty, but she reached over and touched the pillow where there was still a slight indentation where Lindsay's head had lain.

Claudia had lived in the country too long not to understand the ways of a man with a woman, but nothing her mother had told her or the confidences of married friends had prepared her for the eruption of emotion and sensation that Lindsay had awakened in her. In spite of her ignorance, she recognized in him a skillful lover who knew to a nicety how to give her the greatest pleasure with the least pain, and she responded to his every touch as if especially tuned to his skillful playing.

The door to the sitting room was open and Claudia heard a soft knock and then voices. Though she would have been content to lie and daydream of the passion they had shared, she sat up, drawing the sheet up to her shoulders to cover her nakedness.

Lindsay, clad in a wonderfully brocaded dressing gown, appeared in the doorway. Claudia surprised herself a little by being able to meet his gaze without any hint of a blush. There was no need for guilt or shame for what had passed between them.

He sat beside her on the bed and drew her into his arms, kissing her gently. He tugged aside the sheet and kissed each of her breasts in turn. "Put on your dressing gown, sweet, and come into the sitting room. I've had breakfast brought to us."

He drew her to her feet and handed her her dressing gown, which he had taken from her wardrobe, his eyes openly admiring. Claudia felt no immodesty under his gaze, but she was a little disconcerted by the intimacy that had so suddenly arisen between them.

She felt a happiness and contentment that she knew might well be foolish. No words of love had passed between them last night, only a physical hunger, a finally acknowledged need that at last was satisfied. Yet she could not believe that the tenderness they had shared could come without deeper feelings. She examined her own heart and knew it trembled on the edge of falling in love with Lindsay; she wanted to believe it was the same with him.

She put on the dressing gown and allowed him to lead her into the sitting room. A table had been brought into the room, and a small but elegant meal consisting of cold sliced ham, coddled eggs, and a number of other selections awaited them. Lindsay dismissed a hovering footman with a nod and Claudia was glad of it, for she found that her color rose a little when she met the servant's carefully disinterested gaze.

To cover her confusion, she did not wait for Lindsay to draw her chair but sat down at once. "How delightful," she said, lifting the cover of a serving dish and finding the fresh-cut ham. "But it makes a great deal of extra work for the servants," she added, unconsciously voicing a sympathy born of her own days of servitude as a governess.

"For which they are paid handsomely," Lindsay said as he too began inspecting the contents of their repast. "I dismissed Jem because his presence seemed to make you uncomfortable." He paused in the act of lifting a bit of sirloin onto his plate and gave her a sudden, teasing smile. "We are married. Our intimacy is taken for granted, you know."

Claudia returned his smile still a bit shyly. "I know. But I am not used to it yet. Ours was to be a marriage of convenience."

"Do you regret last night, Claud?" he asked softly. "The choice was yours."

Claudia poured out coffee for both of them and handed him his cup without looking at him directly. "Yes," she confirmed. "It was." For all that Andrew set her pulses racing whenever they met, his kisses had not shaken her to her very core as Lindsay's had last night.

They had finished their meal and were discussing whether or not they would ride before luncheon, since they had missed their usual morning lesson, when they were interrupted by a faint scratching at the door. Assuming it was Jem come to remove the leavings of their meal, Claudia gave him permission to enter. To her astonishment and chagrin, Andrew came into the room.

There was no mistaking the intimacy of their circumstances. Andrew checked momentarily on the threshold, and then, with his customary faintly cynical smile, he advanced into the room. "Good morning, Cousin," he said to Lindsay and then bowed over Claudia's hand. His eyes sought hers for a moment, but Claudia glanced up at him only briefly before looking away, unable to meet his eyes. Lindsay was her lawful husband and she had made love with him willingly, but she felt, absurdly, that she had somehow played Andrew false.

"I did not mean to intrude, Claudia, but I thought you wished to see me. Perhaps I misunderstood." He spoke with an odd inflection and his eyes rested briefly on Lindsay as he spoke, causing Claudia to glance at her husband.

Lindsay was regarding his cousin with shuttered lids over his eyes, but there was the faintest upturning of his lips, rather like the smile of a cat. "Perhaps you did, Drew," he said, his voice a soft drawl. He nodded toward an empty chair. "I think the coffee's still warm if you'd care for a cup."

Claudia felt a wave of chagrin, but she had no choice but to second Lindsay's offer. "Please do, Drew," she said, trying to sound as gracious as she could. "There is a great deal more food than we can eat as well. Shall I ring for another service to be brought up?"

Andrew made them a faint bow. "Thank you, but I must decline. I have an engagement at eleven and must change before I go out again." Favoring Claudia with another bow and a smile, he turned and left them.

Claudia, glancing at Lindsay through her lashes as she picked up her coffeecup, saw a smile playing on his lips that might have been described as triumphant. She supposed she could not blame him given the rivalry that existed between him and Andrew, but she disliked the idea of being an object of that rivalry.

She supposed it was just as well. If Andrew knew them to be lovers, perhaps he would finally realize that there was no hope of anything more than friendship between them. She felt a momentary pang of regret for what never could be, but it was not more than that. She met Lindsay's eyes and he smiled at her in a warm way that conversely made her shiver inside at the memory it evoked.

They did ride, and after luncheon Lindsay went out and Claudia very contentedly spent her afternoon with Vivian and Lady Ellacott in the latter's sitting room. As the afternoon waned, Claudia went down to the front saloon, which overlooked Laura Place, and sat at the desk to write to her mother. She took out several sheets of foolscap and mended a pen, but she found it impossible to compose her thoughts in an orderly way. Instead, they returned constantly to the night before.

Claudia was so absorbed in these thoughts that she neither noted nor heard the sounds of arrival and was a bit startled when Andrew came into the room unannounced. She was not as dismayed as she had been earlier in the morning when he had interrupted her breakfast with Lindsay, but she felt a moment of awkwardness as he approached.

He returned her greeting almost curtly and sat in a chair beside the desk. He took a small piece of paper from a pocket inside his coat and handed it to her.

Claudia read it and looked up at him puzzled. "I didn't write this. It isn't even my hand."

"No. I know that now. I suspect it is Lindsay's, sufficiently disguised so that I should not recognize it."

She looked at him uncomprehendingly. "But why on earth would Lindsay send you a note asking you to come to me and pretend that it was from me?"

His smile was sardonic. "Isn't that obvious? He wanted me to walk in on your intimate little *tête-à-tête* this morning, the inference of which would be plain. I have been warned off, my dear." Claudia's brow creased in puzzlement and he clarified his meaning for her. "Either Honora Conniff told him she saw us together, or he drew his own conclusions, but he wants it made plain to me that you are his wife—in every sense of the word."

His eyes on her as he said these words made her uncomfortable. "You have always known I was Lindsay's wife," she said with gentle accusation.

"True." His smile was a bit wry. "But there is a world of difference between knowing and seeing. I had thought . . . I suppose it doesn't matter what I thought now. What does matter is that Lindsay has deceived us both."

Claudia knew that what Andrew had thought was what had been true until last night: that her marriage to Lindsay was in name only. If Lindsay knew that this was what Andrew believed, it was entirely possible that he would wish to refute that belief. She remembered the way that Lindsay had looked when Andrew had come into the room, his smile tinged with triumph. That prospect left her with an extreme distaste. It did not bear thinking of that her husband had deliberately set out to seduce her merely for the sake of the rivalry between him and Andrew. She might have difficulty believing him guilty of such subterfuge if it hadn't been for the duplicity she was certain he had practiced on her the night they had met, which had led her to become his wife in the first place.

Though she was unaware of it, each thought was manifest clearly in her countenance. Andrew suppressed his own faint smile of triumph and said, "I know it is not pleasant to think that Lindsay would stoop to such behavior, but perhaps he had another, greater purpose."

Claudia saw that his eyes searched hers, waiting for her to make some sort of inference from his words, but this time his meaning escaped her. "What purpose?"

"Securing his inheritance beyond doubt." He glanced down at the note and then looked up at Claudia again. "Aunt Jane has said many times, has she not, that the wish of her heart is for you and Lindsay to fill your nursery. She would not show herself ungenerous, I am certain of that."

Claudia felt as if her stomach had become suddenly hollow. There was no question that if she were to bear Lindsay a child, virtually all his aunt's fortune would be secured to them. Lady Ellacott had promised this in Claudia's hearing. "Lindsay would not behave so basely," she said, but her words carried no conviction.

"I have no wish to insult you or give you pain, Cousin,

but your own circumstances must make you aware of the importance he places on securing Aunt Jane's fortune for himself. A timely heir would all but guarantee that he would cut me out for certain.''

Claudia almost winced at his words. She knew far better than Andrew the lengths to which Lindsay had already gone to ensure his inheritance. She didn't want to believe it was true, but she could not dismiss Andrew's charges against Lindsay as absurd, the way she had treated Lindsay's suspicions that Andrew had somehow been responsible for Lady Ellacott's accident. The realization that the night of love and passion she had shared with her husband might have been finely and coldly calculated by him made her mortified to think that she had so easily succumbed to his practiced seduction.

"You know what I am saying is true, Claudia," Andrew prompted as the silence between them lengthened.

"If it is, it is infamous and unforgivable," she said with a sudden ferocity. She stood, too agitated to remain seated.

Andrew rose also and took one of her hands in his. "Perhaps I should not have spoken, but I couldn't bear for you not to know the truth."

Claudia, too, wished that he had not. She was not certain that she believed all that he said, only that she could not dismiss it. "No. You had to come to me, didn't you?" she said neutrally. "I wonder Lindsay didn't realize that you would do so."

He let go of her hand abruptly. "If you think it was to pay him back . . ."

Claudia moved away from him. "Of course it was," she said roundly. "Oh, perhaps you had other nobler intentions," she allowed as he began to protest, "but I begin to think that I am nothing more to either of you than a pawn in your stupid rivalry, which you both would use to see the other bested."

"Dear God, Claudia," Andrew said, astounded by her unexpected attack, "acquit me of such a base motive. You know that the moment I set eyes on you—"

"Please don't" Claudia interrupted forcibly. Even she was

surprised by the strength of her bitterness and realized that she was more hurt than she had thought she could be; Lindsay had touched her heart more than she knew. "If you suppose that this would make any difference to us, you are mistaken. Even if Lindsay has done as you suggested, I still would never betray my vows to him."

"Your virtue does you credit," he said, but with sufficient edge to his voice to make it more of a condemnation than an approbation. "My cousin is more fortunate than even I guessed. He may use you to his own ends and betray you with Sally Hart and yet command your fidelity and regard."

Once before Andrew had hinted that there was more than friendship between Lindsay and Mrs. Hart, but it had not troubled her then and she had put it from her mind. This time his accusation was outright and affected her far more, for now the thought of Lindsay in the arms of another woman made her feel suddenly cold inside. "Are you saying that Mrs. Hart is my husband's mistress?" she said with fragile command of her voice.

"You can't mean you didn't know of it?" he said as if incredulous. "Dear Lord, Claudia, I'm sorry. I thought you knew. Everyone does. It is such common knowledge that it is not even an *on-dit* anymore."

Claudia swallowed a hardness in her throat. She thought of seeing Lindsay with Mrs. Hart in the Pump Room, on the morning of her first lesson and countless other times at private and public assemblies. There was nothing remarkable in his talking or dancing with her so often—he did the same with Kitty Lodder and one or two other young women whom he regarded as friends. But Claudia recalled her own early impression that there was a greater intimacy between Lindsay and Sally Hart, and she knew she had no real doubt of it.

Had she been physically struck, she could not have felt more stunned. But Claudia would not allow her distress to be further manifest to the earl. "Oh, I have heard the gossip," she said untruthfully. "But then I suppose they gossip about you and me as well, and we know it is baseless.

Will you forgive me, Andrew, if I leave you to dress for dinner? Vivian and I are to attend Mrs. Cancort's musical party tonight and we dine a bit earlier than usual.'' She did not wait for a reply but turned and left the room, too upset to trust herself to remain without betraying her emotions completely.

# 8

Andrew was not displeased at the fruit of his revelations, even though Claudia had spurned him once again. He felt his point was scored and he was yet confident of carrying the trick. He spent several minutes in self-congratulations before picking up his hat and gloves from the table near the door. He was about to step into the hall when Vivian came down the stairs and ushered him back into the room.

He raised his well-shaped brows. "To what do we owe this unexpected pleasure, Viv? I thought you despised Bath for a provincial backwater."

She gave him a humorless smile. "Curiosity to see what has kept your interest here so long. It is not too difficult to discern."

"Really? What have you discerned, dear sister?"

"That you are engaged in your usual games. Is it Lindsay alone that you wish to score against, or is it Aunt Jane's fortune as well? There is no guarantee, after all, that if she cuts Lindsay out of her will, she will cut you into it."

Andrew regarded her as if perplexed for a moment and then his countenance spread into a slow smile. "Now, who has been telling tales out of school, I wonder? Kitty Lodder, I'll wager. La Maye is not only the greatest quiz in Bath but she is training her daughters to assure it is a hereditary title."

"Kitty is like a sister to Lin and has his welfare at heart.

But I would have guessed for myself when I saw Claudia running up the stairs all but in tears and discovered that you had been with her. Did you make violent love to her and frighten her? I thought your address more polished than that.''

"I should hope it is," he said, affronted. "I merely pointed out that her husband is no paragon deserving of her unwavering loyalty."

"Did you tell her about Sally Hart in the hope that she would follow his example and give Lindsay his horns? My compliments, Drew. You are wonderfully despicable," she said in mock admiration.

He bowed in acknowledgment. "I do my humble best. Claudia is quite out of the ordinary for a mere provincial. He doesn't deserve her."

"She doesn't deserve you. Put a spoke in it, dear brother, or I shall do it for you."

He laughed and said without concern, "Try, if you think you can."

"You don't seem to be succeeding very well, do you?" she asked forthrightly. "I see no signs that Claudia has fallen victim to your fatal charm the way you intended. If she was upset to learn of Mrs. Hart, it is because she cares for Lindsay."

"My dear sister, you can't have fallen for that absurd fiction of love blossoming in the schoolroom at the home of a friend whom no one had ever heard of before."

Vivian shrugged. "Perhaps not, but I think the truth is moot. Claudia may find herself attracted to you, Drew, but I'll wager even she isn't going to lose her heart to you—or her reputation."

Andrew smiled. "Never underestimate the power of consolation," he said, and giving his sister another ironic bow, left her to return to his lodgings to change for the evening.

At first Claudia fed her anger toward her husband because it prevented her from examining her deeper feelings, which were far more disturbing. But she could not sustain the pitch of anger she needed to keep her other emotions at bay, and even what anger remained was turned in on herself.

Her sense of fairness made her admit that she had wanted and insisted on a marriage that was based entirely on mutual convenience, as much as had Lindsay. It seemed unjust to blame him for her losing her heart to him now that they had made love.

She had known form the time she had felt the first stirrings of attraction toward Lindsay that she would be a fool to let herself fall in love with a man who did not love her and made no pretense of it and had even told her that he wished for a marriage of convenience because he doubted his ability to fall in love. But in spite of this, she had lowered her defenses and love had crept into her heart like a thief in the night, a thief who had stolen her peace and her comfort.

Gradually her turmoil was succeeded by a calm, almost icy detachment. She came to the decision that she would say nothing to him about Mrs. Hart or the note he had sent to Andrew. Instead, she intended to repulse any further advances he might make toward her and make it clear to him that what had happened between them had been merely an episode—an error in judgment. She was reasonably certain that though he might dislike it, he would return to their former arrangement without argument. She did not suppose it would matter to him overmuch.

But she proved not to have the command over herself that she wished for. Lindsay's manner toward her when they met for dinner was as it always was, but when his eyes rested on her, the expression in them that she had earlier in the day taken for warmth, she now interpreted as complacent satisfaction in his successful seduction of her.

There was no opportunity for private conversation between them after dinner, for which Claudia was grateful, and she and Vivian returned early from Mrs. Cancourt's rout party so that Claudia was able to retire before Lindsay's return home. She locked both the door into the hall and the door that communicated with his bedchamber. What he thought of this or if he even attempted to come to her, she had no idea, for weariness, brought about by her emotional confusion, took its toll and she fell asleep almost as soon as she got into bed.

On the following morning, though, a confrontation of sorts proved unavoidable. She sent word to Lindsay through her maid that she would not be riding with him as usual, but instead of accepting her excuse of a headache as she supposed he would, he came into her room. Claudia had just finished dressing and Mary was pinning up her hair when he entered.

Lindsay knew the moment their eyes met by the way that hers quickly slid away that something had occurred to mar the harmony they had so briefly enjoyed. "Are you unwell, Claudia?"

"It is only a trifling headache, but I feared riding might make it worse. Please go without me; I wouldn't wish you to miss your ride on my account." Though she wished she might bite the words back as soon as they were uttered, she could not prevent herself from adding, "Perhaps you will meet up with Mrs. Hart and she may give you company."

Her words put Lindsay on his guard. "Would you leave us for a moment, Mary?" he said, and received a startled look from Claudia. But she did not object and the serving girl left them. "What is it, Claudia?" he said quietly.

"I have been thinking a great deal since yesterday morning," Claudia began, repeating her rehearsed excuses. "I believe that we have made a mistake to forget the nature of our agreement."

"In what way?" he asked levelly.

"What occurred the night before last was merely the result of an unguarded moment."

He smiled. "For whom?"

"For both of us," she said, keeping her voice as cool and unemotional as she could. He crossed the room to stand beside her and she stood, disliking the feeling of him looming over her.

"What has happened since our ride yesterday, Claudia?" he asked after favoring her with a long, appraising look.

Claudia's prepared words suddenly deserted her. "Is Mrs.

Hart your mistress?'' she said, blurting the words out almost without her own volition.

Lindsay didn't answer at once. His features set into hard lines that made him look suddenly older. ''Who has been talking to you, Claudia, Strait? I won't believe it was Vivian.''

''Does it matter? Is it true?''

''Yes,'' he said very quietly. ''I'm sorry you learned of it if it disturbs you, but you must forgive me, my dear. I had no notion that it would matter to you.''

If there was a trace of sarcasm in his words, Claudia made no note of it. ''It doesn't,'' she said at once, and then, to her own astonishment, began to cry.

Lindsay at once attempted to take her in his arms, but she pushed him away. ''Don't,'' she said sharply, and fumbled in the folds of her dress for the pocket with her handkerchief.

He handed her his. ''I had no idea you would be upset in this way,'' he said gently. ''Until the night before last you made it very clear that you wanted none of me. I am not a monk, you know.''

''I don't care what you do,'' she said, her voice muffled by the handkerchief, which she held with both hands against her face. ''It was just so . . . so humiliating to be told that the whole of Bath knows you are deceiving me with that woman. They must all be laughing up their sleeves at me.''

''Oh, I shouldn't think so. Such arrangements are thought too commonplace.''

His matter-of-factness offended her so much that it brought an abrupt end to her tears. She pivoted toward him, her eyes still wet but alight with anger. ''Not to me they are not. But I have not had the advantage of growing up with people of the first fashion. I begin to understand why Mama could be content to leave the life of the *ton* behind her to marry a simple country clergyman. I wish with all my heart that I had followed her lead.''

''But, alas, you are riveted to me instead,'' he said with a faint smile, privately rather pleased by her display of jealousy. "My sweet girl, what else did you expect, in our circumstances?"

"I have no expectations from you at all," she said, gaining firmer control of her emotions and feeling humiliated by her earlier display. "I certainly didn't expect that you would stoop to subterfuge and seduction. Did you think to fool either Andrew or me with the note you forged my name to and sent to him?"

Lindsay gave vent to a soft laugh. "So it was my helpful cousin who pointed out my sins. I must remember to thank him." He looked away from her for a moment. "Sending that note was ill-considered, I know," he said. "When I awoke before you yesterday morning, it occurred to me that I had found a way to make it clear to Strait that his intent to come between us was failing. I thought if he saw us together on obvious terms of intimacy, he would take the hint. I should have guessed he would serve me a backhanded turn."

"Then you admit that as well," Claudia said dully. She sat in a stuffed chair near the dressing table and put her head in her hands. "The surrender of my virtue was nothing more to you than a means of proving a point."

"I have never said so." He knelt beside her and removed her hands from her face. "I admit it was seduction, but Strait had nothing to do with it. You are my wife and I have wanted to make love to you very much for quite some time."

"And get me with child so that your aunt will settle the whole of her fortune on you when you have an heir," Claudia said bitterly.

"Dear Lord! What a delightful opinion you have formed of me." He got up. He was becoming angry in his turn, for though the charges she had leveled against him of having a mistress and of forging the note to Andrew were true, he was innocent of the base motives she ascribed to him and it wounded more than his pride that she could think him so lowly.

"What do you expect me to think?" Claudia demanded, encouraging her own anger to prevent any softer emotions from engulfing her again. "From the night that we met you ahve tricked me and used me to suit your purpose."

"And from that night you have found satisfaction in thinking as poorly of me as possible," he said with considerable bitterness of his own. "If I am such a monster, I wonder that you felt obliged to honor your debt to me."

"I wish with all my heart I had not," she said vehemently, rising with agitation and walking over to the window to look sightlessly onto the garden.

"So do I," he said with such deadly quiet that she was silenced. After a time he said more temperately, "But we are bound together for better or worse. We could make it for the better, but you would rather believe the half-truths of a man who has a clear self-interest in keeping us at odds."

"It is your self-interest that keeps us at odds. Drew didn't forge that note, nor did he cause you to make me ridiculous with . . . that woman."

There was no attempt to hide his emotions for once. His anger flashed clear in his eyes, his smile was a bitter parody of his usual amiable expression. "Andrew the Paragon. You are as consistent in believing well of him as you are in believing the worst of me. Perhaps I am the one who is being made ridiculous."

Claudia understood only too well the implications of his words. Her hand came up without thought to strike him, but he caught it at the wrist and a struggle ensued until he brought her hand down and pulled her, struggling, into his arms. "You are my wife, Claudia. If you forget it, I'll teach you the truth of it."

Such plain, hot anger shone in his eyes that Claudia felt an inner tremor, though she met his gaze with a furious glare of her own. He pulled her against him and kissed her in a hard bruising way that was completely opposite to his gentleness and tenderness on the night before last. She struggled against him, but his embrace was like iron and at last she subsided in resignation. Only then did he release her.

"You may be my wife in pleasure or in wretchedness, but my wife you will be." His eyes held hers for a long moment, and then he turned and abruptly left her.

Claudia leaned against the window as if for support, feeling the cool glass against her hot cheek. Her heart was pounding and she felt almost as if she would be sick. Love, she had always thought, if it came to her, would bring her joy, not heart-wrenching misery. For the first time since the afternoon that she had been dismissed from Bingerley Court, she wished with all her heart that she might be back there with George Bingerley, his ill-behaved offspring and his pampered silly wife, and even Mrs. Ramsett.

Though Claudia's attraction to Andrew had lessened considerably since the night at Sydney Gardens, she turned to him now as a source of comfort and diversion, roles he was only too willing to assume. Now that she knew she was in no danger of losing her heart to him, she was considerably more at her ease in his company and far more deft at deflecting his advances while seeming outwardly to encourage them. Nor was she above enjoying the knowledge that her deliberately flaunted preference for Andrew would annoy Lindsay, even if she hadn't the power to wound him as he had wounded her.

The disadvantage was that her coolness toward her husband and warmth toward his cousin was also necessarily observed by Lady Ellacott, who at last felt well enough to resume her usual activities by the end of the week. At first Lady Ellacott seemed only surprised, but eventually she began to give Claudia the hint that her behavior was imprudent and already giving rise to talk.

Claudia certainly had no wish to offend Lady Ellacott or give the Bath quizzes grist for their mills, but she refused any longer to dissemble before Lady Ellacott or the rest of the world that her marriage to Lindsay was something that it was not. She steadfastly evaded or ignored all of Lady Ellacott's attempts to advise or warn her.

Lady Ellacott was considerably upset by what she observed, and confused by it as well. With Andrew's constantly whispered hints in her ears, she had already begun to wonder if Lindsay's marriage to Claudia was as sound as she had supposed and even if it had ever been a love match, as they claimed, at all.

Direct as she was inclined to be, she hesitated to approach Lindsay on the subject at first, but when Mr. Jolliet sent word to Laura Place that the new settlement papers and will were ready for signing, she put him off again with minor changes. She really did not believe that Lindsay had made a fool of her by deliberately contracting exactly the sort of match that he knew she would abhor, but she thought there was no harm in holding back a bit until she was certain they were not to be cast willy-nilly into scandal and Crim. Con.

Lady Ellacott confided her concern to her niece. Claudia had ceased her morning rides with Lindsay, but she now regularly rode with Andrew or went out with him and other friends on pleasure excursions to notable sites in the surrounding area. It was on a morning when Claudia was engaged on one of the latter that the dowager spoke with Vivian. "My dear, I don't know what to think," she said at the end of her recital of her concerns that Lindsay's and Claudia's marriage was in difficulty and that as a result they might find themselves tossed into a scandal broth.

"There is already talk," said Vivian candidly. "Do you suppose that there is anything in it? I put nothing past Andrew, but I wouldn't have thought it of Claudia."

They sat in the morning room, Lady Ellacott writing out invitations to a small gathering she was planning on having in a fortnight and Vivian embroidering altar cloths she had brought with her from Landgrove. Lady Ellacott put down her pen and gave up the pretense of attention to her task. "Then, what is she about to allow Andrew to live in her pocket whenever they are together? She does nothing to discourage him. Even at the Pump Room they sit with their heads together and stroll with no one else. I am very much afraid that I have been mistaken in her, for I thought her a gentle, pretty-behaved young woman when Lindsay first brought her to me."

"If it is anyone who is deceived, Aunt Jane, it is Lindsay," Vivian pointed out. "I think it unfair to blame Claudia, though. My brother is a rake and an exceptionally attractive man. His address is polished from much practice, and if he were not making a push to fix his interest with her, there would be no threat of scandal at all.''

"What is the point in placing blame with either of them?" Lady Ellacott said peevishly. "I have decided not to sign the settlement papers just yet, and I mean to tell Lindsay that if he does not take proper charge of his wife, I shall not do so at all.''

Vivian's dismay was plain. "Oh, Aunt Jane, I hope you will not,'' she said, also putting her sewing aside. "Lindsay is the sweetest, most even-tempered man in the world, but he can't be pushed, you know that. I shouldn't be surprised if he told you to take the settlement and cast it into the baths.''

"He would never do so,'' she replied with assurance. "Lindsay, however furious he may be, is never a hothead. Thank heaven for that, or he would probably call Andrew out, and then where would we be?''

"Well, Andrew, at least, would probably be dead and Lindsay forced to flee the country." Vivian shivered a little at the prospect. "I won't even permit us to discuss such an odious possibility. Besides, it is very unlikely that Lindsay would so forget himself that he would call out his own cousin. That would be a pretty scandal.''

"But you know as well as I how strong is the rivalry between Lindsay and your brother. If Andrew dares to go too far, who knows where it may lead? Do you think you might have a word with Claudia? You are of an age and I think she might confide in you where she would not do so with me.''

"I don't know,'' Vivian said pensively. "She has been a bit distant with me of late and she would likely resent my interference, and rightly so. But I shall do what I can if you think it will help.''

This appeared to make Lady Ellacott a little easier, and Vivian promised that she would spend as much time with Claudia as possible in the next few days.

On the Friday a fortnight after Claudia had confronted Lindsay about Mrs. Hart and the forged note he had sent to Andrew, she and Vivian went together to a lecture in the Upper Rooms, and there, as usual, Andrew waited, clearly intending to attach himself to their party as they arrived. He checked slightly at the sight of his sister, and his glance when it rested on her was plainly speculative.

The lecture for the evening was on the topic of several lesser-known pastoral poets, and the lecturer spoke in a voice that was nearly a monotone. There was nearly undisguised relief when he at last dwindled to an end and the company was free to seek refreshment and to walk about the rooms and gossip with their friends and neighbors.

Andrew would have singled out Claudia as usual, but with Vivian at her side, Claudia felt the conspicuousness of his attentions and would not permit it.

"What can this be, Drew?" Vivian said with obvious raillery. "No pretty little baggage to take your eye tonight? I can't believe my brother is reduced to spending his evening with a family party. I see Miss Kankaid glancing this way whenever she thinks you are not observing her. You must not let her languishing smiles go to waste, Drew. Claudia and I shall not miss you; we are going to find a quiet corner and exchange confidences."

This was so plainly a dismissal that Andrew was left with little choice but to bow and leave them. They made their way through the room looking for a sofa or two empty chairs together. Claudia had indeed backed away from her earlier intimacy with Vivian, fearing that the marchioness would comment on her encouragement of Andrew's attentions. She saw now, though, that she could not avoid Vivian without being rude and resigned herself to it.

They found a comfortable spot to talk and the next hour was spent in pleasurable conversation until Vivian at last dared to touch the forbidden topic. A parting in the company showed them Andrew in conversation with an attractive brunette unknown to Claudia. From their expressions and postures it was clear that they were engaged in flirtation.

"Andrew is the most shocking flirt," Vivian commented as the throng of people shifted again and hid Andrew and his fair companion from their view. "But, of course, it is hardly surprising. He is such a beautiful man and his address so accomplished. I could not begin to number the hearts he has broken since his first Season.''

"He is attractive," Claudia agreed cautiously. "But he is very amiable as well. I like him very much and consider him a friend.''

Vivian raised her brows skeptically. "Well, perhaps it is so, as you are a part of our family, but it is not my experience that Andrew makes friends of women. He is inclined rather to view our sex as potential conquests. Though Drew's charm and address draw people to him, I would say that he has few close attachments even among his own sex. It is not conceit that sets him apart, I will give him that, but he is signally self-absorbed. I sometimes think there is nothing and no one he does not view solely in terms of how it affects him personally.''

Though her words might have made Claudia suspicious that Vivian had been enlisted to warn her away from Andrew, Vivian spoke in such a matter-of-fact and uncritical manner that Claudia could convict her of no complicity.

In fact, the things that Vivian said against him were similar to Claudia's own thoughts about Andrew since their intimacy had grown in the past fortnight. It was not that he was not constantly attentive to her, but somehow their conversations seemed to revolve around his opinions, beliefs, and feelings.

Claudia began to realize that what had begun as an act of defiance, brought about by the hurt she had been dealt by Lindsay, was becoming increasingly dangerous. Whatever her anger with Lindsay, she still had no intention of cuckolding him with Andrew, and neither did she wish to bring her defiance to the point of open scandal.

Though Claudia did not consciously change her manner toward Andrew, Vivian's comment that he was a rake who would place more value on her conquest than on preserving her reputation had its effect, and she began to place him more at arm's length. Andrew was no fool and knew his sister well enough to guess that his gradual decline from favor was due to Vivian's influence. Vivian was far too sensible to disparage Andrew openly to Claudia, but she made it clear to Claudia that there was little love lost between brother and sister, and such was the attraction of Vivian's own open, sunny personality that the implication of it was not lost on Claudia.

But Lady Ellacott could not contain her impatience to allow Vivian's more subtle methods to work their effect. She only saw that Claudia spent far more time in Andrew's company than she felt was proper and that Lindsay apparently felt no need to check his wife's behavior.

Eventually she could contain herself no longer. Lindsay was neither deaf nor a fool and there could be little doubt that he had heard the gossip about his wife. It was beyond Lady Ellacott's comprehension that he would permit Claudia's flirtation with Andrew to continue in such an open way if he cared anything at all for his wife.

She approached him in her usual straightforward style, which was almost certain to set up his back however much she had his interests at heart. A few days later after her talk with Vivian she drew him into the morning room when he returned from his ride, ignoring his protests that he ought to change and wash before sitting down with her.

"There is not the least need, my dear boy. I shall only detain you for a few minutes," she said, sitting on the sofa near double windows looking onto the garden. "In any case, it is best if I speak to you at once before my courage fails me."

Lindsay knew his aunt's penchant for speaking her mind too well to take her avowed trepidation seriously. "You terrify me, Aunt Jane," he said, his slow smile curling his lips. But the expression in his eyes was guarded. "By all means, tell me at once and put an end to my quaking."

"It is about Claudia and Andrew." She paused, waiting for a response, but there was none at all. "You know I am very fond of Claudia and I would never wish to think poorly of her in any way, but she has lived so much of her life retired that perhaps she is unaware that her friendly manner toward Andrew is being talked about by all the silly Bath quizzes."

"And by quite sensible citizens as well," Lindsay remarked undemonstratively.

Lady Ellacott was genuinely shocked by his apparent lack of concern. "Do you mean to do nothing about it?"

He was slouched a little in his chair, lazily regarding his aunt. "What would you have me do? Ask Drew to name his friends?"

Lady Ellacott was appalled. "Of course not."

"Then, what do you suggest? That I forbid my wife to know my cousin?" He gave a short, ironic laugh. "That would be a pretty scandal in itself."

"You might have a word with Claudia," she said severely.

"You might trust me to manage my own affairs."

"I might if you would make a push to manage them," she returned waspishly. "What has happened to you and Claudia? If you are in love with each other, how can she encourage Andrew to dangle after her in such a way."

"Most women find my cousin exceptionally attractive," he said noncommittally. "Claudia, I suppose, is not immune."

"I am very fond of Claudia. I won't suspect her of more than flirtation, but who knows where that may lead if unchecked? You could not wish to be cuckolded by your own cousin."

"Or anyone else, for that matter," Lindsay said in a dry tone. "It won't come to that."

"Half of Bath already believes that it has." She saw something flash in Lindsay's eyes that made her uncomfortable. "You cannot afford to be complacent."

"No doubt you are right," he said, once again at his blandest.

Lady Ellacott was well aware that she was treading forbidden ground and that Lindsay, though equable in temper, could not be pushed too far. Yet, Lindsay's seeming indifference to his wife's reputation and her own fears of a brewing scandal angered her and made her forget caution. "I begin to wonder if Andrew was not right when he told me that yours was not the love match you claimed but a connection formed in unseemly haste to gain the settlement I had promised you."

Lindsay laughed softly and said self-mockingly, "Married in haste, we may repent at leisure."

"Then it is true?"

"What is true," Lindsay said, "is that Claudia and I have had a falling-out. Not an uncommon occurrence between husband and wife."

"Certainly it is not uncommon between a husband and wife who do not even choose to share a bed. Ellacott and I had our differences too, but lying beside each other at night nearly always made it impossible for us to remain at odds."

Lindsay got up and went to the sideboard, where sherry and glasses were kept. It took all his considerable control not to deliver a deserved set-down to his aunt, but in addition to his liking and respect for her, he was too levelheaded to risk his inheritance for the sake of venting his resentment. It was still fairly early and he didn't really want the wine; his actions were more for the sake of occupation while he fought to keep his temper in check.

Lady Ellacott watched him but drew no warning from his stony silence. "You know I believe in the value of speaking one's mind, Lindsay. You have got to take this matter more seriously. We must think of what we are to do if we are not to find ourselves cast into a scandal broth."

"We do nothing," Lindsay said so shortly that even his aunt could not mistake the hostility in his tone.

"Don't be absurd, Lindsay," Lady Ellacott said with unaccustomed sternness. "Something must be done. We cannot have a scandal of this nature in the family."

"I have told you there will be no scandal," he said shortly.

Unused to open defiance from her usually sweet-tempered godson, Lady Ellacott bridled. "You are being willfully blind. Since you do not seem willing to take charge of your own affairs, I can only draw the obvious conclusion: you have deceived me about your marriage. If it is only my fortune that matters to you, then perhaps that is the means I must use to protect our family name, since you will not. You leave me with no other choice. I shall send word to Mr. Jolliet that I wish to postpone signing the settlement papers and my will indefinitely until I feel assured that your marriage to Claudia is not to end in disgrace.''

Lindsay drank the wine mechanically and placed his glass down again. He turned slowly to face his godmother. "You must, of course, do as you see fit, Aunt Jane. I have no more claim on your fortune than I do on your affections. Perhaps you would prefer that my wife and I leave Bath.''

Though his voice and expression were controlled, Lady Ellacott knew she had gone too far. She was upset herself that her hope of bringing Lindsay to heel had failed so signally. "Surely we may have our differences without permitting them to come between us.'' She moderated her tone to make it more conciliatory. "I have only your best interests at heart, Lindsay, you know that. But I must not permit my affection for you—or for Andrew, for that matter—to cloud my judgment. You know it has always been my intention to make you my heir, and I only urged you to marry because I wanted you to live a settled life, but I fear now there is more danger of you falling into ruin than ever before.''

"If we are indulging in plain speaking, Aunt,'' Lindsay said in a voice carefully devoid of the anger he was feeling inside, "then let us strip the bark from the tree altogether. You didn't urge me to marry, you forced my hand. I've taken the wife you seemed to think I needed, but people aren't puppets with strings to be pulled. The heart is a recalcitrant organ and can't be controlled, even if the strings are purse strings. Shall I tell Storry that you wish someone to carry a message to Jolliet this morning?''

Lady Ellacott could have wept for vexation. She was unwilling to back down, even though she knew his defiance was justified. "Please do,'' she said coldly.

Lindsay made her a stiff formal bow and left her. She was as good as her word and postponed the signing of the papers, but more because she knew that Lindsay would know if she had not than because she had any intention of disinheriting him or refusing him the settlement she had promised. In spite of her ineffectual manner of dealing with her godson, she truly did only wish for his happiness, and though her pride made her carry out her threats, she regretted deeply that they had alienated him.

Lindsay was almost as angry with himself as he was with his godmother. With every fiber of his being he longed to tell her that he didn't give a damn for her money, but he knew that it did matter to him. He was only too well aware of the gossip about his wife and cousin, but that disturbed him considerably less than the underlying and barely acknowledged fear that the gossip was not idle, and his aunt's words served to feed this insecurity.

He knew that Andrew would attempt to seduce Claudia if he could; what concerned him was Claudia's blatant encouragement of his cousin, which at first he had believed was because she had found out about his connection with Sally Hart, but which he now began to fear was a genuine attraction to Andrew that might well lead her to taking him for her lover.

These prickings of doubt were fed, in part, by the bruising of his vanity when she had rejected him so summarily after they had made love. It had surprised him in one sense, and not at all in another. So many marriages of the *ton* were made for reasons other than love that it was commonplace for a wife to make love with her husband as merely a duty to be gotten over with so that she might at last turn to her lover. He tried to banish these thoughts, but he had lived in the world too long to completely dismiss them. The dislike and distaste he had felt whenever he saw Claudia in his cousin's company were rapidly becoming something far more primal, and his own unexpected feelings disturbed him a great deal.

Relations between Lindsay and Lady Ellacott, if not hostile, at least remained cool. If Claudia noted this, or guessed she was the cause of it, she gave no sign. If anything, she made it worse by spending even more of her time in the company of Andrew, who seemed to materialize at her side wherever she was present.

Lindsay, returning to Laura Place after lunching with friends a few days later, found the house empty except for the servants, or so he thought. But when he entered the library to put back a book he had finished the previous evening, he was greeted by a sight too disturbing to continue to ignore.

The door was ajar and he pushed it open silently. Standing by the long windows overlooking the street were Claudia and Andrew. They stood very close to each other, not quite touching but obviously engaged in intimate conversation. Lindsay had a sense of intrusion that was quickly followed by a powerful jealous rage, but it lasted only a moment as base instinct was quickly subdued by the civilized man.

He drew the door shut and opened it again with sufficient warning that someone was about to enter. They had separated, as he had known they would, but Andrew cast him a quick, almost triumphant look as he entered that would have told him what he already knew even if he had not witnessed them together himself.

He gave no sign to them of what he had seen; the mask of pleasant indifference was perfectly in place. But he avoided looking directly at his wife because he wasn't certain he could keep the anger that was simmering inside of him from showing in his eyes if they met hers.

Lindsay prided himself on being a reasonable man of reasonable temperament. He was deeply disturbed not only by the strength of his emotions but by their very existence at all. If they were the result of mere possessive instinct, then he was troubled to think that the patina of breeding and polish was so thin; but in his heart he knew it wasn't that. The physical attraction he had felt toward Claudia had gradually developed into something deeper and more enduring. Since the night they made love, the truth was more difficult to deny and made her rejection of him and obvious preference for Andrew the more difficult to endure.

As the month of June progressed the fetes at Sydney Gardens increased to twice a week and the private al-fresco parties, which were all the rage, were held there virtually every day. The most fashionable of these were the breakfasts given by the principal hostesses of Bath. Lady Ellacott was not one to be behind the fashion, and she was quick to take their lead. On Thursday of the third week in June a select score or two of her particular friends were bidden to break-fast at Sydney Gardens, and the morning dawned as bright and sunny as the dowager had hoped it would.

Lindsay was not in the habit of joining the ladies at such entertainments, but in the circumstances, his absence would certainly have occasioned remark. And so Lady Ellacott's guests were treated to the increasingly rare sight of Claudia gracing her husband's arm as they strolled among their guests to the strains of violins wafting from the musicians' platform erected for the occasion.

Andrew was also present, but the Bath quizzes hoping for scandal were disappointed. Under the vigilant eye of his aunt and in the presence of her husband, Andrew found scant opportunity for dalliance with Claudia.

A sufficient number of the invited guests attended for the party to be considered a success, and Lady Ellacott was in a fine humor. The coolness between her and Lindsay was almost dissipated, and she would gladly have sent for Mr. Jolliet again to bring the settlement papers if Lindsay would only make the least push to prevent Claudia from encouraging Strait. Still she was not without hope that her ploy would prove effective. She knew Lindsay's affection for her was sincere and not for the sake of her fortune, but she also knew that it did matter to him that he was her heir. She observed him and Claudia together and saw that he deftly managed to keep Claudia near enough to his side to discourage any attentions Andrew might wish to pay to her, and yet he did so without obviously seeming to wish to keep her in his pocket.

While the servants were clearing away the last remnants of breakfast, she managed a few words alone with him. "I know you find such entertainments insipid, dear boy," she said. "I am sure Claudia is glad that you have come as well. I have noted that you have been together almost since we arrived. I hope this is the beginning of a new understanding between you."

Lindsay gave her a long look before answering. He knew she was fishing to discover if he intended to bring his wife to heel as she wished him to. He did intend it, but his aunt's officiousness rankled and he would not give her the satisfaction of a positive response. "One must keep up appearances," he said with an inflection that just eluded sarcasm. "But that is not why I am here. Put it down to a sudden wish to commune with nature. Do you think old Grimsby will offer for Miss Rushmore?"

Lady Ellacott took his hint and abandoned the topic, responding to his question about two of their guests instead. But she was not displeased with what she had observed that morning, and when she chanced to see Lindsay and Claudia move away from the gathering down the path that led behind the musicians' platform, she had every hope that their intended *tête-à-tête* was the beginning of a better understanding between them.

Claudia did not share her sentiments as Lindsay led her away from the throng of guests. Their punctiliousness toward each other continued unimpaired, but a wall had been erected between them since they had quarreled, and though there was no open hostility, neither was there ease between them. At the very least she found the prospect of being alone with him uncomfortable.

At first there was little conversation between them. Claudia was quiet, remembering the last time she and Lindsay had strolled along the paths at Sydney Gardens the night she had rejected Andrew's advances and had given herself completely to this man whom she had claimed not to love but who had moved her as no other man ever had. And Lindsay, too, had thoughts to preoccupy him.

Eventually Claudia began to realize that their silence was becoming strained. It was more the awkwardness of two people who had once shared the greatest of intimacies and who now met almost as strangers.

Feeling the need to bring it to an end before her discomfort became any greater, she spoke on the first topic that came into her head, though it was not the most felicitous. "Have you spoken with Mr. Jolliet any further about the house in Landsdown Crescent?"

"No. But then I haven't spoken with Jolliet in some time."

Claudia, who would not be required to sign the settlement

papers, had no idea that Lady Ellacott had postponed this event indefinitely. "Is there some difficulty about the house?" she asked artlessly. "I thought it was all but a settled thing."

"It would have been if Aunt Jane had not rescinded her offer."

"Rescinded it?" Claudia asked with genuine surprise. "But why would she do such a thing?"

Lindsay stopped and turned to her. "I am sure, my love, if you tax your ingenuity, you will be able to find an answer to that interesting question."

Claudia saw that though a faint smile curled his lips, his eyes on hers were steady and unsmiling. She realized that he referred to her in some way, but at first she could not understand him. "Is there some sort of misunderstanding? Have you spoken with Aunt Jane about it?"

"We have already had a rather diverting conversation on the subject. She isn't going to sign the papers, Claudia."

Though she was not sure why, her heart began to beat faster. "Why not?"

Lindsay's smile increased but became no more pleasant. "Because she thinks that our marriage is likely to come to an abrupt and scandalous end. I am not sure she is mistaken."

"Are you suggesting that that is in some way my fault?" she said slowly as she began to be enlightened. "I never wanted to be married to you in the first place."

"You have made that only too plain. But I thought I also made it plain that I would tolerate your other interests only if they were carried out with discretion. Did you really think I would let you hand me my horns in public, and with my own cousin?"

Claudia's eyes flashed with anger. "Why should you expect me to keep my end of our bargain when you could not keep yours?" she demanded. "You gave me your word it would be a marriage in name only, but you could not keep it."

"It wasn't rape, Claudia. I seem to recall a response that could not have been forced from you."

"You took advantage of my inexperience to manipulate

me to your own ends," she said with increasing fury as he reminded her of her foolishness. "I doubt it would have mattered to you if it had been rape."

"Oh, it would have mattered to me," he said with a silkiness designed to irritate. "I hope my technique is more perfected than that." At these words she would have turned and left him, but he caught her wrist in a viselike grip. "If we are to speak of bargains, my love, let us remember that we married to secure my inheritance, not jeopardize it. I've decided to send you to Lovewell. I'll join you there as soon as I've taken steps to repair some of the damage your indiscretion has caused."

Claudia as appalled at his arrogance and the degree of humiliation that he intended to visit on her by sending her away as if he had the right to order her life as he pleased. "How dare you suppose you can chastise me like a recalcitrant child. I have done nothing for you or anyone to reproach me, and I won't be sent away in disgrace to Lovewell or anywhere else."

He released her hand. "Do you imagine that you will find a champion in Aunt Jane, my precious?" He laughed unpleasantly. "She will applaud my unexpected display of backbone, which she has accused me of lacking because I have attempted to treat you as a responsible adult. But you have paid me handsomely for my light hand on the reins, and now I have no choice if everything is not to be lost."

"We always come back to the only thing that matters to you, don't we?" she said bitterly. "You don't give a damn about my discretion or virtue or anything else. Well, your inheritance matters not at all to me, and I won't allow you to use me to gain it any longer. I have kept our devil's bargain. I married you, and to my sorrow I must live with that for the rest of my days."

His lids came down over his eyes to shield their expression. "As must we both, dear wife. What an apt term for a marriage made far from heaven."

"It was what *you* wanted."

"And I am well-served for it."

"I am sorry if you and Lady Ellacott choose to judge me

harshly, but I shall conduct myself as you do, consulting no judgment but my own.''

Claudia felt tears forming and threatening to choke her, though whether from anger of wretchedness she couldn't say. Again she started to walk away from him, but the icy severity of his voice held her. He grasped her shoulders in a not very gentle way. ''You will conduct yourself as my wife,'' he said, almost from between his teeth. She had never heard him sound so implacable before, however hot their previous quarrels. ''If you force me to put you aside, see if even your family will give you welcome then.''

''I won't need to worry about that if I am under Andrew's protection,'' she said, spitting out the first taunt that came to her. For a moment she thought he would strike her, so plain was the rage in his expression, but this time her fury was equal to his and she felt no urge to flinch. ''If you ever touch or threaten me again, you will give me no other recourse. I'll elope with Drew and then see what lengths you will be driven to secure your inheritance.''

To her astonishment he simply released her, holding her now only with his eyes. Somehow his lack of response to her awful threat was worse than if he were ranting. She hadn't meant it, of course, but she saw that he believed it. This should have pleased her, but it did not. Instead, she felt an unaccountable sense of loss, as if something important to her were now beyond her recall. Tears stung at her eyes, but she made no attempt to blink them away. She forced her eyes away from him, turned, and left him, making her way blindly back toward the sound of the music. But her ears were attuned for another sound that she never heard. He did not follow her down the path.

# 9

The sights and pleasures of Bath that Claudia had delighted in no longer pleased her, the friends she had made ceased to amuse her, and at times she felt an emptiness that nearly brought her to tears. When she and Lindsay met the following day, on the surface his manner toward her was unchanged, but there was a hardness in his eyes, a set quality to his expression, even when he smiled, that bespoke his feelings clearly. She wished she had not let her temper get the better of her; she had never meant for Lindsay to infer that she and Andrew were lovers even to punish him for using her for his own ends.

Conversely, now that the estrangement between them was complete, she found it was not what she wanted, after all. She might abandon her hopes that they would one day be lovers in every sense of the word, but she realized that the last thing she wanted was for their marriage to be a sterile truce between strangers who tolerated each other as victims of mutual misfortune. At the very least she had hoped they would be friends of a sort.

Claudia longed for a confidante, but in the circumstances she could not turn to Vivian and there was no one among her new friends that she could entrust with the truth of her strange marriage. She hadn't even the outlet of writing to her mother or eldest sister, for how could she admit to either the enormity of what she had done on no more than the turn of a card.

Though Claudia did not confide in her, Vivian was not blind to her distress, or the cause of it. She saw that her subtle attempts to warn Claudia away from her brother had not succeeded as she had hoped, and efforts to discuss Andrew more directly with Claudia met with polite rebuff.

Yet Vivian's efforts had not failed completely. Claudia had principally engaged in her outrageous flirtation with Andrew in defiance of her husband and in hurt over his liaison with Mrs. Hart. Vivian had awakened her to the earl's true character, and as she saw him for the self-absorbed, rather vain man that he was, even her physical attraction to him began to wane. If it were not that it would seem that she was bowing to Lindsay's commands, Claudia might well have brought an end to Andrew's presumption.

As it was, Andrew found her perceptibly cooler toward him, particularly when they were alone or unlikely to be overheard, which caused him to guess that her encouragement was at least in part to punish Lindsay. He did not precisely object, for Claudia's motives mattered little to him, but as he realized his power to attract her was lessening, his vanity was piqued.

In spite of his vanity, nourished by his easy successes with the fairer sex, he was not blind to his limitations and he recognized that though Claudia might skirt the edge of ruin by encouraging his advances, she would not slip easily over that edge as he had hoped, but would have to be firmly pushed. Yet Andrew was not yet prepared to admit defeat.

If it were merely a question of her values, he was certain that success would already have been his. If she were in love with Lindsay, his task was much harder, but not, he felt, impossible. What was necessary was for him to erode her feelings for Lindsay, to turn her against him if he could, for he had no doubt at all that he could persuade her to turn to him if he succeeded.

When he saw Claudia that night at Lady Silverdale's party, he asked her to ride with him the following morning, and Claudia happily accepted. Since her estrangement from

Lindsay, they had given up their early-morning rides and lessons, and now the only time she was able to enjoy the exercise that she had truly come to love was when she occasionally went out with Kitty Lodder or as part of a party to explore the neighboring countryside. But since Mrs. Lodder was a rather diffident horsewoman and the excursions were mostly long, rambling walks, she looked forward to riding again with a horseman form whom she might hope to learn. She gave no thought to the propriety of riding out alone with him, for despite growing gossip about them, she considered such an activity to be too innocuous for reproach.

And so it proved to be. Andrew was on his best behavior, his manner toward her attentive, but not sufficiently loverlike to put her on her guard. It was a beautiful summer morning, the day promised to be quite warm, but the air was still cooled by early breezes that rustled the treetops above them. Sparkling rays of light crisscrossed the path as they rode along it at an easy canter, and there was a freshness in the air that made the exercise invigorating.

Andrew led her in a direction Claudia had never ridden before, to the south and away from the rolling hills where she and Lindsay had mostly ridden. As the fields gave away to a wood and the wood deepened, she felt the first stirrings of trepidation, for she was suddenly very aware of their solitude. But still Andrew's behavior gave her no cause for concern. When they reached a fork in the path, it was he who pulled up and suggested that they turn and retrace their steps.

They did so at a slow trot, which eventually dropped to a walk to cool their mounts. It seemed to Claudia that Andrew was mildly distracted. Several times she noticed him looking about him as if looking for something or expecting to see someone. But there was only the sound of their voices and the steady rhythm of their horses' hooves until they reached the outskirts of Bath. They were passed by a curricule pulled by two bang-up-to-the-mark bays, a farmer's dray, a pair of riders, and a single rather dandified young man on a showy chestnut. Another pair approached them and Claudia recognized the riders almost before she could reasonably expect to make out their features. It was Lindsay and Mrs. Hart.

Though she saw them together in company quite regularly, it was very different seeing them alone in such a way. Again the memory of the meeting the day that Lindsay had first begun to teach her to ride returned, even more forcefully perhaps because they were again on horseback and with belated feelings of humiliation to think that he had left her to go off with his mistress.

Andrew saw her pale and suggested that they turn away and avoid the meeting, but Claudia shook her head and refused. "By all means let us meet. They must have seen us by now and it would look quite peculiar if we turned back in an obvious way."

Lindsay, who might have had cause to blush, greeted them with perfect equanamity, seemingly upset neither to find his wife with his cousin nor to be discovered in company with his avowed mistress. "Are you on your way back from your ride? We'll join you, then. If we go down Argyle Street instead of the North Parade, we can see Sally to her door without going much out of our way."

This suggestion pleased no one. "There is no need," Claudia assured him hurriedly. She was horrified that he would even suggest such a thing. Perhaps it was a part of marriage *à la mode* to behave with such insouciance, but she was not equal to it.

"No, not the least need," Andrew seconded with equal alacrity. "We would not hear of you interrupting your ride to accommodate us."

"We had planned to ride to Rowden Wood," Mrs. Hart said with a hint of annoyance. "If Lady Lindsay and Lord Strait do not mind, surely we may still do so. It is one of our favorite rides, is it not Lin? You do not mind our little excursions, I hope, Lady Lindsay," she added with an arch glance cast at Claudia. "Lin and I have been friends since we were in leading strings."

Claudia saw the lines set around Lindsay's eyes and knew that he found Mrs. Hart's words as distasteful as she did.

Succumbing to a justifiable lack of charity for the other woman, Claudia said, "I hope I would not be foolish enough to mind what Mr. Hart clearly does not," and received the satisfaction of bringing a flush to Mrs. Hart's cheeks.

"We have been out for over an hour and I think we may put off our ride to the wood for another time," Lindsay said without any discernible change in his humor, and turned his horse in the direction of town to end any further argument.

It was an uncomfortable ride for everyone, but outward appearances were kept and a flow of conversation, though far from spontaneous, was maintained. Andrew, after reminding Claudia pointedly that she had promised to go driving with him after luncheon, parted from them soon after they had left Mrs. Hart in Lansdown Crescent and Lindsay and Claudia traveled the short distance to Laura Place almost entirely in silence.

As they turned into Laura Place, Lindsay said quietly, "I am sorry for that. I had no idea you rode out that way."

"Did you have to force us to return to Bath together?" Claudia demanded coldly, seeking in anger to hide her unhappiness.

Lindsay took in his breath deeply, letting it out again and ending with a soft mirthless laugh. "I wish I understood what you want from me, Claudia," he said with genuine puzzlement. "You insist that you want no part of me and that you care nothing for my affairs and yet you object when faced with them."

"It isn't that," Claudia said, not looking at him.

"What is it then?"

"It hardly matters what I think. We have agreed to living our separate lives." He would have spoken again, but she would not permit it. She spurred her horse for the few remaining yards and was already dismounting willy-nilly as he came up behind her. A footman came out of the house to take her horse and there was no opportunity for further speech between her and Lindsay, which was what she intended.

Claudia felt treacherous tears welling in her eyes and

closing her throat, but she would not cry again before him. She gathered up the full skirts of her habit and went quickly into the house and immediately up the stairs.

Vivian was just coming out of her own bedchamber at the end of the hall as Claudia entered it, and at once saw her distress. She called out to Claudia, but Claudia ignored her and continued into her room. Vivian entered without bothering to seek permission and at once went to Claudia, who was sitting at the foot of the bed, her head bent against the post, not crying but breathing heavily in dry sobs.

Vivian went to her and placed a gentle arm about her rigid shoulders. "What is it, love? Have you and Lin been quarreling?"

"There is nothing for us to quarrel over," Claudia said bitterly. "Ours is a purely business arrangement." She had not meant to say such a thing to Vivian, but in her distress her tongue was unguarded.

Vivian said nothing for a moment. "Was there any truth at all to the story that Lindsay told to us about your long-standing attachment when you came to Lovewell House?"

Claudia's innate sense cautioned prudence, but anger was her uppermost emotion and would not be denied. "None at all."

"But I thought, for a time at least . . ." Vivian said as if puzzled, and then broke off, asking abruptly, "Are you in love with my brother?" Claudia cast her a swift startled glance and Vivian continued, "It is an *on-dit*, Claudia, you must know that."

"It isn't true," Claudia said, and walked away over to her wardrobe. She opened the doors and began sorting through the contents with savage unconcern for the creases her carelessness was creating.

"I'm sorry," Vivian said, coming up to her again. "I didn't wish to upset you further, but I thought if we got it out into the open, we could talk and maybe it would make you feel better."

"There isn't anything to talk about," Claudia insisted, turning her back on Vivian once again. Even a week ago she might have been grateful for Vivian's offer, but her emotions were in such turmoil that the solution went beyond speech. She had thought she had control of her feelings for Lindsay, but riding with him in company with Mrs. Hart had made her feel so empty and ravaged inside that she knew it had only been self-delusion. She had fallen foolishly, hopelessly in love with a man who made no pretense of loving her, who could use her to his ends without a blush, and who thought nothing of parading his armours about her publicly.

Vivian was not impervious to the rebuff, but she genuinely cared about Claudia and was willing to risk Claudia's rejection if she could break through her defenses and help her in any way. If it was true that Claudia and Lindsay had lied about their marriage being a love match, she could imagine how difficult Claudia must have found it living such a lie with no one to confide her true feelings to. "Is it Lindsay, then? Has he done something to hurt you?"

Claudia had to put a check on her tongue to keep from snapping at Vivian. However well-intentioned, Vivian was bringing her perilously close to tears. "Andrew and I met Lindsay and Mrs. Hart this morning."

"What is there in that?" Vivian said, though cautiously. "Did Lindsay object to you riding with Andrew?"

"No one, least of all Lindsay, has the right to object to how I chose to conduct myself," Claudia said fiercely as she pulled a cream linen driving dress from her wardrobe, nearly ripping the material in her vehemence. She then spoiled the effect of righteous anger by saying in a voice that almost choked, "Mrs. Hart is Lindsay's mistress."

"You should not leap to conclusions," Vivian said in a conciliatory way.

"Lindsay has admitted it quite freely."

Vivian's brows shot upward. "Has he really? It is not like him to be so graceless."

Claudia stepped out of her habit and cast it onto the chair. She went to her washstand and poured out water that had long since cooled, and began to wash off the dirt from her ride before she trusted herself to speak. "Even you know of it!" Claudia cast the damp towel on top of her habit, heedless of staining it. "And condone it, I suppose. Lindsay informs me that such arrangements are not thought at all remarkable.''

"In some ways they are not," Vivian agreed cautiously. "When a marriage is for the sake of convenience, it is regarded as inevitable.''

"Then why does the world remark at my friendship with Andrew?" Claudia demanded. She sat down in her petticoats in front of her dressing table and began to pull pins from her hair to redress it.

"It is not the same thing precisely," Vivian acknowledged, aware of Claudia's rage and knowing it was not unjustified.

"In what way?" Claudia persisted, turning and looking up at her. "Why should Lindsay be able to please himself with impunity while I must mend my ways or be condemned?"

Vivian knew her answer was not likely to be placating. "For one thing it is a matter of the relationship to which Lindsay and Andrew stand to each other. It is not at all the thing to form a liaison with a connection of one's husband, and then it is also a matter of discretion.''

"Discretion?" Claudia said, her voice rising. Her anger at last effectively routed her tears. "Is it discretion for Lindsay and that woman to meet openly in public and to ride unescorted beyond the city?"

"Isn't that what you were doing with Andrew?" Vivian said with more truth than tact. "It is not as if Sally Hart were of the demimonde. She is received everywhere and we have all of us known one another since our nursery days.''

"I knew there would be no point in talking," Claudia said, turning back to the mirror and looking resolutely at her own reflection, avoiding Vivian's gaze.

Vivian made no comment to this, aware that her worldly philosophy had not reassured Claudia. She might have read into Claudia's behavior that she was distressed about Mrs. Hart because she was in love, after all, with Lindsay, but to set against this was Claudia's open encouragement of Andrew. "Are you going out again?" she said after a bit.

"I am going driving with Andrew just after luncheon," Claudia replied with the satisfaction of knowing that Vivian would probably disapprove. "We are going to Wraxworth to see the priory ruins."

"Alone?"

"Quite alone," Claudia said in such a bellicose tone that it was clear she was challenging Vivian to object.

But Vivian did not. Instead, she got up and went over to Claudia. Touching her arm lightly she said, "We dine at seven tonight because of the Sellington ball. You'll enjoy the ruins, I think. They are very picturesque."

When she left her, Claudia felt a little nonplussed and some of her feelings of angry defiance evaporated. She had meant to cry off from the excursion with Andrew, an engagement she had made with him some time before, until they had met with Lindsay and Mrs. Hart. She had little desire for the drive, but while her husband dared to flaunt his mistress all over town, she would not hesitate to show the world that she was free to pursue her own interests, whatever Vivian might say of it being a different matter. She only hoped that at least half of their acquaintance would see her in Andrew's curricle.

At a quarter-past seven Lady Ellacott glanced again at the clock on the mantel and said pointedly, "I think we must suppose that Claudia does not mean to join us for dinner tonight. Cook frets terribly when dinner is left so long that the food is half-ruined, and quite frankly I am of a like mind. Shall we go in?"

Vivian agreed and rose from her chair. "It is probably some mundane thing like a tossed shoe that delays them," she said, but inside her concern was very much greater. She alone knew the defiant mood in which Claudia had left for her drive with Andrew.

Lindsay, too, took his wife's absence in more serious part, but his outward manner was as untroubled as Vivian's. Only Lady Ellacott displayed any outward concern for Claudia's failure to return to Laura Place in time for dinner. "I certainly would not wish Claudia and Andrew to meet with any accident," she said, rising also, "but I confess I would hope it is some minor mishap that delays them rather than a disregard for our comfort and, I might add, all propriety. It is really almost beyond the line for Claudia to go alone with Andrew beyond the boundaries of the city, even in an open carriage. I wonder you choose to permit it, Lindsay.''

Her attack was not unexpected, and Lindsay's control on his temper was sufficient to permit him to smile and say without concern, ''Claudia is a big girl. She is quite capable of ordering her own conduct.'' Storry came in to announce dinner and Lindsay offered his aunt his arm, which she accepted without further comment.

Vivian, with her gift for light chatter, saved dinner from being a somber meal, but she found the task wearing. In spite of herself she kept glancing at the door, half-expecting Claudia to come rushing into the room full of apologies. But dinner came to a merciful end and still Claudia made no appearance.

Lady Ellacott at last rose from the table. ''Since we are only a family party and we are a bit late as it is, I hope you won't linger over your wine tonight, Lindsay. I'll have Storry fetch our cloaks, Vivian, and order our carriage for a quarter-hour from now.''

Vivian did not follow her immediately. ''I am sure it is some silly, but easily explainable mischance that keeps them,'' she said, pausing beside Lindsay's chair.

He looked up at her with a half-smile. ''Quite.''

Vivian subsided into Lady Ellacott's vacated chair beside him. ''You can't think she has eloped with him.''

''No. Of course not. But between that desperate course of action and a mere drive to visit ruins there are several unhappy mediums that suggest themselves.''

''I don't believe they have been lovers,'' Vivian said frankly. ''Claudia is attracted to him—few women are completely immune to my exquisite brother—but even while permitting him to flirt quite desperately with her, she keeps him at a little distance.''

''What would you expect her to do in your company?'' Lindsay said, his smile turning sardonic. He turned the wineglass idly by the stem. ''Did you know that we quarreled today?''

She nodded. "She was upset about meeting you with Mrs. Hart. Surely you could have avoided that."

"I don't think the meeting was chance," Lindsay replied, but would not elaborate when she asked him to.

Though she was not precisely breaking a confidence, Vivian hesitated to speak her mind. "Claudia told me that you lied about falling in love," she said finally, deciding that the circumstances warranted it. "She said that you married only for your inheritance."

Lindsay laughed with self-mockery. "And much good has that done me."

"But you care for Claudia, don't you?"

He looked up quickly, as if startled by her question, and in that unguarded moment her question was answered before his heavy lids again concealed his emotions from her view. "I had thought for a time that we might have something more than a sterile business agreement. I think, though, that I was mistaken." He drank deeply from his glass and would have poured more, but Vivian put her hand over his on the bottle.

"I think Claudia may be in love with you," she said, surprising herself. She was not certain she thought that at all.

"With me?" He smiled, but not with humor. "You are clearly not in her confidence if you believe that. It is Strait who has the gift of attaching women without effort."

"In the most shallow way. Would you want to be thought a libertine like my brother?"

He pushed back his chair and stood up. "I should make a wretched libertine. I can't even seem to attach my own wife," he said with a grim little smile. He held out his hand to Vivian and they left the dining room to join their aunt.

It was a warm night for the exercise of a ball, but fortunately Lady Sellington had no qualms about fresh air and draperies were drawn back from open windows and the several doors leading out to a raised terrace that overlooked the garden were flung wide so that anyone wishing to step out into the cooler night air might do so. Even so, ladies coming off the dance floor fanned themselves vigorously and the most expertly starched points of the gentlemen's collars had begun to wilt.

Vivian, who had the gift of finding pleasure whatever her circumstances, was enjoying herself very much, only occasionally feeling a brief dampening of her spirits when she wondered what had become of her brother and Claudia and what would be the outcome of it when they finally did return.

Lindsay was not the sort of man to give away his innermost thoughts, but Vivian knew he was deeply disturbed by Claudia's apparent flaunting of her attraction to Andrew, and she knew Lindsay well enough to know that his equable temper could be pushed only so far.

It wanted only two sets before supper when Claudia, on the arm of the Earl of Strait, entered Lady Sellington's ballroom and set the gossips abuzz. Vivian, seeking to be helpful and never supposing for a moment that Claudia would come to the ball on her own, had made Claudia's excuses, pleading the headache. When she saw Claudia, for once her usual good humor deserted her and she silently castigated Claudia as a fool.

Claudia, who had spent a wretchedly uncomfortable day, well paid out for her defiance of her husband, would have agreed with Vivian if she had known her thoughts. She had gone driving with Andrew principally to punish Lindsay, but the lateness of her return had nothing to do with intent. The day thus far had been a waking nightmare for Claudia and she was so out of humor she was having considerable difficulty maintaining her civility with Andrew, who had insisted on escorting her to the ball despite her protests.

They had viewed the ruins extensively, though this had been somewhat wasted on Claudia, who was too preoccupied with her tumultuous thoughts to give them the attention they deserved, and afterward they had stopped at a small inn to refresh themselves with lemonade against the warmth of the day. It had taken them some time to be served and Claudia began to be concerned about the length of time they had been away from Laura Place. If anyone were marking the time, it would be obvious that they had been gone far longer than was usual for such an excursion.

In spite of her wish to cast her friendship with Andrew

in Lindsay's face, she had no intention of creating scandal, and she was utterly dismayed when their journey was further delayed by a minor accident. They had slid into a ditch on a sharp turn as they had been overtaking a farmer's wagon, and had cracked a wheel. Claudia had been vexed almost to tears, and the time it had taken for the wheelright to come to them and to repair the damage had seemed to her interminable.

Andrew, wisely, since she was so clearly on the fret, took no advantage of their extended *tête-à-tête*. Claudia was annoyed, but not with him. His purpose in taking her out for a drive had been to divert her and she could not justly give him the blame for their misadventure.

Claudia was not surprised to find that Vivian, Lindsay, and Lady Ellacott had already gone to Lady Sellington's when they finally reached Laura Place. She might have simply gone to her room and retired for the night, a course her common sense urged her to take, but sleep was far from her and the last thing she wanted was an evening of solitude.

Her mistake, though, was in voicing her intention to go to the ball aloud to Andrew. Nothing she could say about not wishing to inconvenience him or the ease with which Storry could procure a chair to carry her to the ball, could deter him from his intent of conveying her there himself. It was not until they entered the ballroom and so many eyes seemed to swivel their way and become quickly averted that Claudia realized how particular it must look for her to arrive so late, and in his company, when her own husband was already in attendance.

Lindsay came up beside Vivian. He too had witnessed Claudia's entrance. He had meant to behave with his usual civility toward Claudia whenever she did return, but his iron self-control was weakening. Though he was unaware of it, he was now tasting exactly the same hollowness and emotional upheaval that Claudia had felt when she had met him with Mrs. Hart earlier in the day.

Vivian touched him lightly on the arm, a comforting gesture, but he only gave her a bland smile and then left her to go to Claudia. The other guests within earshot gave no appearance of interest in the meeting, but there could be no doubt that all ears were carefully tuned to catch any exchange.

Claudia had meant to be calm and dignified in her explanation of her tardiness, but under her husband's cool, slightly ironical gaze she found herself stumbling over her words as if she had cause for supposing she would not be believed.

Lindsay's listened without comment, but when he spoke, his lip curled faintly. "Quite so. Passing a farmer's wagon might well test one's driving skill." Both his tone and his words were an insult.

Andrew appeared unaffected. "Devilishly ticklish turn," he agreed. "Might have happened to anyone, even you, Lin, if you'd tried it."

"I daresay." He turned to Claudia, still evincing neither disapprobation nor outright anger. "Aunt Jane was quite worried about you. I think we should find her and put her mind at rest."

He held out his arm and Claudia had no choice but to take it, though she dreaded what he would say to her once they had parted from Andrew. But her husband surprised her by uttering only commonplaces while they skirted the perimeter of the room. Nor did Lady Ellacott heap recriminations on her head. She seemed only relieved to discover that Claudia had met with no serious mishap, and the matter was not referred to again.

# 10

Claudia's late arrival did not go unnoticed by her admirers and she was quickly claimed for the next set by Colonel Amworthy and promised to go into supper with Mr. Talent. She was also soon engaged for the sets after supper, and she might have found the evening very pleasurable if it were not for the fact that in the back of her mind was the knowledge that the events of this day would yet have repercussions.

At the end of the third set after supper, Claudia began to feel the heat of her exertions. Her partner was Andrew, and though she knew she only added to her imprudence, she permitted him to persuade her to step out onto the terrace, where it was a bit cooler. It was not a great imprudence, after all; the terrace was in full view of the entire company and any number of couples had wandered outside during the course of the evening.

There were a half-dozen or so other guests on the terrace and Andrew drew her a little to one side as far from the others as they could be. "Was Lindsay very difficult about our returning to town so late?" he asked with concern.

"No. He said nothing at all beyond what he said to you."

"He doesn't believe it, you know."

Claudia did not understand him. "Doesn't believe what?"

"That there was any accident at all. He thinks we were at some trysting place and lost track of the time."

Claudia found this prospect disquieting. "Why should he think such a thing?"

"Because he believes we are lovers," Andrew replied patiently.

Claudia knew this was likely, but at the moment she was almost glad of it. What difference did it make what he thought? He had Sally Hart to comfort him. But she did not say so to Andrew. "There is no reason for him to think so beyond his own imaginings," she said.

"Alas," Andrew said with a soft, self-mocking laugh. He moved a little closer to her. "Since we are accused without cause, perhaps we should be hung for a sheep as well as a lamb."

Claudia had the balustrade to her back and he stood before her; she looked quickly to where the others had been standing, thinking he would never be so daring as to kiss her in front of strangers, but the music had begun again and they were quite alone.

She said firmly, with just a trace of annoyance in her tone, "I thought we understood each other, Drew. I like you very well, but it is not more than that."

"Still determined to be the virtuous wife? What is it serving you, Claudia? You don't suppose it matters to Lindsay more than as a point of pride? You know his interests lie elsewhere."

Claudia felt a stab of pain at the reminder. "It doesn't matter," she said coldly. He was standing so close to her that they were nearly touching, and this made her very uncomfortable. She no longer cared if she offended him. She only wanted to return to the house and the safety of lights and numbers. "Neither Lindsay nor I consult each other in matters of conduct."

Ignoring her obvious displeasure, he put his hands on her shoulders, restraining her. "You are such a warm, beautiful woman, Cousin," he said, bringing his face very near to hers. "I can't believe you are all ice inside."

Claudia tried to avert her face, but he grasped it in his hands and his mouth came down on hers, hard and insistent. She didn't struggle, but she became completely rigid lest any residue of the purely physical attraction she had felt for him betray her into a response as it had the last time. She thought her coldness would be sufficient to put him off, but he continued to kiss her as if her response were everything he could wish for, and his caresses became increasingly urgent and intimate.

It was impossible to imagine that he would force himself upon her here, but Claudia's heart was hammering in her breast and her reason was overwhelmed by fear that if she didn't stop him she would find herself violated. She managed to get her hands against his chest, but his strength was greater than hers and it took all the energy she possessed to finally push him a little away.

His expression was neither surprised nor dismayed. In the feeble light of a half-moon she could see that he smiled, though it was hardly a pleasant expression. "Release me," she said imperiously, though she was still quaking inside.

He ignored her, his smile spreading and becoming even more unpleasant. "If I don't, will you scream for help, Claudia?" he asked. "Would that be wise, do you think? Several people saw us come out here, not to mention those who were already here before the set formed. Half the world already thinks you are my mistress; they are far more likely to think it a lovers' quarrel than a ravishment."

Claudia struggled for a moment but abandoned it as undignified when he continued to hold her fast. She was genuinely frightened, but she was even more frightened of letting him see it, fearing that he would use it against her. "Let them think what they will," she said defiantly, unhappily aware that it was much her own fault that she was judged so by the world.

"And in the process complete the ruin of Lindsay and yourself. By all means, my dear. Call for assistance." His lips came alarmingly near to hers again, but Claudia merely averted her face and did not cry out. He laughed. "I thought you would not. Then I think we should step out into the garden, it is too public here for making love, don't you agree? It is a warm night and we should find a spot that is more to our comfort."

"You really don't want me, do you?" Claudia said, her fear forgotten for a moment as she acknowledged what she supposed she had already known for some time. "It is only to ruin me and, through me, Lindsay, that matters to you."

"Not true. Or at least not entirely. I do think you beautiful and desirable, quite unworthy of my bland cousin Lindsay. There really is no need for this to be unpleasant, you know. Whether you admit it or not, Little Miss Virtue, you are not indifferent to me and I am told I am quite an accomplished lover."

As he spoke, one hand pushed down the already low bodice of her gown and sought her breasts. Claudia scarcely noticed the physical intimacy. His words and tone chilled her; he clearly intended to make love to her tonight whether by choice or by force. One way or the other, her ruin was certain.

Whatever the outcome, she knew she could not let him rape her. His touch, once desired, now made her flesh shrink. She began to struggle in earnest, aware that her gown was becoming disheveled and the pins were loosening from her hair. She was not without strength and she nearly succeeded, but as she pushed past him, he caught her wrist and pulled her against him again, his lips crushing against hers so brutally that she could taste blood.

Her common sense told her that he would not rape her nearly in view of two hundred people. She knew her only hope was not to panic; she could not let him drag her from the terrace, but she was almost physically ill with the fear that his determination went beyond reason. She knew that there was no choice left to her: she would have to cry for help, whatever the consequences.

But quite unexpectedly, Andrew's embrace was eased and she struggled quickly out of his arms. She felt the wall at her back, but Andrew was not pursuing her. He was on his knees, looking up, but not at her. Lindsay stood in front of him, his expression tense and rigid as stone.

Andrew rose slowly to his feet, his smile growing equally unhurriedly. Blood began to drip from his nose. "A lucky punch, Cousin," he said to Lindsay so matter-of-factly that he might have felt nothing at all. "You would not have been so successful if my guard were up. But I will allow it was not unjustified and not give you the retribution you deserve."

"Name your friends, Strait," Lindsay said in a low voice entirely devoid of expression.

Andrew appeared momentarily nonplussed and then he laughed. "You can't call me out now, Lin. You've just planted me a facer. It would be my choice now, and as I've said, I'll allow that it was not undeserved."

"Meet me, Strait, or I'll see to it that everyone knows you would not."

"You're bluffing. Everyone would know why you called me out, and that would bring down enough scandal on your head not only to ruin your wife but to ruin any chance you still have of being our damn-fool aunt's heir."

Claudia, effaced against the house, was virtually forgotten by both men. The men spoke in low, level voices, but the tension between them was so intense it was palpable, and Claudia knew it wasn't just male bravado. They were in deadly earnest, and in spite of the calm of his voice, she sensed that Andrew was frightened. She remembered Lindsay's comment to her about his renowned skill with the pistol, and she understood Andrew's fear. There was no doubt in his mind, or for that matter in Claudia's, that Lindsay was determined to use his skill to exact his revenge.

Claudia felt as if her stomach dropped; the rivalry between them was of long standing, but she was the cause of it coming to such a violent head and two lives—three, for what would her own be like if Lindsay shot Andrew and had to flee the country—might well be destroyed. Knowing she was casting herself between two deadly sword points, she went to Lindsay and grasped his arm. "Lindsay, there is no reason for this. Nothing has happened."

He broke the icy stare between him and Andrew reluctantly and looked down at Claudia. His eyes were hard and without expression. "Go inside, Claudia. We'll speak later."

"No. You can't fight a duel with your own cousin, Lindsay. Even I know that. You'll ruin us all."

He carefully removed her hand from his arm before

answering. "That is already in a fair way of being accomplished."

"I know I have been foolish," she said, more than willing to take the blame if it would prevent tragedy, "but now it is only gossip. If you and Andrew do this thing, it will be disgrace. If you don't care about me or yourself, think of what it will do to Aunt Jane and Vivian. What if there is an accident? What if one of you is killed?"

He transferred his gaze back to Andrew and smiled in an unlovely way. "One of us shall surely be killed."

There was no mistaking his meaning and a sudden wave of fear washed over Claudia, so intense that she felt nauseous again. She realized that argument was pointless; Lindsay was beyond the point of listening to reason. She turned away to leave, feeling that she might actually be physically ill if she remained, but Lindsay caught her arm and stopped her.

"Say nothing of this to Vivian or Aunt Jane, Claudia," he commanded, his voice like stone. "It is nothing to do with them. It will change nothing and will make matters worse rather than better."

It was an unnecessary warning. Claudia had been too well-versed by her father in the tacit rules of honor not to know that such an action would be considered unpardonable. She might have breached the code that most women felt scarcely applied to them if she thought it would prevent the meeting, but she was well-acquainted with the strength of Lindsay's will and determination, and she knew that he meant to meet Andrew no matter what.

To make it worse, if she were to go to Lady Ellacott, she would have to admit to what degree she had deliberately flirted and encouraged Andrew for it to have come to this pass, and she shrank from that humiliation when she did not even believe it would serve any purpose. For the first time Claudia realized how foolish her defiance and denial of her feelings for Lindsay had been and in what unflattering light they had placed her.

She smoothed her gown and tucked a straying curl back under its pin and returned to the ballroom. Somehow she made her way through the company, smiling and saying a word or two to acquaintances as she passed. The set was just ended; even as she entered the room she saw couples drifting toward the terrace and wondered how Lindsay and Andrew would conclude their quarrel, but in an abstract, almost detached way as if, having left them, she was no longer a part of the scene she had just witnessed.

She found Vivian seated with Kitty Lodder, and Vivian, seeing the strain behind her smile, quickly excused herself and took Claudia's arm and walked a little way with her before speaking. "Is anything the matter, Claud? Did you and Lindsay quarrel again?"

Claudia shook her head. She wanted to unburden herself, but she would not betray Lindsay. She shook her head and forced a smile. "No. But I have the headache. It has been a wretched day. I should never have come."

This last was said with considerable feeling and Vivian silently concurred. "Where is Lindsay? Perhaps it would be best if we left."

Claudia ignored the first question, feeling quite unequal to any answer. "There isn't any need for you or Aunt Jane to come with me. I'll have a footman call me a chair."

"Nonsense. Aunt Jane is having a marvelous time playing whist for pound points, but I am quite fatigued myself and would welcome an excuse to leave. Just let me tell her that we are going. She can tell Lindsay when she sees him."

Vivian left her, but Claudia did not wait for her return. She did exactly as she said she would and returned home alone by chair. She felt quite unequal to conversation, which would require dissembling, and even silence was not without danger. She felt so wretched that she feared a kind word or the slightest encouragement might well betray her into confiding the whole sordid mess her life had become.

When she returned home, Claudia went up the stairs and to her room almost at a run, curtly dismissing a startled Mary, who arrived shortly afterward to help her undress. She sat in one of a pair of chairs before the empty hearth, too wretched even to cry, though she felt more desolate than she had ever recalled feeling before in her life.

She could not help imagining horrors, her mind bouncing

back and forth between the fears that Lindsay meant to kill Andrew or that perhaps Lindsay's skill was overrated and it would be he who lay dead on the grass in the feeble morning light. This prospect was so devastating that she sobbed aloud and at last began to cry. The only sensible thought that occurred to her was to return to her mother, but with disgrace on her head and the unlikelihood of ever finding another post, she would be more of a burden to her family than ever.

As her weeping abated, she heard sounds of movement in the adjoining room and supposed that Lindsay had returned. She had no idea what she would say to him, but she got up at once and entered his room without ceremony. But it was Lady Ellacott who stood in Lindsay's room beside the bed.

The older woman's bosom rose and fell with strong emotion and Claudia had no doubt that somehow she had discovered what was afoot. "If anything should happen to either Andrew or Lindsay, I hold you entirely to blame," the dowager said without preamble. "I hope you shall be able to live with blood on your hands."

Claudia had no notion how she had discovered their intention to duel over Andrew's attentions to her, and she didn't bother to speculate. She had no intention of succumbing to an equal melodrama and said simply and with obvious pain, "I don't know how I shall support it."

Her acceptance of the blame seemed to take the wind out of Lady Ellacott's sails. "Didn't you realize it might come to this?" she demanded in a much leveler tone. "Why did you do it? Andrew is a pretty fellow and many foolish women fall in love with him, but he hasn't half of Lindsay's worth."

Claudia nodded agreement, unwilling to contribute more for fear that she would again begin to weep. She had a sudden, all but overwhelming impulse to unburden herself at last of the truth to Lady Ellacott and had to bite her lips to keep the words from forming on them.

"If you know that," said Lady Ellacott angrily, "why have you taken Andrew as your lover and forced Lindsay to this desperate course to save his honor?"

Claudia's eyes were bright and there was the hint of a tremor in her voice. "He is not my lover," she said vehemently. "He is *not* my lover."

Lady Ellacott, seeing Claudia's desolate expression and hearing the anguish in her voice, felt some of her righteous anger melt away. "What has happened between you and Lindsay to bring you to such a state?" she asked in a desperate tone. "If you loved each other when you were married . . ." She broke off as Claudia, who had buried her head in her hands, looked up and shook her head slowly in denial.

"It was not love that brought us together," she said, bringing out the words at last. "I have been a terrible fool, but not in the way that you think." It was not just the weight of her misery that made Claudia confess everything since the afternoon at Bingerley Court when she had left that house in disgrace and had met Lindsay at the Red Doe, but the need to abandon the subterfuge and deception that she now believed was the underlying cause of all that had occurred on this wretched night.

She had no expectation that Lady Ellacott would think better of her than she did now; in fact, she thought she would lose what good opinion of her that remained, but she was mistaken. "Oh, my poor dear," Lady Ellacott said when she had heard most of Claudia's story. "How alone you must have felt. Am I such an ogre that you couldn't trust me with the truth?"

"How could I?" Claudia said as she dabbed at her eyes in which tears intermittently formed and spilled over onto her cheek. "Lindsay told me that you would disinherit him if he married for any reason but love, and what would have been the point of going through with it at all if I were to lose him the only thing that mattered to him in the first place."

"Andrew tried to hint to me that there was no love between you and Lindsay, but I thought it was just the jealousy that has always existed between them. Even when I threatened to change my will again if Lindsay did not prevent your flirtation with Andrew, in my heart I believed it was only a lovers' quarrel that had gotten out of hand. I never had any idea Lindsay would go to such lengths for his inheritance,'' Lady Ellacott said, a puzzled frown creasing her brow. She stood up and moved about the room in an agitated way. "You know he has always been as a son to me. I never supposed he would stoop to deceiving me for my fortune.''

Claudia thought the criticism unjust, since it was the conditions that Lady Ellacott had set up that had engendered the deception in the first place. "Perhaps if you had not put him under the constant threat of disinheritance if he didn't do as you wished," she said, her frayed nerves making her imprudent, "he would not have done so.''

Lady Ellacott bristled. "I never urged him to do anything so improper as to marry a woman he had met in a common inn,'' she said, making Claudia wince. The dowager said more temperately, "I'm not blaming you for that, Claudia, at least not very much. You must have felt your situation to be most unhappy, and the temptation to have position in the world must have been great. It may even be that you have the taint of your father's gamester's blood. If you are breeding, I only hope it doesn't come out in your children.''

Almost wearily Claudia said, "I am not breeding, nor is it likely to happen now.''

Incredibly, Lady Ellacott seemed disappointed. "If you are not in love with Andrew . . .''

"That's of no consequence," Claudia said fiercely. "Lindsay is not in love with me.'' With more reluctance than she had admitted marrying Lindsay in payment of a wager, she acknowledged that she had come to fall in love with her elusive husband and had turned to Andrew believing that Lindsay cared nothing for her. "I know I've been foolish. I even wish I had never left Bingerley Court," she said with a watery, mirthless laugh. "Even that fate would have been preferable to knowing that Andrew and Lindsay are going to try to kill each other in a matter of hours.''

"I trust they will not," Lady Ellacott said with such certainty that Claudia's tears were at last arrested. "When I left the Sellingtons' Vivian was going to have a word with Lindsay to try to talk sense to him. If anyone can do it she can; he listens to her before he listens to anyone else.''

"How did you learn of the duel?"

"Andrew told Vivian." She saw Claudia's surprised expression. "Oh, not on purpose, of course. He made some comment to her and she had the truth out of him and came to me. It is a pity that he is the challenged and not the challenger. He would be sunk beneath reproach if he refused to meet Lindsay, but he doesn't want to fight is own cousin. It is Lindsay who won't listen to reason.''

Claudia thought that Andrew was already sunk beneath reproach, but she held her tongue. It was obvious to her that he had deliberately given Vivian the hint, hoping that through her or his aunt the meeting might yet be stopped. And perhaps it would be. Claudia might hold Andrew in contempt for his obvious cowardice, but if his tactics worked, she would be grateful to him. "I only hope that Vivian is successful," was all that she said.

But it was soon obvious that Vivian had failed as Claudia herself had. It was only a few minutes later that Lindsay and Vivian returned to the house. He came into his room and, seeing Claudia and his aunt, checked his progress at once. "The devil! Are you lying in wait for me? It won't serve anything. You may ask Vivian if I am to be deterred.'' Walking past them, he went to his wardrobe, pulled out an appropriately somber black coat, and began to strip off his silk evening coat.

Vivian came into the room behind him and stood framed in the door; she looked over at her aunt and shook her head unhappily.

Lady Ellacott rose from her chair near the hearth and went over to Lindsay. "Claudia has told me everything, from the first time you met at the Red Doe,'' she said in a flattened voice. "It is absurd for you to behave like an outraged husband in the circumstances.''

"It is an affair of honor. Our circumstances have nothing to do with it,'' he said tersely as he pulled a fresh shirt from his cupboard and then went to the bell by his bed to ring for his valet.

"You can't do such a thing, Lindsay,'' his aunt said

vehemently. "Whatever the outcome of such a meeting, it would mean tragedy and disgrace for us all."

He stood quite still while she spoke, his eyes focusing unwaveringly on hers. "I shall tell you what I have told Vivian. The challenge has been issued and the challenge stands. If Andrew chooses not to meet me, then the disgrace is his."

"If you call a halt to this absurdity right now, there need be disgrace for no one," Vivian said in the tone of one who has said the words many times before.

"If I call a halt to this now, I admit the wrong."

"There is no wrong," Claudia said quietly. "Or if there is any, it is mine." Lindsay turned to her, really looking at her for the first time since he had come into the room. She saw a shaft of emotion come into his eyes, quickly banished to give away none of his thoughts. She could readily guess these, and this brought a flush to her cheeks that was not entirely free of shame, for she knew that she had given Andrew the encouragement that had led to this tragedy. "Nothing has occurred between Andrew and me," she said, not with heat but with appeal. "Not in the way you are thinking."

He went over to her and cupped her face with his free hand and raised her head till she looked directly into his eyes. "But then you don't know what I think."

Silent tears welled in her eyes, and for once she had no desire to banish them. "Please don't do this. We'll all be ruined if you do."

"All will be ruined if I don't," he said enigmatically. He turned away as his valet entered the room. "Fetch me water to wash, Rush, and put out a clean breeches as well. I'll be going out again as soon as I change."

"You are meeting Andrew this morning," Lady Ellacott said, horrified. "How will you have time to arrange for your seconds or a doctor to be present? It can't be an honorable fight if it is so irregular."

"All matters are being seen to," Lindsay said over his shoulder as he stood before his dressing table divesting himself of his neckcloth.

Vivian walked slowly into the room and went over to her aunt. "It is pointless to argue, Aunt Jane. Nothing will change his mind. I don't know what will be the outcome of it, but there is nothing more we can do."

"There is something I can do," Lady Ellacott said, incensed that Lindsay was impervious to reasonable argument. "If you go through with this disgraceful meeting, Lindsay, you shall never see another penny from me either now or after my death."

Claudia looked swiftly to Lindsay to see his reaction, and their eyes held for a moment before he turned to Lady Ellacott. "I have told you before, Aunt Jane," he said with perfect calm, "it is your fortune to do with as you please. But whatever you choose, I shall still meet Andrew."

"This is not a time to defy me, Lindsay," Lady Ellacott said in a minatory way. "I mean what I say."

Lindsay gave her a level look. "So do I."

Lady Ellacott looked as surprised and pained as if he had struck her. "We shall see how you regret it. I'll send for Jolliet this very morning to change my will. I'll leave it all to Andrew."

Lindsay's smile was grim. "I should wait at least until you know the outcome of our meeting. Dead men have no use for legacies."

Lady Ellacott caught at her breath and fled the room. Vivian, after a moment and moving with unusual dis-spiritedness, followed her. Rush returned carrying a brass can full of hot water. His eyes flicked over Claudia as he added the hot water to the cool he poured out of the pitcher.

Lindsay pulled his shirt free from his breeches and began to unbutton it. Claudia could not help recalling the last time she had observed him undressing, but this time it brought no blush to her cheek. "You really mean to do this thing, Lindsay?"

"Yes."

"Because of me?"

"Because it is necessary. We have much to discuss, Claudia, but not now."

"Will we be able to discuss anything at all after this morning?" she said bitterly.

He took off his shirt and went over to the washstand. "I devoutly hope so," he said, flashing a quick smile over his shoulder.

"This is serious, Lindsay, deadly serious. I need to talk to you alone."

His smile flashed again. "Your timing is a little inappropriate, but the sentiment is not unappreciated. We may be as private as you like when I return. We'll even scandalize the staff by not coming out of our room for luncheon."

Claudia knew he was deliberately interpreting her request as sexual to discomfit her, but she would not be deterred. "Please, Lindsay," she said, going up to him and lightly touching his arm. He turned to face her, and before she could realize his intent, she was caught in his embrace and his mouth was on hers. She stiffened, but only for a moment, and then she melted against him, returning his kiss with full fervor. His skin felt warm and smooth beneath her touch, his mouth tasted faintly of wine, and she suddenly wanted him more than she had ever wanted anything before in her life.

Lindsay released her with obvious reluctance, removing her arms from about him and taking her hands in his. He brought them to his lips and kissed each in turn. "We will talk, Claud, I promise you, but not now." He saw that she was about to protest and put two fingers to her lips. "Don't try to dissuade me, you can't do it. This is something that goes beyond us and has to be played out, whatever the consequences."

A footman came and informed Lindsay that Mr. Merton had arrived to see him. "That will be Strait's second, come to see to the proprieties. Let me dress, Claudia, and have this thing be over with."

He was so gentle that for the first time she had hopes that he wasn't prepared to cast her off for causing this dreadful state of affairs. She didn't accept his insistence that the meeting with Strait was unavoidable, but she recognized the finality in his tone, so she left him to dress.

When she returned to her own room, she found her maid, looking frightened, waiting for her. She rejected the offer of her nightdress and instead had the girl put out a morning dress for her. There was no hope for sleep and she needed to be dressed and feel prepared for whatever might happen in the next few hours.

She heard Lindsay leave his room and go down to meet Mr. Merton. Shortly after this, Vivian came to her room. It was not yet dawn but would be soon, and in spite of the time of year, Claudia felt an early-morning chill and had Mary kindle a fire in the hearth.

Vivian sat in one of the chairs near the fire, hugging herself slightly as if she were cold. Claudia put the finishing touches on her toilet and sat across from her. Vivian in repose was an exceptionally pretty woman, but it was her vibrance and animation that usually gave her the appearance of great beauty. Claudia had never seen her looking graver, or plainer, and she bridged the distance between them and took her hand between her own.

"Is Aunt Jane gone to bed?"

Vivian nodded. "Though it will be wonderful if she can sleep. I gave her some of the laudanum left from her accident and it seems to have calmed her at the least. When I left her she was crying one moment because it is all her fault, and the next she damns them both as hotheaded fools and washes her hands of them both. But mostly, I think she is just scared. I'm scared, Claudia. Drew is a care-for-nobody and he is self-centered and can be cruel when he chooses, but I don't want him to die, any more than I want to see Lindsay hurt."

Claudia leaned over and squeezed her hand for reassurance. "No one is going to die. However great their rivalry, neither one would carry it to such a length."

"Lindsay is considered one of the finest shots in the kingdom. I have known him all of my life and I have never seen him like this, Claudia. He is determined to settle the score between them once and for all."

In spite of her fears, Claudia had never really accepted in her heart that it would be a killing affair, only that it might be if anything went amiss, but the patent fear in Vivian's tone, the complete depression of her spirits, began to infect her. She felt a sudden gripping sensation in her stomach, but she refused to regard it. "Don't tease yourself, or me for that matter, with such a notion. It won't come to that." Vivian made no comment, but her eyes said plainly that she did not agree.

Claudia stood abruptly and took an agitated turn about the room. "This can't be happening. We can't let it happen. I can't let it happen, because it is my fault. If Lindsay . . ." She broke off as a wave of despair swept over her. The thought of Lindsay dying was so unbearable she could not even think of it, but Lindsay shooting Andrew was almost equally uncomfortable to imagine. "We must do something," she said with sudden decision.

"There is nothing to be done," Vivian said in a flat voice. "Andrew would be only too glad to avoid the meeting, he let me guess at the truth in the hope that I could convince Lindsay against it. But Lindsay is adamant and Drew's reputation would be destroyed if he refused to meet him."

"Is it better that he should lose his life?" Claudia said caustically. "If only we knew where they were meeting, perhaps we could think of something to prevent it before it begins."

Vivian looked doubtful but said, "I know where they are meeting. On the rise near the south gate of Sydney Gardens."

Claudia crossed immediately to the mantel but midway through the action of pulling the bell she stopped. "I think we had better walk. Very likely Lindsay has gone to the mews to have his curricle made ready, and if I send for the town carriage, he will know of it."

"What could we hope to do by going there?" Vivian said fatalistically. "We're better off staying here and waiting for Lindsay to return."

The thought, *if he returns*, came unbidden into Claudia's head and was instantly banished. "You may stay if you wish, but I'm going." She had no idea what she could say when she got there, but she hoped the very irregularity of her presence would prevent them from fighting at least for now, and give Lindsay time to regain his more usual temperate nature.

"You would never find a chair at this hour."

"I said I would walk." Claudia had already gone to her armoire and was pulling out a shawl.

"Alone? You can't take your maid on such an errand."

"I don't intend to." Claudia found a poke bonnet that was ill-suited to her dress, but that concealed her face from casual inspection of passersby.

This roused Vivian from her dejection. "Don't be absurd," she said tartly. "You can't go traipsing about Bath in the middle of the night without any escort. It isn't even safe."

"It will be light before I get there," Claudia said with a glance at the mantel clock. "If you are concerned for me, come with me. I would be glad enough for your company, but whether you will or not, I'm going."

Vivian bit at her lip in consternation but quickly made up her mind. She spread the folds of her silk evening dress and said, "I can't go like this, we'll likely be taken for light-skirts as it is." Before Claudia could protest about the delay, she ran quickly from the room and returned in a remarkably short time changed into a cotton walking dress.

Her mercurial smile returned for the first time. "I am sure I look a perfect quiz. I just pulled out the first thing that came to hand, and I blush to say I haven't dressed myself since I came out of the schoolroom. Lovewell would be astonished to know that I could be ready for anything in under a quarter-hour."

She made no further attempt to talk Claudia out of going to the meeting place, and as quietly as they could in a house that was just stirring awake as the servants arose to begin their morning routines, they let themselves out the front door onto Laura Place.

Used to amusing herself with long walks in the countryside, Claudia set a brisk pace, but Vivian kept up with her, only once or twice being forced to trot a little when some inner spur caused Claudia to quicken her steps a bit more. Even so, it seemed to Claudia an endless distance to Sydney Gardens as the horizon gradually lightened and day began to break. The duel would likely take place as soon as they felt it was light enough to proceed to avoid the likelihood of being interrupted by chance by some passerby. The last quarter-mile she nearly ran, heedless of Vivian panting gamely behind her.

They had nearly reached the gate before Claudia saw them, five men on a slight rise near a large spreading tree, the pastoral setting an ironic contrast to the deadliness of their purpose.

At first she thought they had arrived in time, but even as she began to run toward them, Lindsay and Strait stood back to back and began to pace the agreed-upon distance. So intent was she on the tableau before her that she caught her foot on a root and stumbled, going down on one knee. She tried to rise, but was tangled in her skirts. Vivian, coming up to her, helped her to her feet.

But there was no point in going on; as they watched, the two combatants turned and the sound of a shot rang out. At first Claudia didn't believe what she had seen. Lindsay was still in the act of turning when Andrew had fired. For one horrified moment she expected Lindsay to fall, but he continued to turn and then his pistol was aimed squarely at his cousin.

It was Vivian who cried out, though for a moment Claudia thought the silent wail in her heart had been uttered without her volition. If anyone heard, they paid no heed. Each second seemed a minute in duration, and Claudia expected Lindsay's arm to come up to delope. She prayed fervently as if to will him to do it. But the hand with the pistol remained outstretched and then he fired.

The earl was a deathly white as if he had been shot, but he stood as firm as Lindsay; incredibly, Lindsay had missed. He dropped his arm and stood still, his eyes never leaving his cousin's ashen face. Strait turned away abruptly, stumbled a few feet away, and was sick in the grass.

The realization that it was over and both men were miraculously uninjured swept over Claudia in a wave of relief. Vivian urged her to come away, since there was no cause for them to be there any longer, but Claudia shrugged her off and continued toward them.

Lindsay turned toward the others and Claudia heard Mr. Merton ask Lindsay if he felt his honor was satisfied. What he thought of the earl's dishonor or Lindsay's sudden want of skill was not discernible either in his voice or in his expression. Nodding, Lindsay turned toward Sir Michael Dray, his own second, who was not so practiced at dissembling and who looked distressed and disgusted. Lindsay then walked over to the third man, obviously a doctor, who turned and headed toward Sir Michael's phaeton.

Victor Merton was the first to notice Claudia and Vivian standing by the gate, and he broke off what he was saying to Sir Michael and spoke to Lindsay, who then turned and saw them.

Lindsay strolled toward them without urgency. "You shouldn't have come here," he said evenly. He turned to Vivian and spoke with considerable curtness to her. "I told you you could best serve me by keeping watch over Claudia and Aunt Jane."

Vivian bristled at what she felt was an unjust criticism. "Did you imagine I could stop Claudia from doing as she pleased? God knows I tried," she said defensively, "but she would have come alone if I had refused to come with her."

"You shouldn't have been witnesses to this."

"Andrew fired before the signal, didn't he?" Vivian asked bluntly.

"His pistol misfired, yes," Lindsay replied, but Vivian shook her head slightly, denying his assessment, which they both knew was untruthful.

Claudia understood the implications of what had occurred, but it was over now and all that mattered to her was that somehow she had to bridge the chasm that stretched between her and Lindsay. "What difference does it make now? It's ended."

"Not entirely. Michael will drive you back to the house."
Without waiting for their acquiescence, he turned and began
to walk away.

As if impelled to do so, Claudia ran after him and caught
his arm. He stopped and looked down at her, his expression
far from encouraging. Claudia pushed down a sudden urge
to cast herself on his chest and weep. "Aren't you coming
with us?" she asked, because she had no idea what to say
to him.

"No," he said abruptly, and then softened it by adding
in an easier way, "There are still matters to attend to."

"Andrew tried to kill you," she said quickly, unwilling
to let him walk away from her just yet.

"He was badly frightened. Frightened men do foolish
things."

Claudia knew that what Andrew had done had dishonored
him whatever Lindsay might say to mitigate it. "You are
being very generous."

His smile was brief and wry. "At the moment I can afford
to be. Go back to the house, Claudia. Aunt Jane needs
someone to be with her."

Finally, Claudia could not prevent tears from forming in
her eyes and spilling over. She had had more cause to weep
in one day than she had since her father had died. "I'm sorry,
Lindsay," she said, somehow keeping her voice steady. "I
know I am to blame for what has happened. Andrew merely
responded to the encouragement I gave him. I never meant
it to go so far."

There was a subtle change in his expression and his eyes
became shuttered. "I'm sure you didn't," he said in a quiet,
level voice. "Andrew did. It was always his intention. Go
home, Claudia."

He walked away from her, but Claudia stood there for
another minute or so, silently weeping, until Vivian came
up behind her and put an arm about her, leading her toward
where Sir Michael's curricle stood waiting.

With the melodrama played out, Vivian's spirits began to
return and she made several comments about the loveliness
of the morning and plans for the day, but she received

virtually no response from Claudia, who was too preoccupied with her thoughts to even dissemble an interest outside of them.

This time she feared she had at last accomplished what she had seemed bent on doing almost from the start of her marriage. Afraid of loving a man who she knew had no strong feelings for her, she had consistently behaved in a manner designed to keep her husband at a distance and protect her from succumbing to the undeniable attraction she felt for him. But she had not successfully preserved her own vulnerability; there was an ache inside of her that only Lindsay could soothe, and all that her defensive actions had contrived was to create a situation that she had no doubt had given him a complete disgust of her. And yet she was not ready to entirely abandon hope. When he returned to the house, they would talk and perhaps somehow they would begin to unravel their tangled affairs.

But Lindsay didn't return to the house. Lady Ellacott, relieved that neither of her nephews had succeeded in killing the other, was inclined to forgive and forget, and advised patience for Claudia. "You know, my dear," she said to Claudia, "whatever has occurred between you and Lindsay, you must not give up hope. He is very sweet-tempered, you know, and never stays angry or upset for long. You are still his wife, and if you will both just make a little effort, in time I am certain you will find happiness together."

Her words were meant to be encouraging, but as the hours passed and Lindsay did not return to Laura Place, Claudia had to make a conscious effort not to appear as depressed as she felt.

In light of this, she recalled everything he had said to her that morning and divested it of all hope, teasing herself that he stayed away deliberately because he did not want to see or speak with her again. Her anxiety was doubled when she saw Rush going out of Lindsay's room carrying a small valise that she had no doubt he was taking to his master. At first she had only supposed he was with Sir Michael, but a new anxiety began to gnaw at her; she feared he had gone for comfort to Sally Hart.

She would have been glad enough to have remained in her room nourishing her anxieties, but Vivian would not permit it. "Sir Michael and Victor are discreet, but there are bound to be rumors after last night. If we all stay at home and avoid meeting people, we'll not only confirm their suspicions, but give rise to a speculation that results in the worst sort of gossip."

"If I go with you to Mrs. Carrington's assembly, the whole world will know that there is something amiss the moment they set eyes on me," Claudia told her plainly. "I couldn't meet anyone tonight and pretend otherwise."

"Yes you can," Vivian said firmly, going over to Claudia's wardrobe. "Wear the peach silk tonight. It makes your skin glow, so you won't have to fear that you will look too pale."

Claudia continued to protest, but her resistance was considerably less than it had been in the morning and ultimately she found it was easier to agree than argue. Somehow she did get through the evening, though the memory of it when they returned home was a blur. Lady Ellacott complimented her on her aplomb, but Claudia scarcely knew if she had acquitted herself well or not. If any of the other guests had been whispering behind their hands, she failed to note that as well.

By the next morning, though she was still feeling dispirited, her good sense reasserted itself and she did what she could to put Lindsay from her mind. Eventually he would have to return to Laura Place, but he would do so in his own good time and teasing herself into such a disordered state would accomplish nothing.

Accordingly, though her inclination was to remain at home, she agreed to accompany Lady Ellacott on her morning visits instead of waiting about for Lindsay to return. At Lady Seton's an invitation was issued and accepted for them to remain for luncheon, so it was late afternoon before they returned home.

Vivian met Claudia in the hall outside her bedchamber and

informed her that Lindsay had come home some time ago. "I haven't spoken to him, though. I've no wish to concern you, dearest, but he looked so forbidding that even I didn't dare approach him beyond the barest civilities. Perhaps it would be best if you left him to himself a little longer. He'll get over his ill humor; Lindsay always does."

But Claudia was not as sanguine, nor could she bear any further delay with its attendant anxieties. Discovering from Vivian that Lindsay was to be found in the study, she went to her own room, and after assuring herself in the cheval glass that she was not looking creased or hot from her excursion, she decided to go to him at once.

The face that looked back at her in the mirror wasn't dour, but there was a hollowness about her eyes and a general sagging to the features that bespoke her inner feelings. She tried to force her expression into more pleasing lines, but the smile was strained and her eyes were untouched by it. Giving it up, she went down to the ground floor and went into the study without bothering to knock.

Lindsay was sitting in one of a pair of leather chairs flanking two tall windows that looked out onto the street. A book was open in his lap and his eyes were downcast, but Claudia had the impression that he hadn't read anything on the printed pages before him in some time.

Though her entrance was not made with deliberate quietness, he was slow to look up at her. He closed the book without reluctance, placed it on the table to his right, and waited for her to approach him.

Claudia sat in the chair beside his. She had rehearsed a dozen different openings she could have made, but sitting so near to him, yet not near enough to touch and not yet daring to close the breach, every one of them seemed stupid and contrived and she could not bring herself to utter the words.

Lindsay saw her hesitation and the corners of his mouth turned up a little. "Bereft of words, Claudia, or gathering your resources?"

"Is everything settled now?"

"Ambiguous questions usually garner ambigious answers.

The sawbones was paid handsomely to keep his budget closed and Sir Michael and Victor may be counted on for their discretion. It may occasion some talk when it is learned that Strait has left Bath so abruptly, but it won't be wondered at that he preferred to visit Brighton, where most of his friends are now.''

"Is that where he's gone?"

"So Victor told me. I didn't speak with him myself."

"Not at all?"

"It was kinder, don't you think?"

"He must feel wretched for what he has done."

Lindsay shrugged slightly. "Perhaps. I don't rely on it."

"He felt bad enough to leave Bath," Claudia said, an automatic defense of Andrew that she wished unspoken as soon as she had said it.

There was a cooler note in Lindsay's voice. "He hadn't the bottom to face me again. I suppose you could call that remorse of a sort, or at least regret. He knows I won't forget his dishonor."

"You could have killed him, couldn't you?" Claudia said, searching his eyes for an answer before he could even reply. "You missed him on purpose."

He gave a soft laugh. "Don't credit me with nobility. My inclination was thoroughly primitive, but I didn't fancy leaving the country to escape the consequences of the act."

Claudia smiled a little. "I don't believe you. You aren't like Andrew."

"Is that meant to be to my credit?" he asked so softly she was not certain she heard him correctly. He saw her surprise and said, "Most of the comparisons you have made between us were not."

"I never meant . . ." She broke off and looked down at her hands in her lap. "I-I'm sorry. I've been a fool. I don't know what to say to you."

Lindsay stood and drew her to her feet as well. "So have I. I didn't come home yesterday because I wanted to think what was best to be done. It isn't possible for the marriage to be annulled any longer, and divorce would mean greater ruin for you than for me. I know you don't want to be married to me and never did, and I apologize for drawing you into my mad schemes. It wasn't even to any purpose, was it? Aunt Jane has completely disinherited me, which I have come to think is no worse than I deserve for my duplicity. But it is the harm I have done to you that troubles me most. What can I do to make it up to you, Claudia? I haven't a fortune or even the hope of one now to make you a settlement."

"I don't want money," Claudia said, looking at her hands in his rather than meet his eyes.

"I can't give you your freedom without hurting you worse than I already have."

"I don't want that either," she said in a small voice, and then, when he was silent, the need to know his reaction gave a boost to her courage and she looked up at him.

He regarded her in some puzzlement, but there was another emotion in his expression that was less decipherable. "If you're willing to stay with me, we could try to make the best of our absurd bargain. But if you do, I don't promise to keep my word to you any longer. I don't want a marriage in name only. I find I can't continue to live with you on those terms. I never supposed it would happen when I made you my proposal, but I have fallen in love with you, Claudia."

He dropped his eyes as he spoke, but then raised them again to hers. "If you will let me, I promise to do my best to make you happy and to make you forget Drew."

Claudia listened with growing astonishment as he spoke. She had meant to throw herself on his kindness and beg him not to set her aside, but to give her a chance to be a proper wife to him! She was not certain she would have dared yet to admit to him that she, too, had fallen in love with him, but in her growing wonderment, her fear of her own vulnerability began to evaporate.

"You won't even have to try. I was attracted to Andrew, but I was never in love with him. I know you think I have been his mistress, but I swear to you I have not. There is only one man I have ever wanted to make love with, and that's you."

She had barely finished this speech before she found herself enfolded in his arms and soundly kissed until they were both left quite breathless.

"We are very fortunate, I think," he said between nuzzling kisses on her throat and hair. "Not many people who make a start as bad as ours get a second chance to make it right again." He pulled back from her a little. "I want you to know that I saw Sally Hart yesterday evening. I told her plainly that I wouldn't be seeing her again and that it would be best if even the friendship were curtailed. I'm sorry you ever had to know of that."

"I'm glad that I did," she said perversely. "I couldn't bear to think of you with her, and it made me realize how much I wanted you myself."

He kissed her again and they were lost in this pleasurable activity for a considerable time until the opening of the door at last separated them.

Vivian came into the room and when she saw them, she laughed. "I am so delighted," she said, hugging Claudia first and then Lindsay. "Whatever silly scheme you hatched between you, I knew from the moment you brought Claudia to Lovewell House that she was the perfect wife for you, Lin. Aunt Jane sent me to be certain you hadn't come to blows. I think she is very sorry for the things she said to you both yesterday. She has sent for Mr. Jolliet again, but to sign her will, I think, not to change it."

Both Claudia and Vivian thought that Lindsay would be delighted at the prospect that he might be reinstated as his godmother's heir, but his response surprised them both and particularly pleased Claudia. "I'm not fool enough to whistle a fortune down the wind, but if Aunt Jane wants to make me her heir again, it will be without condition. I won't be controlled by it again."

Vivian left them to tell Lady Ellacott that her hopes had been realized, and perhaps to give her the hint that she would find Lindsay less biddable.

"Will you mind very much if Aunt Jane doesn't care for my independence?" Lindsay asked Claudia as they made themselves comfortable on the one small sofa in the room. "I am not a pauper, but I can't keep my promise to keep you in the style I told you I would when we made our bargain."

"I am not surprised," Claudia said with mock severity. "You have already made it clear to me that you are not a man of your word. But I shan't hold you to this promise any more than the other," she added handsomely, and kissed him.

After a time Claudia rested contentedly in Lindsay's arms, but she could not resist quizzing him a little longer. "I suppose I am fortunate that you did not stand up to your godmother sooner. If you had told her to leave her fortune to the devil before that night at the Red Doe, I would likely be governess of Lady Convers instead of Lady Lindsay Alistair."

"Do you know, the more I think on it, the more convinced I am that I am being hasty. She is very rich, you know." He stood and held out his hand to her.

Claudia took it, and when she rose, he tucked her hand in his arm and led her from the room. "Where are we going?" she demanded.

At the door he stopped, turned, and gave her his most disarming smile. "To fulfill Aunt Jane's fondest wish—or at least to see that it is fulfilled by next spring."

Claudia blushed a little at the implication of his words, but she made not the smallest objection and followed him contentedly out of the room.

# SIGNET REGENCY ROMANCE
## COMING IN FEBRUARY 1990

---

*Norma Lee Clark*
THE INFAMOUS RAKE

*Mary Balogh*
A PROMISE OF SPRING

*Gayle Buck*
HONOR BESIEGED

---